Praise for Flo

"Masterfully crafted and wickedly funny, Paul Wilborn's delightfully dark, comic adventure glitters with witty dialogue and crisp, clever prose. Wilborn's tale of offbeat outsiders in search, in flight, and in love is an acerbic, delicious treat featuring the magnificent swampland of Florida in all its quirky glory."
Natalie Symons, author of Lies In Bone

"Steeped in 1980s film and horror culture and basking in Palm Beach's neon glow, Paul Wilborn's rollicking ride of a novel **—Florida Hustle—** is fully immersive, wildly entertaining and as authentic as it gets."
Steph Post, author of Miraculum, Lightwood, Walk in the Fire, Holding Smoke and A Tree Born Crooked

"**Florida Hustle** begins with an imagined screenplay, and the entire story is camera-ready (be alert, streaming services). The hues of Wilborn's home state suffuse the setting; the action is rapid and the plot twists many. Most important, he's created characters who continually surprise us with their complexity as well as their doings. It's entertaining and more —a romp with heart."
John Capouya, author of Florida Soul and Gorgeous George

"If you're a fan of Hiassen, Dorsey and other practitioners of the rollicking Florida Escapade genre, I bring good news: there's a new, wholly original voice you won't want to miss. In his first novel, **Florida Hustle**, former journalist Paul Wilborn takes us on a thoroughly entertaining romp through upper-crust Palm Beach to the seedy side of West Palm to the swampiest of the Everglades. Filled with plenty of twists and turns, it brims with a cast of misfits and miscreants, including seventeen-year-old Michael Donnelly, whose obsession with a slasher film star prompts his father to try to lock him in a psychiatric hospital before he becomes another John Hinckley Jr, relentless-but-lovable con man Cavanaugh Reilly and ambitious seductress Lola Fernandez Famosa. **Florida Hustle** has a lot of fun with its oddball characters but never looks down on them, making this a novel with a ton of heart."

Jane Heller, New York Times and USA Today bestselling author

....

Vivid characters. Delicious dialogue. A smart, funny, wild ride you won't be able to put down. Love, love, love this book.

Tom Flynn Screenwriter (GIFTED, TOGO)

....

...Relentlessly clever plot... It's an antic, very Floridian tale, populated with larger-than-life characters and full of Carl Hiaasen-style dry humor and Elmore Leonard–style sharp descriptions. The characters all have penchants for funny one-liners, and a kind of zany logic binds their very strange separate worlds. Wilborn packs a lot of fun and human insight into a slim number of pages.

An irrepressible Florida frolic filled with lost dreams, forlorn love, and horror movie lore.

Kirkus (starred review)

Published by St. Petersburg Press
St. Petersburg, FL
www.stpetersburgpress.com

Design and composition by St. Petersburg Press and Isa Crosta
Cover design by St. Petersburg Press and Chad Mize

Paperback ISBN: 978-1-940300-48-1
eBook ISBN: 978-1-940300-49-8

First Edition

Florida Hustle

By Paul Wilborn

The way you walked was thorny, through no fault of your own...

———

Maleva, The Gypsy Woman,
The Wolf Man **(1941)**

Sometimes I think I've figured out some order in the universe, but then I find myself in Florida.

———

Susan Orlean

For Cavanaugh Murphy III

How Much For that One?

—

Closing his eyes, Michael conjured his establishing shot:

EXT. - Palm Beach - Day
Tight on a long black Cadillac cruising streets as smooth as alabaster. The camera pulls back, the B/G music soft but with a steady beat. The limo's graphite-gray windows give away no secrets as it glides past rigid hedges, putting-green lawns and coquina-colored privacy walls.

A title card superimposes over the action for five seconds:

Palm Beach
January 1982

The shot pulls back as the limo makes a left onto a four-lane avenue, lined with coconut palms, the east and west traffic divided by a lushly landscaped median. Small knots of extras - costumed in pastels and carrying shopping bags - sashay along wide sidewalks, lined with shops and restaurants that wouldn't be out of place on the Italian Riviera.

Roll main titles as the limo crosses an ornate, old-world drawbridge. On the west side of the bridge, the tone shifts from **The Great Gatsby** *to* **Serpico**. *The buildings along the waterfront are shiny and solid, but the downtown beyond is all for-rent signs and empty storefronts. A bleary-eyed drunk, rousing himself from an inset doorway, raises a bony finger as the limo turns north onto an urban thoroughfare thick with cars headed somewhere else.*

Hold on a final card: **"A film by Michael Donnelly."**

"Stop!" Michael shouted from the back.

The driver dutifully stomped the brake, tossing the aspiring 17-year-old auteur off the leather backseat and onto the floor, as other drivers – shouting curses and pounding horns - dodged around the suddenly stationary limo.

Michael had snapped out of his film reverie just as the Cadillac passed a strip center housing Larry's Discount Liquors, Soap and Suds 24-hour Laundry Palace and Horror Time Video, its picture window painted black and plastered with posters for Friday The 13th, Halloween, The Omen II and a dozen more blood-soaked titles.

"Sorry about that," the driver said, calmly looking over his shoulder at the empty back seat. "You okay?"

"Fine," Michael whispered, from the black-carpeted floor. "But you passed it."

"Don't worry, kid," he said. "I got this."

The man at the wheel, Randy Stewart, was currently a resident of the Donnelly pool house. He was Alex Donnelly's best friend, tennis instructor and the bass player in Alex's Tuesday night jam sessions. He also drove the limo when the regular driver was off. At 39, Randy's tight curls had gone salt-and-pepper, but he still looked like an athlete - tanned and muscled, and always dressed in tennis whites and sneakers. A ranked player in the early '70s, Randy was most famous for a U.S. open quarterfinal when Ilie "Nasty" Nastase frisbee'd a racket at his head.

While he was still an excellent tennis player, Randy was a terrible driver. To get back to *Horror Time Video*, he attempted a U-turn that immediately blocked all four lanes. As more horns blared, the limo bumped over a curb into a motel parking lot. Randy's driving mantra was "speed trumps safety," so he didn't bother to check for oncoming cars when he bounced back over the curb onto the highway, setting off another round of horns, screeching tires and angry shouts. Michael pulled himself up off the black-carpeted floor and back onto the leather seat.

Punching the gas pedal, Randy made a hard right into the

strip center parking lot. Too fast now, he again slammed on the brake, sending Michael tumbling off the seat a second time. When the limo finally stopped, the chrome grill was extended across the front sidewalk, two feet from *Horror Time's* poster-filled picture window.

"Jeez, sorry, kid," Randy said, seconds later, as he held open the back door and stared inside at the boy on the floor. "Let me help you up."

Michael waved him away.

Stepping back, Randy watched a gawky mantis of a kid, with a spiky mass of brown hair, unfold from the car, his bony six-foot frame swathed in black jeans and a gray *Psycho Killer* T-shirt.

"You okay?" Randy asked, pulling out a pack of Salems.

"I'll live," Michael said, already striding toward the store and not looking back.

Randy lit a cigarette, leaning back against the driver's door as he exhaled.

"Take your time, Mike," he said. "I got all day."

The wooden front door of *Horror Time Video* was hidden behind a life-size black and white cutout of Boris Karloff's *Frankenstein*. Pushing the door open set off *Horror Time's* version of a door chime – a woman's terrified SCREAM!

Pausing inside the door, Michael sniffed the store's acrid bouquet of mold and burnt wicks. Ray, the owner, favored ambiance over commerce, so his horror video store was lit by thirty-six candles flickering atop a half-dozen Liberace-style candelabras set on tables around the low-ceilinged room, the tarnished bases gloved in pleated jackets of wax. Stepping from a sun-washed Florida day into this shadowy den, Michael felt like he was nervously descending a basement staircase in *The House On Haunted Hill.*

God, he loved this place!

He picked up one of the silver, baton-style flashlights Ray provided for customers on a table by the door, the pale beam revealing racks of VHS boxes garish with Godzillas, teenagers from outer space, and masked slashers waving hatchets or ma-

chetes. Poster board knives, dangling from strings, pointed out
Horror Time's various specialty sections, each blade marked
with a jagged, hand-lettered inscription: CORMAN, HITCH-
COCK, WHALE, 5Os SCI-FI, SLASHERS, VAMPIRES, WITCHES
AND WARLOCKS, JAPAN'S FINEST and more.

Michael bypassed the video racks, heading directly to the
checkout desk in the back. Ray had called the day before saying
he'd located "something I know you're going to really like. I got
it all wrapped up for you."

Ray Villadonga, a horror film savant, who appeared to be
gestating triplets under his grimy T-shirts, was the closest thing
Michael had to a friend. Crystal Donnelly had home-schooled
her son, and until her untimely exit, she had been his main
companion and confidant. Now, except for occasional trips
to a mall movie complex or *Horror Time Video*, where he and
Ray jousted for hours over arcane bits of horror movie history,
Michael was at the drafting desk in his bedroom, sketching out
storyboards for the fright films he was certain would catapult
him from Palm Beach to Hollywood.

A toad-like teenage clerk, his cheeks dotted with fresh con-
stellations of acne, hunkered on a stool behind a blood-red
counter reading the latest *Conan the Barbarian* by flashlight.
The clerk hadn't looked up when the door SCREAMED. He didn't
notice the restless customer idling in front of him.

"How much for that one?" Michael finally asked, his flashlight
focused on the promo poster for the upcoming *Slasher High*,
featuring the screaming face of Dawn Karston, the film's blonde
teenage star.

The clerk's head made a lazy swivel, following Michael's flashlight beam to the wall behind the counter. He quickly returned
to his comic.

"Not for sale."

"But I want to buy it."

Setting his own flashlight on the counter, the clerk closed
his comic book with feigned care, taking a long breath before
looking up.

"You can want to buy it, but you can't. It's not for sale. The movie isn't out until next week. We got old posters in the corner." The kid nodded in that direction before going back to *Conan the Barbarian.* He didn't see Michael pull a fat roll of cash from his pocket, but his head jerked up when Michael slapped a fifty hard on the counter.

"I want to buy that one."

"It's not..."

Another fifty slammed down.

The clerk aimed his flashlight at the bills, just to be sure. Then, setting the glowing baton back on the counter, his hand crept crab-like toward the bills, thick digits fluttering briefly above the face of Ulysses S. Grant. The decision didn't take long. His hand came down on the crisp fifties, sliding them back across the counter and into the pocket of his jeans.

"You want me to roll it up in a tube? Or what?"

"Yes. In a tube. Did my order come in?"

"Who are you?"

"Look under the name Bava. Mario Bava. Where's Ray? Or Tony? They know me here."

The clerk searched under the counter and came back with a VHS tape, wrapped in a sheet of lined notebook paper with "BAVA" scrawled on it. Snapping the rubber band that held it and crumpling the paper wrapper, the clerk shined his flashlight on a video box for *Bay of Blood – Collector's Edition.* On the cover, a screaming woman, the tops of her breasts breaking the surface of a bloody pool, was about to be stabbed in the throat by a curved blade wielded by an unseen attacker. There, just below the title, was the director's credit: *Una pelicula de Mario Bava.*

The clerk lowered the video box and shined his light in Michael's face.

"You don't look like a Mario to me. You made these movies?"

Looking away from the light, Michael pushed a hand through his unruly hair. He couldn't believe this.

"Let's just say I'm a fan," he said, reaching out. "Can I have it now?"

The clerk aimed the light back at the blood red cover.

"So who is this Mario guy?"

"He's the goddamn Fellini of gore!" Michael almost shouted, as he reached out again for the tape. "Can I have it now, please?"

"Hmmm." The clerk hummed, turning the box over and reading the back. "Never heard of him."

"How'd you get this job?" Michael barked, his patience gone. "This is *Horror Time Video*, right? Bava's the father of modern horror. There's a knife with his name on it right over there. Friday the 13th was a direct rip-off of *Bay of Blood...*"

"Yeah, *Friday the 13th* was cool," the clerk said, still eyeing the back of the box.

"No. It wasn't," Michael shouted. "It was shit. Does Ray know you work here?"

"You mean, Uncle Ray?" the clerk asked, holding the box out to Michael. "Yeah, he knows."

———

The master bedroom of the Donnelly waterfront mansion was outfitted with expansive "his" and "her" bathrooms. At 6:45, after a long day at the office, Alex sat on a porcelain throne reading the *Wall Street Journal*, a pair of white silk boxers gathered around his ankles. A tiny television on the marble counter across from the toilet was tuned to the evening news. Alex kept lowering the paper to watch.

Truth was, Alex read the *Journal* because he had to. Before his father's heart had imploded in the boardroom of Donnelly Avionics and Alex was called back from a post-college tour of Europe to run the business, he was absolutely sure his garage band, a mash-up of The Kinks and The Animals, would soon have theaters full of teen-age girls screaming and fainting for them.

Instead, he found himself the CEO of a major defense contractor, with a corner office that overlooked two vast parking lots, a few miles northwest of West Palm Beach. Sitting down behind his father's wide, teak desk on his first day, Alex was terrified. This was Jack Donnelly's world, not his.

"How the hell am I going to do this?" Alex asked the man standing across the desk.

"We'll take it one day at a time," Dick Adams told him. "Here's lesson number one."

Dick stepped over to a coffee table where the local and national papers were splayed out. He picked up a copy of the *Wall Street Journal* and placed it in front of Alex, his hand sliding lovingly across the paper to ease away the crease.

"Read this every day," Dick told him. "You do that and you'll sound like you know a lot until you actually know a lot. In the meantime, I'll take care of everything."

Jack Donnelly and Dick Adams had built Donnelly Avionics together. Jack was the salesman, a scratch golfer who liked closing deals over stiff cocktails at the proverbial 19th hole. He was often mistaken for an astronaut with his star quarterback physique and sandy crew cut. He came to work most days in a polo shirt with the logo of one country club or another on the chest. Dick was the square-jawed numbers guy, in custom-made suits and dress shirts, accessorized with monogramed cuff links and Countess Mara ties. Darkly handsome, he was clearly a man of substance, and more than a little sex appeal, his wavy black mane slicked back like some modern-day Valentino.

Taking over for his father, Alex did as he was told. And after 20 years of reading the *Journal* and working with Dick, he knew a lot.

In the comfort of his pale blue bathroom, Alex was skimming an article on defense appropriations for the aeronautics industry. He looked up when Tom Brokaw introduced the next story - an in-depth analysis of the attempted assassination of Ronald Reagan.

Alex peered over the top of the paper. An image of the White House quickly cut to a replay of the chaotic, black and white video of the shooting outside the Washington Hilton Hotel six months earlier. The picture on the tiny screen began to roll and Alex leaned forward, wiggling the spindly rabbit ears until the TV settled down. As it did, he saw the face of Reagan's failed assassin – a teenage boy named John Hinckley.

"Hinckley's obsession with Jodie Foster and the film *Taxi Driver* went largely unnoticed by his parents," the announcer said. "Much of Hinckley's plot was developed in his bedroom of the family home in a plush North Dallas suburb."

The rest of the commentary was drowned out by the gurgling blast of a flushed toilet.

Washing his hands, Alex thought his mirror image looked bleak in the harsh bathroom light. His hair more Marine drill sergeant than aspiring rock god; his mouth starting to sag to the south; spidery lines creasing the skin around his eyes. How did this happen to me, he thought?

His son was no Hinckley, Alex was sure of that, but the boy was in a particularly dark place since his mother had - Alex struggled with the S word – since she had taken action. Irreversible action. Somehow, their grief over the loss of a woman they both loved hadn't brought them closer together. Not that he and Michael had been best buddies. But Crystal Donnelly's death six months before had turned them into polite strangers padding about in a sprawling, hollow house.

Alex could see the blame in his son's eyes on the rare times they talked. It was Alex who had insisted on the new doctor, a doctor who prescribed an experimental drug to level out Crystal's increasingly volatile mood swings, a drug that didn't work as planned.

Alex shook the thoughts from his head. Moments later, wearing a silk robe covered in swirling paisleys, an anniversary gift from Crystal, he knocked on the door of his son's second-floor bedroom, a long hallway away from his own.

When Michael didn't answer, he tested the knob. It was unlocked.

Alex hadn't been invited into Michael's room in months and the change was drastic. The west wall was the same - all floor-to ceiling windows that opened onto the churning black expanse of the Intracoastal Waterway – but the other three walls looked a lot like the inside of that West Palm Beach horror video shop he had once visited with his son. The wall behind the boy's teak-framed double bed was papered with posters from '80s horror films – *Homecoming In Hell, Sorority Slasher, Frat House Fiend* - all with images of the same young screaming star, Dawn Karston.

A second wall was home to vintage posters of Mario Bava's '60s and '70s films, *Kill Baby Kill, Blood and Black Lace, Bay of Blood* and *Baron Blood*, and a poster for *Suspiria*, by Bava's artistic heir, Dario Argento. When they were talking, in the months before Crystal's suicide, Michael had described his love for Bava's surrealistic horror films. When Alex and Michael watched one in the mansion's home theater, Alex had a flashback to a bad acid trip he and Crystal had taken in the early years of their marriage. As Alex recalled the film, frightening things were happening, but none of them made any sense.

The third interior wall – behind Michael's drafting table - was covered in corkboard and 11-by-17 sheets of paper, anchored by white-tipped pushpins. On each sheet were multiple hand-drawn images of movie scenes, some bursting with balloons of dialogue, looking like pages from a giant, monotone comic book.

Moving closer, Alex took in a series of drawings set during the French revolution. He recognized Marat, the French revolutionary, in his bathtub, and his assassin, Charlotte Corday.

BLOOD REVOLT
Draft 3

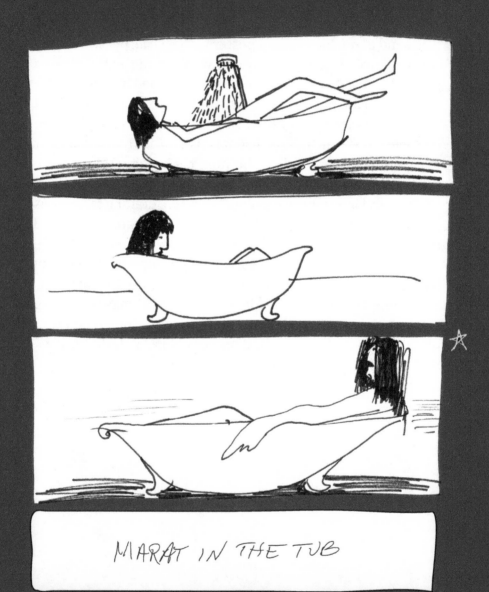

MARAT IN THE TUB

CHARLOTTE RAISES A LARGE
BUTCHER KNIFE.

CHARLOTTE SLAMS THE KNIFE
INTO MARAT'S NECK.

CHARLOTTE, BLOOD DRIPPING, WALKS AWAY.

MARRY, RAISING THE KNIFE,
FOCUSES HIS DEAD EYES ON
HIS SCREAMING ASSASSIN.

When had his introspective young son become obsessed with horror movies and violence? He had tried to be a loving father. He came home every night after work, hugged his son, and forced the boy to play catch in the backyard. And what about his huge donation to PBS for that one-on-one visit with Mr. Rogers? Michael was so excited he had literally peed his pants, and Mr. Rogers, ever gracious, had pretended he didn't smell a thing.

This was clearly Michael's mother's fault: the home schooling, the Puccini operas on her stereo each afternoon, the gallons of chardonnay, the manic mood swings, and her final selfish decision in the tub of the master bathroom.

Still, blaming a dead woman didn't feel right to him. He was shaking the dark thoughts from his head, when the door squeaked behind him.

"Dad?" It was Michael. "What are you doing in my room?"

Alex turned quickly, his face flushed, feeling like he'd been caught at something. His son stood framed in the doorway – so tall now, but still a boy in Alex's eyes – a boy clutching a black-handled butcher knife.

"I just wanted to say hi." Alex said. "The door was open. What's with the knife?"

"Just doing a little research. So, do you need something?"

"Is everything okay, Michael?" Alex stepped closer, his eyes moved from his son's placid face to the knife dangling in his fingers. "Would you...maybe...like to talk?'

"Everything's good, Dad. Thanks for asking." Michael stepped out of the doorway. "Listen, I gotta get back. I'm working on something. Okay?"

Alex put his hand on Michael's shoulder, leaning toward his son.

"You're not...you're not. Um. Michael, listen, I gotta ask - how do you feel about Satan?"

"What?"

"I mean, you're not one of those kids worshipping Satan, are you? There was a story in the *Journal*. It's apparently a thing."

"Dad," Michael said, suddenly smiling. "We're atheists, right? You and Mom and I talked about it. There is no God. That's what we all agreed. Remember?"

"I do. But – "

Michael waved him quiet.

"So no God. No Satan. They're kind of sold as a set, you know? Dad, I'm in the middle of something here. Okay?"

"Right. Sure. I'm still your favorite dad, right?"

"Absolutely. Maybe we can talk more tomorrow? Okay?"

"Okay then. See you tomorrow. And, you know, be careful with the knife."

"Yeah, I will. See you tomorrow."

Stepping into the hallway Alex turned back to look into his son's bedroom as Michael closed the door in his face, the lock clicking into place. Alex leaned forward, pressing his forehead against the door. The feel of the wood against his skull was comforting somehow. He held that pose a long time before padding back down the wide hall to his bedroom.

———

Michael stared at the door until he heard his father's footfalls moving off. He hated it when his dad got that "I'm worried about you..." look on his face. And now Satan worship! Michael was glad he hadn't laughed.

He had told Alex more than once that he wanted to make horror movies. He had a million story ideas. He had trouble getting them all sketched out. And when he sat in a darkened movie theater hearing Dawn Karston scream, he knew she would understand his vision. She was wasted in all that second-rate, high school slasher shit. He would make her a horror star people would remember. And if a romance developed, what was wrong with that? Directors dating their leading ladies was a Hollywood tradition, right?

A classified ad in *Fangoria*, the quarterly horror bible, promised to "locate your favorite stars." Michael had sent a check and received an address in Venice, California.

He'd been mailing his sketched story boards – the cinematic scenarios all leading to Dawn's demise - to the Venice address for a while, but had only gotten a response to his initial postcard. A signed copy of Dawn's headshot had arrived in an envelope with the Hollywood address of someone named Ben Hoffman.

Michael was excited about the Marat-Charlotte idea. Dawn would be perfect as Charlotte. But he knew you didn't get ahead in the movie business waiting for someone like Dawn Karston to respond. Stars were busy people. Distracted with lots of important matters.

Dawn was coming to Florida in two weeks to make a movie. That was his chance. He'd find her and convince her in person.

Just the thought of standing next to Dawn on the film set gave him a tingle he couldn't quite describe. The feeling didn't seem to be in his head or his chest. It was lower down. He liked it.

He walked over to the Dawn blow-up doll. Last summer, he had slipped $200 to a movie theater ticket-taker, who helped him sneak the doll outside and stuff it in the back of the family limo. Now Michael raised the knife, bringing it down repeatedly around the neck and shoulders of the screaming Dawn doll.

"Join me! Join me!" he shouted. "Join me!"

When he was satisfied with the scene, Michael set the butcher knife on his drawing table. Settling onto the tall stool, he pulled out the Mont Blanc fountain pen he had filled with blood-red ink and scrawled a single sentence on a sheet of parchment paper. After unpinning the Marat and Charlotte scenes from the wall, he carefully folded the story sheets and the note, slipping them into a manila envelope.

Standing at the west windows, Michael let his imagination slip through the glass, across the pool deck and over the seawall. An hour and change to the west, Florida's flat, palm-lined coast turned wet, lush and mysterious. Mosquitos teemed. Gators lurked. Battalions of birds rose in shuddering explosions of wings. Michael envisioned the Everglades as a giant film set, teeming with primordial beasts.

Dawn would be there soon. So would he.

Staring out into the gathering dusk, Michael raised the envelope to his mouth, moistening the glued flap with his outstretched tongue.

May God Bless You Too

—

A cluster of stoplights dangled at the corner of Quadrille and Dixie Highway in West Palm Beach, where four lanes braided together. A red Volkswagen Beetle was first in line, waiting to turn right. As the driver's window jerked down, a Black woman in her early 20s reached out, a dollar bill pinched in her fingers.

The white man who rolled up to the window in a wheelchair was reedy and regal, with a hawk's nose and a thick silver mane combed back from a wide forehead. A tiny American flag, taped to the back of his chair, flapped in the brisk breeze pushing in from the Intracoastal four blocks away. The woman couldn't tell from the man's tanned and deeply creased face if he was 60 or 80. He wore a white dress shirt and tie – both slightly frayed. He used his left hand to roll the chair forward; his right fist clutched a hand-lettered sheet of poster board: "*Shattered legs. Busted wallet. Can you help a WWII vet - now a writer - out of a rough spot? Thanks!*"

The woman snapped a mental image of the old man – watery blue eyes, explosive eyebrows, jutting jawline, a snatch of red-and-white plaid slacks peeking from beneath the thin blue blanket tossed over his useless legs.

As he pocketed the proffered bill, Cavanaugh Reilly smiled beatifically, showing off a fine set of teeth – save one missing incisor. He followed the smile with the *adieu* he offered to all his drive-by benefactors: "God bless you. And may God bless America."

The woman returned his smile, happy she'd helped out this

weary traveler.

"And may God bless you too, sir," she said.

———

A few blocks away, a squat gray Mercedes, looking more than a little like a spit-polished WWII tank, lurked on a side street, facing North Olive Avenue. Through the tinted windows it was possible to make out a man's head and shoulders in the driver's seat, and then, the figure of a woman slowly rising up in the passenger seat.

The driver was lean, with taut, unlined skin, his stomach flat beneath a Palm Beach Polo Club pullover, though the wrinkles around his eyes and hint of a flap just below his chin were evidence that the facelift was starting to sag. A veteran of these roadside rendezvous, he reached down casually and eased his zipper up. He watched as the woman slipped the pair of twenties he had set on the seat into a tiny gold purse. She was younger than he'd thought, and quite thin, her angular face framed by a cascade of thick black curls. She might have been pretty, but her features were drawn, her eyes bleary and bloodshot. Clearly, street corner sex work was extracting a toll.

The young woman smiled grimly, then leaned close to his ear, her fingers gripping his pale blue polyester golf slacks just above the knee. Looking down, he noticed her red nail polish was chipped, her nails bitten down.

"Could I ask you something?" She whispered.

Her English carried only a glimmer of an accent. Hispanic, he thought, likely Cuban. He hadn't noticed that earlier when they were negotiating a price. But that whole exchange had been settled without a lot of talk.

He always dreaded the after-part, when the girls wanted to have a conversation or ask for a loan or a lift somewhere.

"Sure," he said. "But I've got to get going in just a minute."

"This won't take long. I just want to ask — are you happy with your current income level? Would you be interested in earning two to three thousand dollars a month in your spare time?"

"What?" He laughed. "I gotta say, I'm pretty happy with my income level."

"Well, maybe you know somebody?" She passed him an embossed business card: *Lola Fernandez Famosa/American Dream Representative.*

"I'll keep you in mind," the man snapped, waving the card in her direction, hoping his terse tone made it clear the conversation was over.

After she got out, he watched Lola Fernandez Famosa, American Dream Representative, in the rear view mirror, teetering on gold high heels, tugging the hem of her clingy, black dress until it covered the tops of her thighs. She looked up at the traffic moving along Olive Avenue, then pulled a pack of cigarettes from her purse.

——

The sun had dropped deep into the western horizon when Cavanaugh Reilly, still in his wheelchair, rolled up to his ground-level room at the Blue Marlin motel, a paper grocery sack on his lap. At the door, whistling a jazzy version of *Georgia on My Mind*, he stood on two perfectly workable legs and did a quick soft-shoe. From his pants pocket, he pulled an oversized plastic fish with a room key attached.

His motel room was narrow and dark, lit by two windows that opened onto the parking lot. The ceiling, just six inches above Cavanaugh's head, regularly shed wafers of paint that gathered in the corners like fallen leaves. There was room for a double bed, a side table, and a roll-top desk by the front window – all long past their sell-by date. Along a back wall, next to the bathroom door, was the "kitchen," a single counter with a hot plate and a microwave, next to a wall-hung sink and a squat, dorm room refrigerator.

If he took three steps from the sink, Cavanaugh would bump into a small cocktail table, with room for just two chairs. The room's white walls, yellowed by years of cigarette smoke, were collaged with pinned-up covers from *Time* and *The New Yorker*, a half-dozen nude Playboy centerfolds, clipped images of Buddha, Gandhi, and Saint Francis of Assisi, and a large, gilt-framed portrait of Cavanaugh himself, 25 years younger, in a blue suit and tie, with the Georgia state flag and Old Glory hanging on separate golden flagstaffs in the background. In this professional portrait mailed with press releases during Cavanaugh's days as director of public relations for three different Georgia Secretaries of State, he looked like a smart and sober family man.

Fresh from a shower, Cavanaugh wrapped his pink, sagging skin in a frayed, emerald-green towel, his hair wet and combed back. His outfit for this special evening was laid carefully across the bed – blue blazer, white linen shirt, maroon ascot, and wrinkled white dress pants. Easing his hand under the mattress, Cavanaugh drew out a silver pocket watch and checked the time.

Moving quickly now, as the light outside his front window faded from gold to gray, he set a table for two – a tarnished silver creamer and sugar set, porcelain salt and pepper shakers, two chipped china plates and cloth napkins, one blue, one red. Snapping his chrome Zippo, Cavanaugh lit the two tapered candles rising from a tarnished silver candelabra.

Cavanaugh soft-shoed over to the whirring microwave, humming Cole Porter's *Night and Day*. Bending low, he stared through the smoked glass door where two Cornish game hens and two Idaho potatoes circled slowly. He stepped back, just as the power snapped off.

Carrying the birds and the potatoes to the table on a platter, Cavanaugh set them beside a bowl of salad and an open bottle of chardonnay.

Rubbing his palms together in anticipation, he danced to the window, pulling back the flimsy nylon curtain. After a few seconds of staring into the darkness, he let the curtain fall back into place, pulling the pocket watch from his pocket.

She was late.

———

At another dingy roadside motel just a couple of blocks from Cavanaugh's feast, Lola rapped on a metal door. She was still wearing the short black dress, but her hair had flattened and her lipstick was smeared. In her hand was a single-item brown bag.

Lola heard two clunks, as the dead bolts were turned. The door eased open a crack; a pointed nose, a pair of caterpillar eyebrows and a cleft chin appeared. After a few seconds, the door opened an inch more and she saw two charcoal eyes dance her way before ticking left and right, scanning the walkway and the empty parking lot.

"Dio, it's just me," Lola said.

The man who warily eased open the door was as thin and skittish as a greyhound. His skin was caramel-colored. Curly bristles of black hair sprouted from a receding jawline.

Stepping inside, Lola took in the tiny, but incredibly tidy room. She had been here plenty of times before, but was always struck by the formality of the furnishings and the overarching aroma of Lysol that hung in the air. Dio had covered his two tiny windows in flowered silk curtains. Hand-knitted doilies rested on the crest of a honey-colored leather club chair. More doilies clung to the arms of an antique couch, upholstered in chintz – large pink roses on green stems.

It seemed like the middle-class home of a white, Midwestern grandmother, not the cheap motel room of a swarthy Dominican drug dealer.

"Hey man, you're late," Dio told Lola, once the door was double-locked. "And you look like shit. Careful where you walk. I'm almost done."

A bucket of suds rested at his feet and Dio held a mop deftly, just inches off the floor, looking to Lola like a ballroom dancer waiting to swing his partner across the parquet.

"Sorry. Busy day," Lola mumbled, as if she hardly had strength left to talk. "Payday at the brewery. Dow up 50 points. That's always good for my business."

"Dow who? No, don't tell me. Just tell me you brought my stuff."

Lola nodded at him. His eyes kept dancing as he backed away, leaning the mop against the wall. Lola noticed his hands quivering a bit as she waved the bag in front of him.

"Dio, come on, have I ever let you down?"

Dio's bony arm jerked out, but Lola, suddenly excited about the transaction, stepped back, still swinging the bag.

"Come on!" Dio pleaded, his sandpaper voice rising like a tenor going for a high E. "I really gotta have it! I'm desperate here!"

"Where's mine?" Lola smiled slyly, drawing the bag back toward her chest.

Dio's house-cleaning outfit was a white karate Gi, cinched by a red belt, over a baggie pair of sand-colored, drawstring pants. Lola noticed the toenails of his bare feet were brushed with silver polish. After rustling around in the large pocket, he drew out two plastic baggies, each holding a chalky crumble of white powder.

Stepping forward, Dio waved the baggies in Lola's direction. She raised her paper bag, and in a halting, slow-motion *pas de deux*, they made the exchange.

Dio tore open Lola's bag, pulling out a dark bottle of some kind of cleaning product. He looked closely at the label.

"Toilet Magic," he whispered. "Very cool."

"That should handle the rust stain in your bathroom," Lola assured him. "But we really need to talk."

"You talk." Dio skittered toward a tiny cabinet next to his kitchenette sink. "I gotta get the scrub brush."

Lola watched as Dio, his knees on the wet floor, rummaged in the cabinet, tossing out sponges, rags and a bottle of Clorox.

"Right now, you buy retail," Lola said. "If you'd make an investment of say, two-twenty-five, I could bring you in as a level two and you'd get your product at half-price. Then, when you bring in another level two, a cash bonus comes to you from every sale."

"Are you saying...?" Dio swiveled, looking up toward Lola.

"I'm saying that for a small initial investment..."

"No! I heard you. What you're saying if I'm part of your crew, I get my shit wholesale and sell retail. And if I bring in another dude, I get a cut of his action. Right?"

"In a very basic way, yeah, that's how *American Dream* works."

"Damn girl." Dio was standing now, holding a blue plastic stalk that rose to a floret of white bristles. "Sounds a lot like my business."

He lifted the bottle of Toilet Magic up toward the tiny chandelier above his head, staring hard at the glowing, honey-colored liquid inside.

"You sure this shit ain't illegal?"

———

An hour later, Lola was stretched across the wide seawall on the west side of the Intracoastal, nodding a bit, a forgotten cigarette dangling in her fingers. She loved this spot at the eastern end of the Flagler Bridge. Lit by dozens of golden globes, the gently arching bridge always looked to Lola like the gateway to a magic kingdom. In a way, it was. Licking the last residue off her fingertips, Lola rubbed her fingers across the hem of her dress. She could taste the astringent remains of the powder deep in her throat.

Turning back to the water, she saw the lights of a dozen waterfront mansions glittered at her from across the churning bay. Lola snubbed out the cigarette, then held out her arms, her fingers extended and wiggling, in the direction of Palm Beach's twinkling stars.

———

Three hours after dinner was served, only one of the candle stubs still flickered. The wine bottle was empty. One dinner plate held bones and a few shards of potato skin. The other meal was untouched. Cavanaugh, his eyes at half-mast, sat over a full ashtray. The butt of one last cigarette, protruding from an ivory cigarette holder, threw off a lazy curlicue of gray smoke.

With his free hand, he reached out and wiggled two fingers around the flickering candle, feeling the heat. He looked once more at the door, then licked his index finger and thumb before pinching out the lone candle, leaving only the faint glow of the cigarette to light the room.

Jodie Foster Money

—

Majestic Tower, a 1930s Art Deco office building on Holly-wood Boulevard, had once been a classy Los Angeles address, all eight stories full of managers, agents, publicists and producers. But those tenants were long dead and the current building directory – a black, glass-covered rectangle marked with white, press-in letters - listed two private detectives, *Senora Novia's Tarot and Palm*; *Young and Hot Asian Massage*; *Hollywood Legal Aid*; *Tommy's 24-7 Bail Bonds*, and *Ben Hoffman, Talent Management and Consulting*.

Ben's office had a film-noir vibe, due mostly to the used furniture and slatted light seeping through the dirty Venetian blinds. The faded green shag, flattened by the footfalls of thousands of passing soles, resembled the surface of a particularly rank bog. On the walls were a dozen framed 8-by-10s of Ben posing with people who might have been almost famous in 1973. The poster of Dawn Karston from the upcoming *Slasher High* was mounted on a metal easel opposite the scarred wooden desk that the real Dawn Karston was pounding with her tiny fist.

"You gotta get me out of this!" Dawn shouted, her eyes red and ringed with tears.

"Dawn, sweetie, be calm and...breathe..." Ben whispered, remembering how his first wife, a yoga instructor named Trudy, had spoken to him when he was on a similar rampage.

"Ben!"

He tried to lean his desk chair back to put a few more inches between him and his angry client, but his chair was already at full tilt.

"You're not breathing," he said, in what he considered his best breathy, guru voice. "Come on. Try it. In...out...nice...and...easy."

"Dammit! Stop!"

With his tousled blonde hair and matching moustache, and the Hawaiian shirt he wore over a pair of faded Levis, Ben Hoffman looked more like an aging Laurel Canyon folk singer than a Hollywood talent manager, It might have been a good look for a thinner man, but Ben hadn't been thin since 1969, when the blotter acid he was swallowing most days, laced with speed, kept him wide awake, and very manic, but − on the plus side − seriously svelte.

Michael Donnelly's manila envelope was open on Ben's desk; spread out beside it was a creased sheet of paper the size of a medicine cabinet mirror, edge-to-edge with comic book style illustrations and word bubbles.

Dawn leaned over the desk, getting her face as close to her manager's mug as possible, given the width of the desk, Ben's backward angle in his chair and the fact that Dawn was only about an inch over five feet. She was often blond in her movies − slashers love blondes − but her real hair was thick and red, the perfect waves framing her pale, china doll face. For this visit with her manager, Dawn wore very tight jeans, a sweatshirt pulled off one shoulder, platform heels covered in silver glitter, and enough makeup to do a TV special if one came up unexpectedly.

"There's no way I'm going to the fucking Everglades to do this movie!"

Ben refused to acknowledge such an absurd statement. His clients did not turn down jobs. He had already cashed the deposit check from the producer of *Swamp Fiend II*. It would be at least two more months before he had to worry about the repo men coming for his Bahama Blue Beetle convertible. He started to OOOOHHHHHMMMM, the way Trudy used to, when the drugs and his 15-hour-a-day gig painting film sets had him spinning out of control.

"Come on...OOOOOHHHHHMMMMM. Now breathe."

"I'm fucking breathing. Okay?" Dawn slapped the envelope on his desk. "And I'd like to keep breathing. You gotta get me out of this."

"We have a signed contract. They sent a plane ticket and a deposit. There are things I can get you out of. But not this."

Dawn collapsed into the white plastic lawn chair that Ben provided for guests and clients. She wiped her eyes and gathered herself.

"Ben, please?"

She sniffed, her voice suddenly gentle and shaking slightly, as she tapped into a particularly touching moment from her last Meisner class.

"I'm really at the end of the rope here," she said, tears puddling in her eyes. "I need you on my side. OK?"

"Dawn, kiddo, I'm sorry, but you are doing this picture."

She dropped the vulnerable bit and sprang up again, grabbing the paper.

"This is un-fucking-believable." She pushed the sheet in front of Ben, stabbing at it with her index finger. "Did you see his latest?"

"Yeah, I agree. Un-fucking-believable."

Ben scanned the heavy paper, bringing it up close to his face so he wouldn't need his reading glasses.

"I mean, the fucking French Revolution. Nobody would make that movie. Nobody would watch that movie."

"This freak wants to kill me."

"Come on, now," Ben said, lowering the paper and rising with more than a little effort from his chair. "We don't actually know that. He could just be a misguided fan."

"HE WANTS TO KILL ME!" Dawn was shouting, her fists hammering down.

Ben ignored the pounding, focusing instead on the constellation of adorable peach colored freckles on the back of Dawn's hands.

"Dawn, kid, sit down."

Dawn crumpled into the seat as Ben eased himself back into his office chair, clutching the edge of his desk for balance.

"Look, Gary checked him out. He's a 17-year-old rich kid living in Palm Beach. Dad's company's got a silo full of military contracts. Mom slashed her wrists last year. Apparently the kid sees himself as a budding horror film director. But Gary says he's harmless."

"This is your definition of harmless? Look at this!"

She jumped up again, her hand disappearing inside the manila envelope. She pulled out a sheet of notebook paper and waved it in Ben's face, her index finger jabbing at the blood red scrawl: THIS IS HOW YOU SHOULD REALLY DIE!

"And my personal manager is sending me to a film set right in this psycho's backyard."

"Okay, technically, the set is 74.5 miles from Palm Beach," Ben said, his voice soft and reassuring. "In a giant fucking Florida swamp with no address and plenty of security. He won't find you."

"He found my home address."

"Dawn, I told you, I'm on it. I got Gary talking to the dad's lawyer today. We'll handle it. But you gotta make this movie."

"Is that what Jodie Foster's manager would tell her?"

"When you start making Jodie Foster money I'll tell you anything you want to hear. Until then, you get a job, you do the job. Let me worry about this kid. Look, I'm in your corner. If you die, I lose my favorite client. I can't make my alimony payments or pay my bar tab. Now *that* scares me."

"Not funny, Ben."

Dawn brushed back her tears.

Ben stood again, his voice soothing, his arms outstretched, rising and falling – palms up – as he whispered, "Breathe. Breathe."

Instead, Dawn slumped deeper into the chair and sobbed, real tears this time, her nose running, her makeup smudging, her porcelain face flushed. Ben almost felt sorry for her. His young client was no longer a budding B-movie starlet. She was a scared teenager.

Ben stepped slowly around the desk, his knee throbbing from the motorcycle accident twenty years earlier, when he chased the acid with Seconal and decided to see how fast he could get to Vegas. He took Dawn by the shoulders and brought her to her feet. Gently, he wrapped her in a fatherly hug. He actually patted her shoulder.

"Trust your Uncle Benny. Okay?"

———

The offices of the CEO and the COO at Donnelly Avionics were connected by a mahogany interior door so the two executives could meet without passing the secretaries or using the executive hallway. Dick Adams had slipped into his partner's office a minute earlier, still wearing his suit jacket at noon and carrying a single sheet of paper. He hadn't knocked.

He found the company CEO alone at his desk, working his way through a tuna fish sandwich, with a copy of *People* open to a story about the zoo and carnival rides at Michael Jackson's Neverland Ranch.

Alex didn't notice his business partner standing on the other side of his desk until Dick cleared his throat.

"Oh, hey, Dick. What's up?" Alex glanced up briefly, returning quickly to the magazine. "Can you believe this? Jackson's got a theme park and a zoo at his place. It's like he's having the childhood he never had."

Dick didn't answer. Instead he slapped down a Xeroxed copy of the storyboard sheet Michael had mailed to Dawn Karston.

"Have you spoken to Michael about this?"

"We aren't talking a lot at the moment," Alex said, looking at the paper, then up at Dick. "I mean, I'm talking, but he's not really answering. You know, he's just 17. And he really hasn't processed his mother's...you know...ah...incident."

"'I'm sure he hasn't. Who could?" Dick settled into a teak office chair across the desk from Alex. "You know I like Michael, but this thing is beyond critical."

"What do you mean?" Alex tried to sound oblivious, though he knew sending a young movie actress a hand-written note in blood-red ink saying THIS IS HOW YOU SHOULD REALLY DIE! was clearly a problem.

"Look, I'm afraid it's too late for a simple father-son huddle," Dick said. "Shooting starts tomorrow out in the Everglades. There's an L.A. lawyer rattling a sharp sword. We've got seven-figure exposure here. The kid does something stupid and they come after us and the business."

"Come on, what's he really done? Send a girl some comics? He isn't a violent kid," Alex said, trying to erase the image of Michael standing in the doorway with the butcher knife. "He wants to direct movies. I've got him brochures from USC and UCLA."

Dick waved away Alex's comments. "This note, sent via the U.S. mail, qualifies as a threat on her life. That's a felony. And they've got dozens of other notes, all just as incriminating. Even if they don't sue, the kid could be arrested. And the headlines – after the Hinckley thing – you'd be famous and not in a good way."

"So. What do we do?"

"I've got a plan."

Alex knew something bad was coming. Dick had always done the hard stuff at Donnelly Avionics. While his dad had been in D.C., wooing generals and politicians, Dick had developed this remote, high-security complex two miles west of I-95. He made sure Donnelly Avionics jumped through all the hoops required of companies with multimillion-dollar government contracts. Alex was officially the CEO since his father's death, but his biggest business decisions had been selecting the décor for his office – a Flying V Strat once played by Jimi Hendrix and the Hofner violin bass that Paul McCartney played at the Hey Jude rooftop concert, along with framed posters from Fillmore East and West, advertising psychedelic shows by Moby Grape and Country Joe and the Fish.

"Dick, he's a kid," Alex said, trying to sound fatherly and wise. "Come on..."

"He's a kid who is going to spend the next three weeks in

the comfy confines of Palmdale Haven." Dick pulled a pamphlet from his inside jacket pocket and read from it: "Palmdale Haven, a safe and supportive therapeutic community for all ages."

"What are you saying?"

"It will be like a vacation. Until this Dawn Karston girl is back in L.A."

"Jesus. I can't do this to him. You put somebody in an institution like that and it follows them the rest of their lives."

"There's nothing official about this stay. It's just a few weeks of live-in counseling. A vacation with therapists and no access to cars or the U.S. Mail."

"And if I say no?"

"Too late for that," Dick said, giving Alex his "trust me on this" look. "Think of it like this – you're protecting his inheritance, his future. He'll appreciate it later."

Alex knew fighting with Dick, even about his own son, was a losing game. And Michael might actually benefit from a few weeks of counseling. He really hadn't been the same kid since he walked into that bathroom six months before and found his mother dead in the tub, the butcher knife she used to slit her wrists sunk in a pool of blood on the floor.

"So what will happen?"

"Don't worry about it. It's handled," Dick told him. "Just make sure he's home tomorrow morning at nine."

———

Alex Donnelly was home when the phone rang that evening. But he was in the music room adding his own guitar licks to a live recording of Derek and the Dominos' *Bell Bottom Blues.*

The volume of the Fender twin-reverb was at 8 and he didn't hear the ringing or notice the blinking red light on the wall phone.

Instead, it was Michael who picked up.

"Mr. Donnelly?"

It was a female voice.

"Who's calling?" Michael asked, holding the kitchen phone with one hand and spooning some chicken potpie – left by the family's cook – onto a china plate.

"Hi. This is Helen, from Palmdale Haven. This is just a reminder that we'll be picking up, uh, Michael, tomorrow at 9 a.m.," she said, sounding like she was reading from a schedule. "You'll make sure he's home, right?"

Michael lowered his voice.

"Absolutely. He'll be home. And thank you so much for calling."

Michael left the potpie on the kitchen table. He slipped through the dining room, then the sitting room, and around the corner. He pressed his ear to the door of the music room and heard his father singing along with Eric Clapton: "It's *all wrong, but it's alright.*" He sprinted back to the two-story entry foyer, running up the wide stairs to his parents' room. He didn't linger in the pale blue bedroom and made certain not to look toward his Mom's bathroom. Instead, he went directly to the cavernous walk-in closet. His father's clothes were hung in rows, above and around built-in chests of drawers made of teak.

He knew Alex's soft leather wallet was in the top drawer. He also knew Alex always kept at least $1,000 in cash. Michael extracted all the cash, along with a shiny gold American Express card. He had been pilfering small amounts of his father's cash for months, in anticipation of Dawn's arrival in Florida, but he figured he needed all the financial oomph he could muster since he was now going on the run.

He slipped out of his father's room, but not before looking both ways down the wide halls to make sure Alex wasn't around. He ran past the five other bedroom doors that separated his room from his father's.

The time had come and there was much to do.

Again, I Hate This Plan

—

Crystal knew her last manic episode had been a bad one.

Alex and his business partner had gotten wind of her plan at the very last minute, interrupting the closing before Crystal had officially agreed to spend $2 million on an abandoned warehouse on Race Track Road.

The plan had seemed so logical at the time: Buy the warehouse, spend another $2 million or so to transform it into a working film studio so Michael could make the movies he was so excited about.

It would be a gift to him on his 18th birthday. A gift that would have taken most of the money her parents had left her, but she HAD to do it. It was for Michael.

Afterwards, Alex had insisted on a new doctor. And the young psychiatrist, fresh out of her residency at Duke, had been hopeful.

"We're going to try this new medication," she told Crystal and Alex. "I've seen some real successes with it. I think we can help you level things out."

Crystal was at the bottom of the cycle then. She didn't really hear what the doctor said. She had taken pills since she was a teenager that were supposed to keep her off the emotional roller coaster. But none of them worked for long. She knew the ride by heart: the slow, relentless climb to the heights; the hurtling crash to the depths. This new prescription was just another in a long line of tiny plastic bottles with her name on the front.

But it wasn't. This time the peak had been higher, the air thinner. And when the cascading thrill ride bottomed out, she found herself in a sulfurous valley of guilt and loathing, the path out obscured by a foul mist.

What did it matter anyway? She was 42. Old. Used up. Her son was 17 now and didn't really need her anymore. Staring into her bathroom mirror, her blunt-cut blonde hair tied back with a white ribbon, Crystal counted every wrinkle around her eyes. Spreading her mouth into a scary, Joker-like grin, she thought her skin looked like cellophane as it stretched across her cheekbones.

God, she thought, even my ears are ugly.

When she couldn't stand to look at herself any longer, she closed her eyes, but all she could see was her naked body on the day bed of the pool house, her back arched, screaming obscenities at the man laid out beneath her. Goddammit! Randy Stewart was an asshole and a low-rent lothario. She had always laughed in his face when he tried to flirt. But she was at the top of the ride that morning and all by herself. Michael, trying to avoid his Mom's mania, had gone to the movies in the limo. Alex had left early for the office, taking all the other car keys with him, leaving Crystal to pace the house like a restless prisoner. She hoped a swim would focus her racing thoughts, but before she could dive in, she saw Randy kneeling on the red clay court, restringing a loose section of the netting, his legs and arms muscled and tanned, a days growth of beard on his cleft chin. Some overpowering hunger had gripped her. She dove in and stroked to the bottom of the pool, the pressure a single ringing note in her ears. She kicked hard to the surface, suddenly desperate to reach the silver pool ladder and get to the man on the tennis court. Still soaking wet, she literally pulled Randy through the French doors of the pool house, pushing him down on the day bed, and threw herself on top of him. She caught herself before she sank her teeth into his neck.

Crystal had done a lot of things to make Alex miserable during their marriage, but she'd never cheated on him. What had possessed her? Forty-eight sleepless hours and ten hot baths couldn't remove the smell of Randy. No amount of Valium could blot out the image of the two of them rutting like farm animals.

She'd gone too far this time. And there was no way to walk it back.

When she opened her eyes the solution was right there, a message so clear it could have been written in red lipstick on the mirror.

Seeing the way forward had calmed her. She took a day to prepare. Made sure everything was just right.

The next day she settled Michael in front of a movie, taping a sealed note to his bedroom door. Moments later, Crystal was chest deep in the steaming bath, pulling a black-handled butcher knife from a tie-dyed kitchen towel. She pressed her pink enameled toes against the window at the end of the tub and settled deeper into the hot water. The knife seemed to move on its own, making deep, vertical slices while Crystal stared out at the family pool and beyond that, to the Intracoastal, white-capped by a stiff breeze and decorated with a dozen tilting sailboats.

This bathroom was her favorite spot in the big house. Italian tile, hand-painted with pastel wildflowers covered the walls and floor. She grew up in this house the only child of a Great Lakes shipping magnate and his second wife, a striking Russian émigré who claimed a royal pedigree with only the flimsiest of evidence. Her parents had died together in a helicopter crash outside Aspen while fifteen-year-old Crystal was spending a month at a place called Palmdale Haven.

Her parents had indulged their troubled daughter, but her mother had been adamant about one thing — it was important to be thoughtful when dealing with the help. So the tub was where the deed would be done. The blood — Crystal knew there would be lots of blood — would wash easily down the drain. Annabella, the day maid, could wipe away the rest of the mess with a wet sponge.

———

If he'd been more awake, Randy Stewart might have seen the irony of the situation. Barely six months had passed since his afternoon with Crystal, and he was again a reluctant participant in a Donnelly family misadventure.

Randy's tiny truck was idling on the cul-de-sac at 7 a.m., hidden from view of the Donnelly house by a leafy, nine-foot hedge. The van from Palmdale Haven was due in two hours. He heard the iron gates tick apart and watched Michael emerge carrying a backpack, a small suitcase, and the zippered leather satchel that held the binders and pens the boy used to create his story boards.

"Again, I hate this plan," Randy said, as Michael approached his car window.

"You're backing out?"

"I said I hated it. I didn't say I wasn't doing it. I'm here, right?"

The news of Crystal's death had come as a kind of relief for Randy. He hadn't planned to sleep with his best friend's wife, but hell, she's the one who came on to him. Okay, maybe he'd encouraged it a few times, but it was Crystal who pressed her lips to his, then pulled off her bikini and pushed him down on the day bed.

She was so lithe! So blonde! So naked! What was a guy to do?

Two days later, when the secretary at the tennis school handed him a PLEASE CALL ME message from Alex, Randy was sure Crystal had confessed. But when he finally summoned the courage to call, Alex was distraught, telling his best friend that Crystal was dead.

"What happened?"

"God, Randy. She's gone. I mean, she had talked about it plenty. But this time, she actually did it. Please. Please! Can you come over?"

At the funeral, Randy mentioned he was looking for a place to live – he didn't say that his girlfriend had booted him out after discovering many of his "private lessons" didn't involve tennis. A tearful Alex begged him to move into the pool house – "for as long as you like. Michael and I can use the company right now."

Randy was grateful for the posh living arrangements and that Crystal had taken their secret to her grave. But Randy was still

Randy. Within a few days, he was again naked on the day bed, this time with the teenage daughter of one of the maids, and later, with the young wife of the Mexican gardener who lived with her husband in two rooms over the garage.

Alex was oblivious, but Michael had recorded Randy's liaisons on his Pentax. He had originally been interested in the images cinematically. He hadn't realized the black and white prints would be useful for another purpose. A few hours after intercepting the call from Palmdale Haven, Michael had knocked on Randy's door.

"I don't think my dad would be too happy if he saw these," he said, fanning out the pictures in his hands.

Randy looked at the images a long time, a hint of a smile on his lips. He looked good in the pictures, he thought. Still in shape.

"I'm guessing you want something. Do I need to move out?"

"No. Stay as long as you like. I think it's good for my dad. But I need you to drive me somewhere tomorrow in your truck."

Eight hours later, Michael was standing outside the window of Randy's small white pickup.

"So, where am I taking you?"

Michael hadn't worked out that part of the plan in advance. Before he intercepted the Palmdale Haven call he had planned to leave his house for the Everglades in a hired car, not sneak away before a van arrived to carry him to the nut house.

"I was thinking about the Hilton on Okeechobee," said Michael, remembering the Hilton as one of the few decent hotels on the west side of the bridge around downtown. "I need to stay somewhere a few days while I put things together."

"I'll take you there, but that's the first place they'll look for you," Randy said. "As someone who's had to disappear before, I suggest maybe going someplace...ah...well...a little more below the radar."

Michael remembered the old motels around *Horror Time Video*.

"Drive to that video store on Dixie. I think I know a place."

Michael climbed into the truck bed with his luggage, stretching out flat as a corpse for the ride across the Flagler Bridge into West Palm Beach.

—

At exactly 8:55 a.m., the gate intercom buzzed and Alex, looking down from the upstairs window, pressed the button on the remote.

The iron gates slowly parted at the center, allowing a cream-colored van with *Palmdale Haven* stenciled on the doors to ease up the curving driveway.

Sammi Washington, the woman behind the wheel, was a veteran of these Palm Beach pickups. Her partner, Sheila Sims, still a relative newcomer to the job, was in the passenger seat.

After eight years at Palmdale, Sammi was convinced every one of the families living on this fabled island had a crazy relative or two hidden away somewhere. It was kids, mostly, suffering from too much privilege, too much neglect, or something worse. Some days it was a bipolar aunt, a schizophrenic brother, or a grandmother diving deep into dementia. Sammi and Sheila had been dispatched the day before to gather up a 71-year-old society matron who had come downstairs for cocktails without her clothes, spewing graphic curses at her daughter and son-in-law. Sammi found the famous hostess the next day on a lounge chair in her nightgown, chatting with her dead husband and casually tossing cucumber canapes into the pool.

At Palmdale Haven, or as her bosses called it, "The Facility," patients were medicated and generally docile. But the pickups could be ugly and violent. Very few of her clients went into the van willingly. She got the job because at 6'2" and 285 pounds, Sammi was prepared for just about anything. A karate black-belt and a competitive power-lifter, her thighs could pass for the columns supporting some Palm Beach porches.

Despite her size, Sammi was gentle in her private life. At home she favored flowing caftans and gilded slippers and she wore her Afro like a dark halo. But at work she pulled her hair back in tight cornrows and pasted on her "I can beat the shit out of you" face.

Sammi had met Sheila at the old boxing gym in Riviera Beach, where Teddy, the slightly punch-drunk owner, paired them for a sparring match. Turns out the women had more in common than just being in the same weight class. A week after that bout, Sammi and Sheila were living together. Two months later they were adorning new Egyptian cotton sheets with an "S&S" monogram. At three months, Sammi convinced her bosses at Palmdale that she needed a second for these dangerous pickup runs.

From above, Alex watched what looked like two female bodybuilders, one black and one white, emerging from the van in cream-colored polo shirts and khaki pants, both outfits about to burst at the seams. They marched, shoulder to shoulder, toward the front door.

Jeez, they sent the lesbian goon squad, Alex thought. What had Dick told them about Michael? But it was too late to turn back. He opened the front door and offered a nervous smile.

"I guess I know what you're here for."

"His name is Michael, right?" It was Sammi, in her quiet, all-business voice, looking down at a small notebook she'd pulled from her back pocket. "Michael Donnelly, 17. Possibly homicidal. Will we need any restraints?"

Alex stepped outside and closed the door behind him.

"Hey, look, I don't know what they told you, but my son is a quiet kid. He's not, you know, crazy like that. He's just...well... he's got a few minor issues but he's basically a good kid."

"I can't tell you how many good kids have pulled a carving knife or a razor on me in houses just like this." Sammi didn't raise her voice. She had been in the business long enough to know you stayed calm until the circumstances called for another course of action.

Sheila smiled at Alex, showing off a perfect set of teeth. She reached out, pressing five granite fingers into the fleshy part of his arm, just below the shoulder. "If he's gentle, we'll be gentle.

No need to worry at this point. OK?"

Alex nodded. Nothing to do now but go through with it, he thought.

"And he's where right now?" Sammi asked.

"He's still asleep. Just upstairs."

Alex opened the door and led them up the stairs to Michael's bedroom. He started to knock, but Sammi caught his hand and pulled him away from the door

"Look, let us take it from here. It's really better if you're not directly involved at this point." As he looked up at her, Alex noticed that unlike her body, Sammi's features were soft, almost girlish, her coffee-colored skin glowing in the hallway light.

Sammi turned the knob slowly and eased open the door. She and Sheila looked across the room to the large bed, lit by a few seams of sunlight that had pushed through the break in the thick curtains. The boy was there, wrapped in a mass of blankets and pillows.

She looked back at Alex.

"He likes to sleep late," Alex whispered.

Sammi and Sheila crossed the room. It was too dark to make out the movie posters or the storyboard sheets pinned to the walls. Watching from the doorway, Alex thought the women looked like two marble statues towering over his sleeping son.

"Michael?" Sheila spoke gently. "Sorry to bother you but it's time to wake up."

Michael didn't move. The partners looked at each other, then Sheila reached down and lifted the edge of the blanket, slowly pulling it back, as Sammi flicked on a small flashlight. Under the covers the Dawn Karston punching bag stared up at them.

"I'm thinking this isn't the person we're supposed to pick up?" Sammi had turned back to Alex. He could see she was trying to suppress a laugh.

Alex walked over. He had been worried about this morning and how Michael would react. But now he was mad. He didn't know how he was going to explain this to Dick. His son had always seemed oblivious about what was happening around him, but maybe he *was* up to something sinister.

"DAMMIT! MICHAEL!" Alex shouted at the plastic doll nestled in the covers where his son should have been.

His right fist rose over his head and came down hard into the soft middle of the doll's cartoon cheerleader outfit, just above the place where the skirt appeared to flair out in pleats. Alex gasped and Sammi and Sheila leapt backwards as the blow-up Dawn emitted a metallic but still very piercing SCREAM!

Be Fruitful
And Multiply

—

The motel's neon sign was operational, mostly, beckoning drivers along U.S. 1 with a glowing trophy fish with a long, pointed snout, a ridged fin on its back, and a crescent moon tail-fin lit in aqua blue. The fish still leapt from arcs of green neon surf, but the M had been dark for years, renaming the place "The Blue 'Arlin."

The Pakistani woman who sat behind a glass window in the office hadn't looked up at Michael as she took his money and slid a key, clipped to a large plastic fish, through a slit under the window.

"No guests. No pets. Checkout at 11," she told him, as her eyes focused on counting the bills he had passed her. "You stay. You pay. Yes?"

"Yes," Michael said.

The second story roof of the Blue 'Arlin was covered in barrel-tiles, though tiles were missing in some spots, exposing the tarpaper underneath, giving the roof the appearance of a chessboard done in clay and black. A vacation spot for families a few decades earlier, the motel's exterior was faded to dull gray, the chipped concrete balconies overlooking outcrops of steaming asphalt, gouged and cracked like last century's lava.

Michael's room was on the ground floor. He was struggling to get the large fish key holder out of his pocket, when the door of the room next to his swung open and a deep and resonant voice called out: "Pardon me, but would you have any Scotch tape handy?"

Michael looked over as a tall man emerged, his hair gray and flowing back from his forehead, his eyes set deep above a hawk's nose. He could have been an aging film star, except for the outfit – a blue terry cloth robe, pocked with cigarette burns, that fell just below the knee, revealing bone-thin calves and plus-sized feet stuffed into what appeared to be a pair of fuzzy green caterpillars.

The man was holding a pack of cigarettes in one hand and a thick roll of gray masking tape in the other. He waved the tape at Michael. "This really won't do. Too concealing."

"What are you trying to do?"

The man smiled, showing off some marvelous molars, marred only by a single missing incisor.

"Planting bait, my boy. Planting bait. And what's the good of bait if your prey can't see it? *Comprende*?"

"I don't have any Scotch tape," Michael said.

"Ah, well. We'll make do then. Can you give me a hand?" He pressed the pack of Marlboro 100s about mid-way up the wide window of his room. "If you could just hold this right here."

Michael hesitated. The man turned and stared.

"Now! If you don't mind."

Michael set his backpack down next to his suitcase and stepped over to the window. He held the cigarette pack with two fingers, leaving room for the man to apply the narrow strips of masking tape he had cut with his teeth.

Michael eased his fingers off once the tape was in place. The man stepped back to admire the job.

"There. That will have to do for now."

"Why are you putting cigarettes on the window?"

"When you want to lure a woman, my boy, you have to figure out what they really crave. Jewels. Flowers. Food. Sex. Among other things, Lola really craves Marlboro 100s. I put a pack in the window and she knows I still love her and all is forgiven."

"Is Lola your wife?" Michael asked.

"I'm talking about love here, not indentured servitude. Lola and I are real lovers. What we have is passionate and volatile.

D.H. Lawrence love. Madame Bovary love. Epic. Heartbreaking. Face-down-dead-in-the-snow love. Sexy and tragic. The way God intended love to be."

"Oh..." Michael wasn't sure what the proper response should be.

"Have you ever been in love?"

"No. Maybe...I mean, I think so." The image of Dawn coming out of the shower in *Sorority House Slasher* flashed in his mind.

"And what's her name?" The man asked, setting the tape down on the windowsill and pulling a cigarette out of his own pack.

"Dawn," Michael said.

"Lovely moniker. And what does she crave?"

Images of Dawn taking her final, bloody bow in a dozen cheap slasher flicks ran like a highlight reel across the movie screen in Michael's mind.

"Death, I think. She seems to really love death."

The man smiled and lit the cigarette with a chrome Zippo. He inhaled and let the words flow out with the smoke. "Ah... swooning and sickbeds. Dark night of the soul stuff. The orgasm is a little glimpse of death, don't you think? That magical moment when we come unshackled from the tentacles of this mundane life and soar –"

He looked at Michael. "Am I right?"

"Sure," Michael said, though he was far from sure.

"Is she good in bed?"

"What?"

"Dawn. How is she in the sack?"

Michael found himself wishing Randy was still around. He'd know what to say.

"I don't really – "

The man cut him off.

"Ah, unrequited love. Almost the best kind, but hard on the sheets. A man alone must take matters into his own hands as they say. So, staying long?"

"Just a day or so," Michael said, happy to move on to other

topics. "I'm heading out to meet her. Just working out the details."

"Ah, just give me a minute." The man disappeared into his room. A few seconds later, he was back. "If you indeed snare your lady love, you'll need a few of these."

He flicked a small foil packet in Michael's direction. Michael tried to catch the spinning UFO but missed. When he bent to pick it up he could see the packet had a brand name – *Trojan*. Michael looked closely, turning it in his hand.

"That part in the Bible – be fruitful and multiply – it's an advertising slogan for a product you can never return. You can't get your money back and there's no allowance for buyer's remorse. Listen carefully now. That thin plastic membrane is all that stands between you and a life sentence without parole. The name is Reilly. Cavanaugh Reilly. You free later for dinner?"

———

Harvey's, a legendary West Palm Beach steak house, had survived after the downtown around it had emptied out in the '60s and '70s.

The red brick edifice had opened as a bank during the boom days in the 1920s, but the place had been a steakhouse as long as anyone in West Palm Beach could remember. The tall windows glowed with golden light and the Tiffany-glass double doors stood 12 feet high, crowned with red neon that spelled out: HARVEY'S. A cadre of valets was busy out front.

Michael and Cavanaugh were on foot, headed toward the fast food joints just south of downtown, when Cavanaugh paused outside Harvey's and sniffed the air.

"Ah, the wonders of aged, marbled beef. The joys of garlic butter and the cheesy crunch of French onion soup. I do miss a good steak house. But one must be practical here so close to the end of the month. I get a check from my Uncle Sugar, but it's paltry, compared to the time I gave him. "

Michael stared vacantly. He enjoyed listening to this man,

but didn't always understand what he was saying.

"W-W-2? The big war?" he asked, as if Michael had never taken a history class. "Four years of service, six months in a POW camp, and another 25 years of paying tribute to the gods of So-Called Security. And he barely offers enough to keep me in cheap whiskey and low-rent rooms. How are you fixed for cabbage?"

"Cabbage?"

"Greenbacks. Moola. George Washingtons. Cash. You got any?"

Michael eased the pack off his back and pulled a thick roll of green from the front pocket. "I got this. And this." He put the cash back and came out with a shiny gold American Express card.

Cavanaugh beamed, his palms covering his heart.

"Well. Well. Well. This is what I call a beautiful day in the neighborhood."

———

Pushing through Harvey's tall front doors, Cavanaugh and Michael were greeted by a stiff-upper-lipped *maître d'* who quickly stepped around the reception desk to block their path.

David Carson's father had made his living clinging to the strap on a city garbage truck. But David had won a scholarship to the Florida A&M, leaving behind Riviera Beach and the chance to follow his father into the waste collection industry. He was tall and slender, looking like an aging groom in his black tuxedo, adorned with a lilac boutonniere. His salt and pepper hair was slicked back with a fragrant oil. He liked to smell his hands after applying it, the sense memory conjuring up the gardenia bushes in bloom beside his grandmother's front porch.

"I'm afraid we have nothing available just now." David said, stepping forward slowly, which forced the motley pair back, without his having to touch the old man in the shabby sports jacket and plaid pants, or the teenager in jeans and a hooded sweatshirt.

"Perhaps you could try down the street. I believe there is a Denny's," he intoned.

"Oh, but my friend has a reservation," Cavanaugh assured him. "Michael, show him your reservation."

Michael pulled the gold card from his pack and waved it slowly.

"Gold," Cavanaugh said. "The best color for a card, don't you think?"

He leaned close to the *maître d'*.

"Look, this isn't any kid," he whispered conspiratorially, nodding in Michael's direction. "Eccentric young millionaire. Palm Beach. Computers. I'm sure a man in your position is familiar with Reaganomics – the trickle-down theory? Well, this boy is soaking wet. *Comprende?*"

Cavanaugh snapped his fingers and opened his palm in Michael's direction. Michael pulled a fifty from the roll of bills and passed it over. Cavanaugh slipped it into David's front jacket pocket. David nodded solemnly. He'd seen his share of ragged refugees from Palm Beach in his day. They always looked awful, but their money was good.

He led Cavanaugh and Michael to an empty table well out of sight of the main dining room. After placing two menus in front of them, he bowed and backed away.

It's Been Done To Death

—

Michael's disappearance had forced Alex to cancel that night's recording session. He had planned to put a few of his new tunes onto the Marantz reel-to-reel recorder, but there was more important business to be done tonight.

At 7 p.m., when the doorbell chimed, he and Randy were sitting across the long dining room table, working on club sandwiches the cook had left in the refrigerator.

"Randy," Alex said, his mouth full of turkey, bacon and rye. "You mind?"

Randy returned a minute later along with a stocky man in a powder blue leisure suit that had fit him about 25 pounds ago. His meaty hand held a scarred briefcase that was probably new in 1971.

Alex set down his sandwich and pushed up from the table.

"You gotta be Jamie. Right?"

"It's Jaime," the man said, "Like there's an H in it."

"Like Hi-Me?" Alex asked.

"That'll do," the big man said. "Jaime Solano. Solano Investigations."

"Randy said you're the best in town." Alex nodded at Randy, who was back at the table picking up his sandwich. "And my business partner checked you out and he agrees. You're the best."

"I don't know that I'm the best, but I did find *him* once," Jaime said, nodding toward Randy. "Wasn't that hard actually."

"I'm not that good at keeping a low profile," Randy said, before taking a large bite of his sandwich.

"Look, we're kind of in a crisis situation. Did Randy fill you in?"

Jaime nodded. He was a solemn man, balding, his skin somehow dark and pasty at the same time, likely from spending too much time working nights on the cheating spouses beat.

"I'm gonna need a picture," Jaime said.

Alex lifted a manila envelope from the table and held it out.

"It's all here. And the retainer. In cash."

Alex didn't get up but waved the envelope in Jaime's direction.

Jaime had seen this all before. The rich client establishing power over the hired help. After waiting for the brief moment he felt let him keep some shred of dignity, he slowly walked over to the table and took the envelope.

"What's he doing for money?" Jaime asked.

"Who?"

"Your son."

"I'm not sure. He gets a small allowance," Alex said.

"Credit cards?"

Alex stood, pulling his wallet from his back pocket. He opened it and looked at the empty cash compartment, before quickly thumbing through the credit cards slot.

"Shit!" Alex announced. "About $2,000 in cash and my gold card. I'll cancel it."

"Please don't cancel it. Gives us a way to track him," Jaime said. "Now what about this movie star. Got a picture?"

Alex pointed to a corner of the kitchen, next to the pantry, where the Dawn Karston blowup doll was slowly losing air.

"That's her. Take her with you. And, detective..."

Jaime picked up the doll with one arm, pulling it to his side. He turned back to Alex with a weary look.

"We're worried he might do something," Alex said. "Something extreme. Whatever you have to do, find him and get him into that treatment facility. I will make it worth your while."

"I find people. It's what I do," the detective said. "I'll find your kid."

Moments later, with the doll pressed sideways against his waist, Jaime walked down the driveway, ignoring the tropical plants and palms on display on both sides. The wrought iron gate opened with a low hum as he approached.

A beat-up Pinto was parked along the cul-de-sac outside. Jaime stuffed the Dawn doll the into the passenger side, then wrapped it with the seat belt. He lumbered around and, with more than a little difficulty, maneuvered himself into the driver's seat.

———

Dinner was long finished but Cavanaugh and Michael were in no hurry to leave the clubby confines of Harvey's Steak House. Cavanaugh had encouraged Michael to sip from his 1975 French Bordeaux, and now the room had a warm, almost golden glow. The meal had been epic – shrimp cocktail and truffled eggs, followed by Caesar salads made tableside, two Maine lobsters and two aged T-bones, twice-baked potatoes, spinach soufflé.

The restaurant was almost empty. A tuxedoed waiter looked over at his last table, hoping for a request for the check.

Michael ordered key lime pie, but Cavanaugh skipped dessert, preferring Grand Marnier in an oval snifter, his cigarette burning rakishly in an ivory cigarette holder. A pair of battered reading glasses rested on his nose so he could scan a series of cartoon panels on a large sheet of story-board paper.

Michael looked up from his key lime pie, anxious for a reaction from Cavanaugh.

FOREST BLADE
Draft 1

DAWN, TERRIFIED, FLEES DOWN
A FOREST PATH.

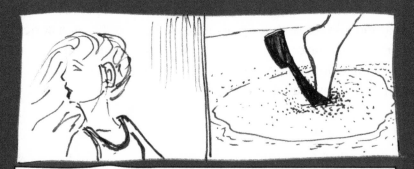

SHE DOESN'T SEE THE QUICKSAND
UNTIL IT'S TOO LATE.

WAIST DEEP AND SINKING,
SHE **SCREAMS!**

A FRIENDLY WOODSMAN SPOTS
DAWN IN DISTRESS,

HE FINDS A FALLEN BRANCH.

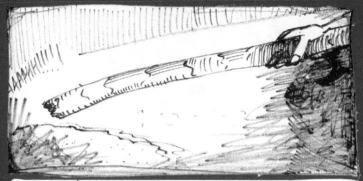

HE EXTENDS THE BRANCH ACROSS THE QUICKSYND.

HE PULLS DAWN TO SAFETY.

DAWN, COVERED IN MUCK, SMILES AT THE WOODSMAN.

SHE RINSES OFF IN A
SUN-GLISTENED POND.

DAWN EMERGES DRIPPING WET,
BARELY DRESSED, SMILING AT
HER SAVIOR.

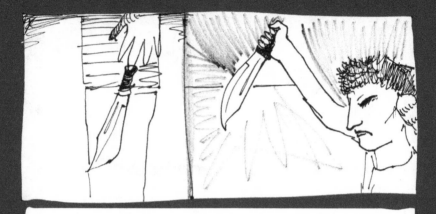

THE WOODSMAN, HIS FACE A KILLER'S GRIMACE, RAISES A BOWIE KNIFE.

DAWN SCREAMS!

Cavanaugh lowered the page and looked at Michael.

"So?" Michael asked, as he forked up the last gooey bit of pie.

"Normally, I would avoid the quicksand scene. It's been done to death – if you'll pardon the pun. But I like this twist on it. She thinks he's rescuing her but he's really the killer. Her salvation becomes her destruction," Cavanaugh said, tapping the page. "A perfect metaphor for our current political situation."

"I'm not sure about politics but I like the idea that the hero becomes the villain," Michael said. "You know the problem with Dawn's movies? The slashers are just killing machines, not real characters. It's always so literal and boring."

"So you plan to kill her with metaphors?" Cavanaugh tapped the ash off his cigarette. "There are worse ways to go. But listen, my boy, it's clear you need serious help."

Michael drew back.

"I'm not crazy!"

"No, of course not. You need help finding your damsel in distress. I'm somewhat of a detective, myself. Read all the books anyway – Hammett, Ellery Queen, and old Edgar Allan, who invented the detective story by the way. For a reasonable retainer and a generous finder's fee, I think I could get you within kissing range. After that it's all up to you."

"I kinda want to do this by myself, but thanks. Really!"

"What about your family? Won't they help?" Cavanaugh asked.

"My Dad, well, he had other plans for me. So, I sort of set out on my own."

The waiter appeared by the table holding a leather folder with a wilted corner of the bill dangling from the top.

"Anything else, gentlemen?"

"I think that's all for tonight, Donald. You were exemplary. For a moment I almost believed I was in Charleston or Savannah, instead of this mosquito breeding ground that passes for a state."

Cavanaugh motioned toward the folder in the waiter's hand, then turned to his companion.

"Michael?"

Michael passed over the credit card.

"If you hate Florida so much, what are you doing here?" Michael asked as the waiter stepped away.

"Let's just say I was blown here by an ill wind. Any day now, I'm gathering my Dorothy, her little dog Toto and skipping down the yellow brick road to Savannah. It's like Oz, only with better bars. Ever been there?"

"No."

"It's a town where a man can find a real drink and a good conversation. A city with history, not just a bunch of strip centers, shopping malls and theme parks trying to pass as an actual place. Lola's going to love it." Cavanaugh savored the last sip of cognac. "I know she will."

People Just Give You Money?

—

Michael's mother had offered her son a sip of her chardonnay now and then, but over the course of the three-hour dinner Michael had taken at least a dozen long sips from Cavanaugh's wine glass. He was stumbling a bit as he tried to match his companion's military pace along the wide sidewalk that led back to the motel. Except for his visits to *Horror Time Video*, Michael hadn't spent any time on the streets around downtown where most of the buildings had gone gray and brittle, like leaves stripped of chlorophyll. In this case, the pigment they had lost was the green of money. Without it, the buildings had withered.

Not that there was no commerce. By night, the dark storefronts, the handful of bars and the derelict motels became specialty shopping centers catering to hungers best satisfied after midnight.

Michael imagined he was walking through some dystopian theme park. Around him, the night people were emerging, like vampires lifting the coffin lid after sunset. Women, in halters and hot pants or clingy knit dresses, leaned against brick walls, staring as cars cruised slowly, the cold streetlight throwing sharp shadows across their faces. Furtive figures in shadowed alleys passed contraband from hand to hand.

Michael pushed down the fear rising in his gut by imagining the scene as a large movie set, and all these shady characters were extras dressed up for a night shoot. Still, he made sure to stay in step with Cavanaugh, who was smiling like a man strolling happily down a woodland path.

At an intersection where two four-lane thoroughfares came together, Cavanaugh pulled up, his hand on Michael's arm.

"This is my corner."

"For what?" Michael looked around for some marker or sign.

"For an appeal to the human heart, my boy. Who can resist? Here's an old man — a war veteran for God's sake — a bit down on his luck." Cavanaugh turned, walking to the edge of the sidewalk, he put out his hand, palm up.

"Couldn't you spare a little silver for a fellow human, who needs a helping hand?" He called out to the street, like an actor rehearsing a part. Then he looked back at Michael, as his thumb and forefinger rose to tip an invisible hat.

"People just give you money?" Michael asked.

"It's not as easy as it looks," Cavanaugh said, the liquor and his full stomach making him philosophical. "Working the streets is a chancy business. It's Russian Roulette. Still, in a few hours I can make thirty or forty bucks, especially if I'm in my chair on wheels. National holidays are the best — particularly Veteran's Day or V.E. Day."

A dark sedan, stuffed front and back with teenage boys, slowed beside Cavanaugh and Michael. The repeated thump of a disco drumbeat drowned out the sounds of the passing cars.

"Hey, Pops, got something for ya," a kid with spiked blond hair yelled from the passenger seat. Cavanaugh stepped away from the curb and, grabbing Michael's arm, eased the boy away from the parked car. "Be ready to run," he whispered.

"Best to be on your way now, gentlemen." Cavanaugh stared hard at the boys in the car, using his deepest baritone. He continued to backpedal slowly, pulling Michael with him. Without warning, a half-finished McDonald's milk shake flew from the car window, landing at Michael's feet, the plastic lid flying off and brown liquid pooling around his shoes. The car screeched off.

"Always good to be wary," Cavanaugh's face relaxed as the car's taillights faded. He smiled at Michael. "A few tossed milkshakes are part of the charm."

"Can I ask you something? Why the streets? This life?" Michael asked. "What are you doing here? You're a very smart man. Anyone can see that."

"I figured we'd get to that question at some point. Read much mythology? Are you familiar with the dark forest?"

Michael shook his head. Cavanaugh wrapped his arm around Michael's shoulder and they began to walk slowly.

"The dark forest? Where civilized people fear to go? It's the Stygian woods, across the black river. It's thick with trolls and demons, quicksand pits, bat-filled caves, and a gingerbread house owned by a very hungry witch. The dark forest is where the wild things are."

"And are you one of the wild things?"

Stepping away, Cavanaugh bowed like a down-on-his luck nobleman.

"Welcome to my world. And now you're wondering why a man like me would choose a life in this haunted forest?"

"You obviously didn't start off here. Right?"

"As your president would say, I sort of trickled down to my current address. I was another dutiful striver but I didn't have the stomach for it. When you leap off the capitalist roller coaster and you don't have a parachute stitched from family dollars to soften the landing, you end up here. But I like it. Except for a firm mattress and an occasional aged Delmonico, I don't miss a thing from the straight world. I quit and I haven't looked back. Besides, the future isn't looking rosy."

"What do you mean?"

"This president, he's the first sign. The tide rolled in after the Great Depression and the big war, but now the tide is going out. It's going to be low tide for a long time, I fear."

Cavanaugh shook himself, stomping his feet like a man coming in from the rain. Soon, he was striding down the sidewalk with Michael hurrying to catch up. After passing a few blocks in silence, Cavanaugh slowed his pace near a cluster of bus benches.

On one bench, three disheveled men were passing a bottle of wine, hidden inside a paper sack. One-bone-thin character, with a face that seemed perpetually startled, pulled the sack to his chest as Cavanaugh and Michael approached.

"Get your own bottle, pal. This one's taken," he rasped in Cavanaugh's direction. His companion on the left, a short man with a jutting Afro and a grimy Miami Dolphins jersey, stared suspiciously in Michael's direction. The third man just gazed forward, apparently oblivious to the newcomers and his companions.

"I'm not taking, gentlemen," Cavanaugh said, his arms extended as if he were planning to walk over and hug them. "I'm giving tonight. My offering is poetic. Something I've been working on this week. I find a lack of conjugal communion inspires my poetic endeavors."

Cavanaugh hopped up on an empty bench next to the trio. There was a streetlight above and, like an aging Shakespearean, Cavanaugh moved down the bench until the light washed across his face. He smiled down at the trio. "This will only hurt for a minute and it's absolutely free of charge."

The drunks stared up at Cavanaugh, now almost eight feet tall atop his concrete perch. He bowed from the waist. Michael sat down on an empty bench as Cavanaugh, rising to his full height, cleared his throat with much gravelly ceremony.

"*The Gandy Dancer By Cavanaugh Reilly.*"

His voice was gritty from too many cigarettes, but it was clearly Shakespearean. King Lear, perhaps, Michael thought, though he'd only ever read a synopsis of the play. He'd seen Gielgud and Olivier as the tragic monarch in film roles. What they had, he thought, was gravitas and a stentorian voice. Just like his new friend.

Here he comes, a smile on his lips
Doin' fine unless he slips
And falls between the cracks
On the railroad tracks.
Got a girl somewhere

A girl who seemed to care
Until she left him there
His heart tied to the railroad tracks.

Cavanaugh was deep in character now. Michael stood up and moved onto the sidewalk, making a football goal with his fingers, as he framed the shot. This is cinematic, he thought.

Cavanaugh was too far into his poem to notice Michael setting up the establishing shot.

He gambols from town to town
A smile to hide his frown
The gandy dancer...
Somehow growing old
A story almost told
The sun about to set
On the most beguiling man
You've ever met

Cavanaugh paused, wiping away a single tear with his index finger. Dropping his fingertip camera, Michael felt a pang of sadness for the plight of his new friend. But then he saw what was really happening. The old man was acting. Chewing the scenery, in fact. Michael moved in a few steps, his fingers rising again as he tightened the frame. Time for the close-up!

The world will be a poorer place
Without his wit, his style, his grace
He's a gandy dancer
A fast and forlorn prancer
Never looking back
Gone...
Down a railroad track."

Michael dropped his hands from his eyes and applauded, as Cavanaugh bowed deeply. The three drunks made no move to applaud. Instantaneous street-corner poetry didn't seem to surprise them. Instead, the skinny one picked up the bottle and took another sip.

"Thank you all," Cavanaugh smiled, as if the bus benches held a cheering Broadway audience instead of three indifferent drunks. "Yes. Thank you all. Most gracious."

———

Ten minutes later, Michael and The Gandy Dancer stumbled past the Blue 'Arlin sign.

The motel, forlorn by day, was more festive as midnight approached. Disco thumped from open doors – *Voulez-vous coucher avec moi, ce soir* – and the light visible through the windows was often blue or red. The parking lot was lit only by the glow of the neon motel sign. Figures, brushed with coral and emerald blue, moved clandestinely along the sidewalks of both floors.

The motel office was a glass-fronted square just off the highway, the front door covered in hand-lettered signs listing various rules. ("NO SIESTA RATES. GUESTS MUST PAY FOR AN ENTIRE DAY NO MATTER HOW SHORT THE STAY!) The asphalt directly in front of the office door was lit by the motel's lone security light. As Michael and Cavanaugh passed by, the office door opened.

"Mister Reely?"

Cavanaugh turned to offer his most engaging smile to the woman who emerged. She was not the same woman who had taken Michael's money that morning. He guessed this woman was in her 50s, her skin the color of milk chocolate, her sari tight around a substantial figure.

She was frowning.

"Saleea, my darling, I've missed you," Cavanaugh almost sang.

"Mister Reeley, we have again had complaints. The music. We have spoken about this and promises were made by you."

"I will promise you anything." His arms reached out toward her.

She stepped back and reset her frown.

"The noise. Remember?"

"But it's James Galway. An Irish pied piper who leads and all one can do is follow."

"But so loud at such an early hour?"

"It's music. Not like that Neanderthal thumping I must endure from some of your lower-class guests on the other side of my paper-thin wall. If you'll listen, I believe you can hear it now quite clearly."

"But Mister Reeley, it is not yet midnight. Seven a.m., while my guests are sleeping, is another matter, am I right?"

"Perhaps if they went to bed a little earlier? But no matter." Leaning closer, Cavanaugh reached out, his fingers just centimeters from her bare arm.

"Saleea, my dear, a woman such as you could never be wrong. And for you, I would gladly give up music, food, breathing, all of it. Later perhaps, you might want to join me for a sip of sherry? We could take turns reading aloud my favorite passages from the Kama Sutra? What do you say?"

"Mister Reeley..." She actually giggled, caught herself, and reset her frown. "No early morning music? Yes?"

"Absolutely," Cavanaugh promised, bringing his hands together and bowing slightly.

The woman shook her head, then turned back to the office.

As they walked through the parking lot, Cavanaugh began to sing – "*Missed the Saturday dance, got as far as the door, they'd have asked me about you...*"

But the song caught in his throat as they neared his room. A figure was slumped in the dark doorway. Cavanaugh rushed forward, dropping to his knees.

Michael heard Cavanaugh whispering – "Lola! Oh my sweet Lola!" He lifted a young woman's head, carefully stroking her tangled black curls. Her arm was limp when Cavanaugh raised it, but Michael could see her fingers gripping the pack of Marlboro 100s Cavanaugh had taped to the window hours earlier.

"Oh, my sweet. My love..."

He turned to Michael, tears ringing his eyes.

"My boy, could you give me a hand with her?"

"Is she okay?"

"I'm afraid it's our routine. My beautiful Lola runs too fast and flies too high, then falls to earth outside my door. Help me get her inside."

———

Lola wasn't heavy, but lifting her dead weight in his slightly drunken state left Michael dizzy. They carried the limp figure to the bathroom. As water thundered into the tub, Michael sat on Cavanaugh's bed, taking in the walls, the books, the entire odd cave the old man had created.

After a minute Michael had to close his eyes to stop the room from spinning. He wasn't sure how much time had passed when he heard Cavanaugh call from behind the bathroom door — "Michael, in here!"

He rose slowly and felt the room spinning again. He stood until the spinning stopped, then walked carefully to the bathroom.

The room was thick with steam. Lit by two flickering candles. Michael flashed on a scene from a black and white Sherlock Holmes film — he was stumbling through heavy fog out on the moors, following the light of a distant torch. As more steam floated out the open door, Michael could make out Cavanaugh and Lola, sitting on the edge of the tub, her head resting on his shoulder, her torso wrapped in a thin gray towel.

Moving closer, Michael found himself staring at the most beautiful female he'd ever seen who wasn't on film. Wet curls reached her bare shoulders, her eyebrows and lashes were thick and black, her nose marked by a slight bump as it curved above a pair of bee-stung lips.

Michael felt dizzy again.

"Let's get her to bed, shall we?" Cavanaugh asked, snapping Michael back.

Cavanaugh rose gently, turning Lola and lifting her from under each arm, Lola's head falling back against his chest. He nodded toward her feet and Michael stepped closer, his hands encircling two perfect ankles.

Lifting her this time, he thought Lola seemed lighter somehow. The thin towel fell away as they stretched her out atop the bed covers. Cavanaugh fluffed a pillow beneath her head. Stepping back, he grabbed a small floor heater with a rusting, cross-hatched grill. Aiming it at the bed, Cavanaugh slowly turned a silver knob. The squat little machine snapped loudly a few times, like a pistol hammer hitting empty chambers, then began to hum, the coils morphing from gray to a fiery orange.

Cavanaugh fetched the burning candles from the bath and set them on the side table. Walking to the front door, he snapped off the overhead light.

Michael stood beside the bed, staring at the fragile, naked creature, her skin washed in the golden light of the coils and the candles. Michael felt dizzy again, before remembering he needed to breathe.

Cavanaugh pulled up a straight-back wooden chair with a quilted blanket folded over the back.

"She's an angel, isn't she?" Cavanaugh said, as he sat. "A fallen angel, to be sure, but an angel nonetheless."

Michael could think of nothing to add, so he just nodded.

After a long moment, Cavanaugh rose. The blanket he pulled off the chair was an afghan, knitted into rust and burnt orange squares. Cavanaugh gently draped it over the girl. Sitting back down, he sighed heavily.

"Thank you for everything tonight," Cavanaugh said, finally looking up at Michael. "Now best to leave us here. I'll stand watch at the bedside."

Hours later, under the covers of his own bed next door, Michael drifted from sleep to consciousness, his vision of the naked creature easing in and out of focus. He felt an odd urgency in his groin. Michael's hand drifted south to investigate, settling around the lighthouse lump rising under the thin blanket.

The image of the girl grew clearer and he could feel her breath on his neck, her fingers tightening around his penis. Suddenly his body was electrified and he felt something pulsing out of him. The sizzling shock of it woke him completely.

Michael took his hand away from the now-moist lump in the covers as the heat began to subside. He lay awake in the dark for a long time, his heart banging away in his chest.

If you're selling, we are not buying

—

It was just after 8 a.m. when Colleen Reilly picked up the yellow legal pad from the passenger seat of her wood-paneled station wagon. *Twin Palms Motel, 4055 Dixie Highway, West Palm Beach*, the note said. Stepping out of the car, she glanced back at the aqua-green neon on the roadside sign that spelled out "Twin Palms" below a pair of arched, Art Deco coconut palms.

She was close. She could feel it. Maybe he wasn't at this address – the one the sympathetic Social Security clerk let her see, upside down on his desk, without actually handing her the change of address form – but Cavanaugh Reilly had been here for certain just two months ago.

Colleen leaned down to the side mirror to check the permed helmet of hair that framed her pale, fine-boned face. It was a bouffant favored by her mother and other Southern Christian women of a certain age. Stepping away from the mirror, she brushed some wrinkles from a flowing, flower-print dress that camouflaged her ample curves. Her mother had called her chubby as long as Colleen could remember. Delia Reilly, a slender and pious woman, had kept her daughter on a series of unsuccessful diets until Colleen was old enough to move away. Now, Colleen's diet plan consisted of avoiding full-length mirrors.

Her father, Cavanaugh Reilly, had fled their home in Alpharetta outside Atlanta twenty-five years before. He didn't leave his wife or his daughter a letter, or even a note. At the state capital where he worked, his secretary had no warning.

He was just gone.

As she grew up, Colleen pined for a letter or a card on her birthday and at Christmas, but the mailbox was always empty.

Less than a year after her husband disappeared, Delia had procured a divorce and married a stern deacon. Colleen didn't take any of it well. By rebellious-teenager standards, she was pretty tame. There was the requisite biker boyfriend, the running away (she always came home), the pot, the pills, and finally, enough booze to fill the baptistery at Alpharetta Assembly of God. She knew her Dad medicated with a bottle.

"I'm my father's daughter," 18-year-old Colleen had shouted at her mother, after arriving home at midnight, stumbling and slurring her words.

"One drunk in this family was enough. Please tell me you don't really want to grow up to be just like him?" Delia almost spit the words.

Colleen didn't have a good answer. Yes? No? She wasn't sure. She just knew she wasn't happy being herself.

Her late teens and twenties were kind of a fog now. Colleen was never a gregarious drunk. Drunk or sober, she was timid and reclusive. She managed to get a nursing assistant certificate and worked odd hours in several Atlanta hospitals and clinics until she was fired for hiding a bottle at work or calling in sick too many times. She rented a tiny garage apartment and consumed soap operas, gin and tonics, and takeout Chinese. After her appendix almost burst just before her 30th birthday, Colleen sobered up. Her mother had visited her hospital room, bringing along Pastor Higgins and a copy of *The Living Bible*, a layman's translation of the Old and New Testaments that the pastor recommended for young people struggling to find their way back to the church.

Turning through the pages, Colleen thought she heard the Lord speaking to her. She wasn't sure what He was saying, but decided to stay sober and listen. After a year of AA meetings and regular church attendance, sharing a pew with her mother and the deacon, she was sure she could hear the Lord speaking clearly, telling her to go and find her father. That same week Pastor Higgins delivered a two-hour sermon, conjuring the requisite hellfire and damnation but also telling his flock if "God is trying to tell you something, you should listen."

Delia had wanted her daughter to find a purpose in life, but not this one.

"He left and didn't look back. Don't waste your life looking for him."

But Colleen was undeterred.

"You remember how Daddy and I used to play hide and seek? He ran but he always let me find him. I think he's waiting for me to find him now."

Delia scoffed. "The only thing your father is waiting for is his next drink."

"Mama, I have to do it. I have to find him."

"And what do you expect to happen when you're face to face with the man? Have you thought about that?"

Colleen didn't have a good answer. The Lord had not been clear on that point. She only knew she would find her father and see what happened next. And now, six months into her search, she was close. South Florida didn't seem like her father's kind of place, but the trail had led here. She felt her hands shaking as she walked toward the motel office clutching the manila folder filled with notes and photos from her search.

Ananya Patel, the woman behind the plexiglass panel in the Twin Palms office, was sure this white woman with the yellow pad in one hand and a large floral-knit purse in the other was not a customer. So she offered the greeting she reserved for non-customers, usually salesmen hoping to make a pitch.

"We're full. No room. If you're selling, we are not buying."

"I don't want a room. And I'm not a salesman. I'm looking for someone," Colleen said, leaning down to talk into the rectangular opening where money and keys were passed through on a plastic tray.

"They're not here," Ananya snapped.

Colleen had met a lot of Indian and Pakistani motel owners

in her search. East Asian immigrants had bought a lot of motels and convenience stores in left-behind urban areas that catered to transients like Cavanaugh Reilly. Colleen knew to smile and be persistent.

"Please, I'm looking for my father."

"No fathers here." Ananya did not look up at Colleen, her cold expression inked to her face like a tattoo.

Colleen tapped the plastic panel. The woman sighed but looked up, meeting her eyes.

"Are you a religious person?" Colleen asked. "Muslim? Hindu? I'm a Christian — Assembly of God — but I believe there's beauty in all religions. And I believe truly religious people share a universal love, one to another. Do you believe that?"

The clerk shook her head and surrendered. She let her face soften into a look that seemed to say "go ahead." Colleen rooted around in the envelope. The 5-by-7 snapshot she pulled out was faded and creased. She pressed it against the panel.

The clerk scanned a black and white family photo, taken on an Easter morning. There was a long green Plymouth in the driveway, with fins that would have looked good on a shark or a sailfish. Three people were posed on the grass in front of it. Squinting into the camera that long ago Sunday was a pretty, helmet-haired mother; a ten-year-old Colleen, already chubby, and a forty-year-old Cavanaugh Reilly, looking like a man who had just run into the picture after setting a timer on a camera pinioned atop a tri-pod.

"That's him," Colleen said. "And that's me. Does he look familiar? I mean, he'd be older now but..."

The clerk's face gave away nothing.

"I'm not sure," she said.

"His name is Reilly. Cavanaugh Reilly." Colleen remained patient. She knew this woman must know him. "He listed this as an address for a couple of months."

"Hmmm..." Ananya was not comfortable being cooperative with anyone. It was a rule that had served her well in the low-rent motel business but here was a daughter looking for a lost father. She didn't get many of those.

"Please..." Colleen said, a tear trailing down her cheek. "I've been searching for him a long time."

"Tell me the name again."

"Reilly. Cavanaugh Reilly."

The clerk reattached her stern face.

"Oh...him. Him I kicked out two months ago. Dirty old man. Very dirty. I would not waste your time searching for such a man."

"Did he leave an address? Do you know where he went?"

"To Hell, I hope," she said. "As a Christian, I think you know the location of Hell? He's probably there. And if you find he's not there – tell him he owes me sixty-two dollars and fifty-four cents."

———

A few blocks south, Michael knocked lightly on Cavanaugh's door.

Cavanaugh eased the door open, putting an index finger to his lips.

"Shhhh," he whispered.

Michael stopped in the open doorway while Cavanaugh returned to his bedside chair. In the quiet of the morning, Michael could hear the soft breathing of the sleeping girl. His friend had likely sat beside the bed all night.

"How is she?" Michael whispered.

Cavanaugh took another long look at the sleeping figure, then tiptoed back to the doorway so he could whisper to Michael.

"Magnificent. Beautiful. Beguiling. And still down for the proverbial count."

"How long does she...sleep?"

"Hard to say but she'll be up any time now. Starving and horny. I'm ready. I've laid in lots of cigarettes. Steaks. Strawberry ice cream. Condoms. Any luck finding your lady love?"

Michael couldn't take his eyes off the tiny figure under the knitted blanket, but he tried to focus on his mission. Last night, as the swelling in his crotch subsided, he had revised his plans. Taking on some partners seemed like a good idea, especially a wise man like Cavanaugh and this beautiful, mysterious creature named Lola.

Michael tilted his head toward the parking lot and Cavanaugh followed him outside, closing the door carefully behind them. The asphalt lot, so busy eight hours before, was empty, the night people now tucked away in their dark daytime places.

"I wanted to talk with you about your offer to help," Michael said. "Do you have a driver's license?"

———

It was 3:30 p.m. and Harvey's Steak House was still an hour or so from its first customer. David, the *maître d'*, hadn't yet knotted his black satin bowtie. Standing at the reception podium, he stared down at a photo of a spike-haired teenage boy and a lean, blonde woman who might be his mother.

"Credit records indicate he spent $271 here last night."

Jaime was wearing his regular detective outfit, a powder blue leisure suit, this time over a Hawaiian shirt in faded aqua and pink.

"Looks familiar, but I'm not completely sure." David stepped back imperceptibly. He was trying not to come in contact with the detective's suit, as if the polyester fabric were radioactive. "Hmmmm."

Jaime pulled a fifty from his coat pocket and placed it carefully on the counter top, keeping two stubby, hairless fingers atop the bill.

"Oh yes," David said. "Now I remember."

Jaime lifted his fingers from the bill and David picked it up, sliding it into his jacket pocket in one swift motion.

"Computer millionaire. Came in with the old man. His grandfather, I figured. Eccentric. Good tipper. "

"Can you think of anything else?"

"I slipped out for a smoke at the end of the night and it seemed odd to me."

"What seemed odd?"

"They didn't have a car. Didn't take a taxi. They were on foot. Headed north up Dixie Highway."

A Dark
And Stormy Dawn

—

Awakened by a thunderous barrage, Cavanaugh slid forward, parting the tent flaps and peering out. The snow had fallen all night, sagging the tent's ceiling, the drifts pushing two feet up the trunks of the trees. The early morning was misty, white and beautiful, until it wasn't. A shell landed, tossing up a wall of flame. He watched a sprinting sentry contort as the blaze engulfed him. Behind the burning man Cavanaugh saw movement in the ivory haze. Seconds later, hundreds of men in black, bayonets affixed, were lock-stepping toward his camp.

Christmas was due in four days and Cavanaugh's platoon, exhausted from two months of non-stop fighting across France and Belgium, was supposed to be resting in a clearing in the Ardennes Forest.

But the war had come to them.

It had happened so fast. Explosions. Death. Surrender. His captors barking orders in chiseled English, thrusting bayonets an inch from his gut. He and the few dozen Americans left alive were ordered to stack the stiffening bodies like firewood. Wide-eyed German soldiers, some no older than teenagers, herded them into a clearing where they stood all day and into the night – with no shelter or blankets – circling up like cattle in the cold, taking turns moving into the center to gather some heat from the press of bodies.

Another explosion shook Cavanaugh. He sat up in bed.

God, he hated Florida storms. They flipped a switch he thought he had disconnected. The thunder became the distant thud of an artillery barrage, the lightning bolts the concussive, flaming explosions that torched the trees.

Cavanaugh's pocket watch said it was 7 a.m., but the room was still dark. He left Lola sleeping in the warm bed and stumbled to the window. Pulling back the thin curtain, he watched the flotsam and jetsam left by the night people tumbleweed across the Blue 'Arlin's parking lot, pushed by the stiff breeze. A January cold front — racing toward Florida — had dispatched an advance team of thunderstorms; a hulking maelstrom of clouds, the color of a day-old bruise, encased the motel.

A white wall of lightning snapped the highway and the buildings beyond into sharp focus, before the world went black again. An angry burst of sideways raindrops staccatoed off the motel window, sending Cavanaugh leaping back, the curtain falling from his fingers.

The raindrops were the machine gun fire cutting down his mates as they fled their tents. On cue, the metallic shudder of a freight train, passing behind the motel, tossed Cavanaugh back into a boxcar that reeked of sweat, blood and piss, the prisoners standing shoulder to shoulder, the sliding wooden doors secured with chain. No food. No water. Rattling along the rail lines for two days, headed east.

Staring out the motel window, wearing only a pair of boxers, Cavanaugh shivered. He could feel his frozen fingers curled over the chicken wire walls of the makeshift POW camp; a metallic curtain of clouds blotting out the sun; the ivory fog of his breath crystallizing in the frigid air. He was waiting — with a hundred other emaciated POWs — for the day's only meal, a dark broth, always cold by the time it was slopped into a mess tray.

He kept these memories in dark rooms behind locked doors that he never wanted to open. In those rooms were the faces of all the friends who died violently in that freezing forest and all the others he saw perish on his long, bloody march across France and Belgium. There was even a room for the Germans who had struggled and died with Cavanaugh's bullets inside them. These weren't the meaningless deaths that filled so many movies and TV shows. Real death – especially when it's violent – resonates.

Sometimes it was Fourth of July fireworks, sometimes a car backfiring. Since he'd been in Florida, it was the tropical thunderstorms that kicked open the door, freeing a blackness that quickly engulfed him. The Darks was his name for this crippling, hopeless feeling. And when The Darks seeped deep inside you, all the color drained from the world.

Cavanaugh shuddered.

"You okay?" Lola asked.

Cavanaugh turned back to look at her. She was rested and beautiful, her back against the pillows, her honey-colored skin set off by a white silk slip. He felt a spark ignite in his gut, the way it always did when he saw her.

"You know I hate these goddamn Florida storms."

Lola, pulling on her first cigarette, patted the bed with her free hand.

"Come on. Sit down. I know you've got a plan brewing. I heard you talking to the boy last night."

"You were asleep."

"My ears still work, even when my eyes are closed. What's going on?"

The old infantryman marched to the bed and sat down, the springs sagging beneath him. Lola passed him her cigarette. He smoked hungrily, the cigarette quivering in his shaking hands. After a few puffs, he felt the nicotine creeping through his veins like a sedative. The memories retreated, the dark cloud slipping under the door, the deadbolt thudding into place. He was in Florida. In a motel room with the right girl. It was January of 1982 and there were plans to make.

Snuffing out the butt, Cavanaugh leaned over and kissed Lola gently on her forehead, then he kissed each cheek, his fingers lingering among her curls. Satisfied she was really there, he leaned back, taking a deep breath.

The world was back in full color.

"I checked his ID and made a few calls," he told Lola. "You

heard of Donnelly Avionics?"

She shook her head.

"Defense contracts. A lot of them. Your favorite president is doubling down on the Cold War and the money is flowing to the fat cats again," Cavanaugh said, his voice a conspiratorial whisper. "I'm thinking we can get the boy to pay us to find the girl. And his Dad will pay us to find the boy. It's symmetry."

"Sounds like another scheme to me."

In their time together, Cavanaugh had hatched more than a few schemes to bring in some quick money. Nothing violent or too hurtful to any single individual, but there was always an angle to be worked.

"Just a business deal," Cavanaugh said. "Not so different than one of yours."

She reached out, fingers pinching his ear lobe. Then, grabbing his shoulder, she pulled him close, her lips brushing his ear.

"I'll play along. Just tell me what I need to do."

They both turned toward the knock on the door.

"Who is it?" Cavanaugh called sweetly.

"It's just me, Michael."

Cavanaugh shot Lola a raised eyebrow. She snuffed her cigarette and closed her eyes, her head sinking slowly into the pillow.

———

A day and night had passed since Michael and Cavanaugh found Lola on the sidewalk outside his room.

In a series of whispered chats, while the girl slept, the old man had offered a simple plan: a car; a drive; a guerilla raid on an Everglades film set that would put Michael face to face with his muse.

It just required a little seed money.

Michael, who had been awake for hours, was too hyped to wait in his room any longer. Wearing his standard uniform – black jeans and the black *Psycho Killer* T-shirt – he took five quick steps through the driving rain to his friend's door.

As he waited for Cavanaugh to open the door, the storm soaked his clothes and flattened his unruly hair, leaving it hanging below his ears like so much straw-colored seaweed.

"Come in, son. Come in," Cavanaugh whispered.

Taking Michael's arm, he pulled him from the rain. Dressed in his old bathrobe and fuzzy slippers, Cavanaugh raised his index finger to his lips.

"Shhhhh...

Michael matched his whisper. "I was just wondering..."

They both looked over at the figure of Lola curled under the knit blanket.

"Is she...?"

"Better?" Cavanaugh said. "Much better, thank you. It's just a matter of time now."

"So, do you think you can get it?"

Cavanaugh smiled broadly.

"The deal is done. All I need now..." He held out a long-fingered hand, palm up. Michael pulled the wad of cash – safely tucked into a plastic baggie – from the front pocket of his jeans. He counted off five hundreds, setting the crisp stack gently on Cavanaugh's palm.

The money disappeared into the pocket of Cavanaugh's robe. They both turned back to stare at Lola.

"Thank you, dear boy. I will take delivery later today, after the storm passes. Oh, there's more news. I've reached out to some old friends in the film industry."

Michael felt his heart jump in his chest. This partnership was already a good idea. "Did you find something?"

Cavanaugh let the moment build before placing his hand on Michael's wet shoulder.

"Dawn Karston and the crew of *Swamp Fiend II* are currently pitching their tents just 75 miles from where we stand."

"She's in Florida now?"

Cavanaugh rubbed his hands together and offered up his best Bela Lugosi cackle. "At this exact moment, your lovely one is enjoying a dark and stormy dawn – in the Everglades!"

As if on cue, a thunderclap exploded, like distant cannon fire, and, seconds later, a sizzling spear of lightning sliced down outside the motel window, whitewashing the room.

———

The booths at Murray's New York Diner were pushed against the tall front windows. The parking lot and the highway beyond it were still wet from the morning's storm, but a midday sun was shining, the sky vibrantly blue. If a passing driver had looked over at Murray's, he'd have seen two figures sitting back to back in adjoining booths.

Jaime Solano was facing south, pushing a spoon into a swirling mountain of whipped cream quivering on a bed of chocolate ice cream, caramel, and chopped nuts, the whole concoction topped with three maraschino cherries, stems up. On the table was the color photo of Michael and Crystal Donnelly.

In the booth directly behind him, Colleen Reilly sat facing north, eating the same dessert, the Reilly family Easter photo smoothed out on the shiny metal tabletop.

Jaime and Colleen had both ordered the signature dessert at Murray's. They called it *The Blizzard*.

A Metallic Magic Carpet

—

Despite its stormy entrance, the Canadian cold front spent its fury as it iced through Georgia and North Florida. Around the Palm Beaches the morning's storm was forgotten by noon. The sky was pastel blue, the air dry and seemingly regulated by a thermostat set at 74 degrees. It was the kind of Florida day when anything seemed possible – the same meteorological miracle that had been luring millionaires, tourists, hobos, con men and criminals to the flat peninsula for the past hundred winters.

Cavanaugh was outside, a song in his heart and a rag in his hand, applying polish to a cream-colored Lincoln Continental convertible now 21 tough years beyond the showroom floor. All that time spent around the salty Atlantic had not been kind. Jagged ridges of rust – shrugging off the previous owner's cheap paint job – had erupted along the doors and the lower edges of the car's body, like a chain of volcanic islands. The red-leather seats were held together with strips of black duct tape.

But on this perfect Florida day, Cavanaugh could see no flaws in this car or in his plan. He was rubbing polish in wide circles along the car's sprawling hood, whistling *Georgia On My Mind*, when Michael's door opened.

"Wow. Nice car!"

"Not a car, my boy. A metallic magic carpet that'll whisk you to your lady-love. And with your blessing, will eventually take Lola and me to *Xanadu*, aka Savannah, the pleasure dome Kubla Khan decreed."

Michael rubbed his hand across the rounded hood that

wrapped the double headlights. He was impressed with what $500 would buy if you knew the right people. And his new best friend, Cavanaugh Reilly, seemed to know the right people. Michael stepped back a bit to take it all in. There was some rust on the front grill, but the car's wide chrome smile, adorned with two tapering steel teeth set a yard apart, glimmered in the morning sun.

"It's great," Michael said.

"And just a bit more than I expected," Cavanaugh said. "They didn't tell me the deal didn't include tires."

"How much?"

"Just an extra one fifty," he said as he returned to his polishing.

The boy nodded, disappeared back into his room and returned quickly with three fifties.

"So how's Lola?"

"I kissed Snow White's ruby lips," he snapped his finger, "and just like that she awoke."

Cavanaugh stuffed the cash into the pocket of his white dress shirt.

"This could be our lady now," Cavanaugh said, as the door to his room eased open.

Lola emerged, moving like a woodland creature stepping warily from the forest into a meadow. She was radiant in a slip of a blue knit dress, barefoot, no makeup, a large red apple in her right hand. When she took a bite, Michael could hear the juicy snap from six feet away.

"Lola Fernandez Famosa, please meet my good friend and benefactor, Michael...uh...Michael...My boy I'm embarrassed to admit I don't know your surname."

"It's uh...Smith." Michael realized he hadn't really thought of a code name to use during this adventure. Smith seemed safe enough. "Michael Smith."

Lola looked him up and down. With the back of her hand, she wiped moist droplets of apple juice from her lips.

"Hi!" She moved closer, her eyes locking on Michael, who

suddenly forgot how to talk. Fortunately, Cavanaugh filled the gap.

"He's loaded. His grandfather was the Smith of Smith and Wesson. I think he invented the trigger."

"Uh...no," Michael managed to say.

"Oh, Mrs. Smith's pies then? Your mother cornered the pumpkin and mincemeat markets."

"No...you see..."

"Smith Brothers? Smith Barney? Smith Corona?"

"Just Smith..." he said.

"Whatever his pedigree, he's a member of the American money-eyed class. And a lovely human being despite that character flaw."

Lola stepped closer to Michael, lifting both of his hands and bringing them together, so she could wrap them in hers.

"Ignore him," she told Michael, leaning in conspiratorially. "He's just jealous of people with money. I'm making a fortune too. Are you familiar with the opportunities in multi-level marketing? It's the future of retail. But you know that, right?"

"Not really, " Michael stammered. "I don't think I do."

"I'll be sure and get you a brochure," she whispered in his ear, her small, cool hands still clutching his.

Michael struggled to say something, but Cavanaugh saved him the trouble.

"Well, my rich young friends, we've got wheels. And this beautiful morning calls for a celebration. Don't you agree?"

———

An hour later, Cavanaugh's blue chenille bedspread, with puffy cotton acorns dangling around the edges, was spread across a khaki square of Atlantic beachfront. Cavanaugh had dressed for the occasion in a floral cabana set from the 1940s, a pink plastic nose cap – a sun barrier last seen in Florida during the Eisenhower administration – resting atop his majestic appendage and a snow-white swipe of zinc across his lips. His daily occupation as a street-corner solicitor had left his skin tanned and weathered. Add the zinced lips and Cavanaugh looked like an escapee from a 1920s minstrel show. He was stretched out on his back, staring up at the cloudless sky. Lola sat beside him in a bikini that barely kept her within the law. Michael hadn't packed for the beach, so his swimsuit was a pair of cut-off blue jeans, which exposed long, hairless legs only a few shades darker than the goo on Cavanaugh's lips.

A wicker picnic basket was open and a plate of cheese, bread and grapes were scattered nearby. Lola broke chunks off the French baguette, chewing happily. Michael tried to keep his eyes on the water, but they kept returning to her honey-colored skin, covered in just three spots by tiny patches of pink polyester.

Cavanaugh held out his hand and Lola put a hunk of torn bread onto his upturned palm. Popping the chunk into his mouth, he washed it down with a sip of bourbon from a silver flask. The mood was pleasant, though Cavanaugh kept goading his girlfriend into minor skirmishes about the current occupant of the White House, Ronald Reagan, who was still on the mend after the attempt on his life.

On politics, and lots of other things, the two lovers' opinions diverged.

"You know what he said to Nancy that day in the hospital?" Lola asked Michael.

Michael shook his head. Cavanaugh jumped in with the answer, his voice a perfect copy of Reagan's folksy baritone.

"Honey, I forgot to duck."

"That's right," Lola said, turning in his direction. "How did you know?"

Cavanaugh pushed himself up onto his elbows.

"Because he stole it. 'Honey, I forgot to duck.' That's what Jack Dempsey told his wife after he got knocked out in a title fight. The Gipper probably had a writer there in the hospital. Man hasn't said a word in 30 years that wasn't in a script."

"Don't start that again," Lola said, frowning. "He's turning our country around."

"In which direction, my sweet, misguided girl? In which direction?"

"Rebuilding the military. Standing up to the Communists who stole my country. Stimulating a sluggish economy."

Cavanaugh huffed. "Reagan's a talking head in pancake make-up and a nice suit, shilling for the corporations and his rich pals. It's all an act. Besides, darling, you're the most stimulating thing in our economy." He raised himself onto his elbows and leaned in to kiss her bare back.

"I want your beautiful stimuli to trickle down all over me," he whispered.

Lola let him nuzzle her a bit, then, as she looked back at Michael, she pushed Cavanaugh away.

"Stop it, baby. We got company, remember?"

Cavanaugh looked up from his nuzzling, but only for a moment.

"Michael appreciates love, my sweet. He's in love himself. Aren't you, my boy?"

Michael had been staring hard at Lola, creating a movie scene in his head starring his beautiful new friend. Hearing Cavanaugh snapped him back to the beach.

"Who is she?" Lola asked.

Michael again found himself having trouble putting words together.

"Go ahead? You can tell me."

Lola reached across Cavanaugh and brushed Michael's leg with her outstretched fingers.

"Well, her name is Dawn," Michael said.

"Is she from your school?"

"Actually, she's in the movies. An actress."

"Wow. Where did you meet her?"

"Oh, we haven't met yet. I just sent her some letters. She sent me a signed photo."

"Movie star. Lots of money in that. How are her boobs? Big?"

"Um. Well. Yeah, I guess so. There was this scene in *Frat House Fratricide*..."

Lola turned to Cavanaugh.

"See. I told you. Boobs sell. I need to buy some."

Cavanaugh shook his head. "Artificially augmented mounds of jelly, from the people who brought you Agent Orange. Flaming deaths. Atomic breasts. There's a metaphor there somewhere."

Looking down at herself, Lola pushed her chest out, brought her hands up to cup the two swatches of fabric that covered her breasts. "A girl can't get anywhere with these. Michael, tell him I'm right." She leaned across Cavanaugh and grabbed Michael's hand, pressing it against her left breast. "Feel that. Nothing, right?"

"Ah...but..."

"In today's economy, a salesperson isn't just selling a product. They are selling themselves. I've got nothing to sell."

Lola released Michael's hand, but it remained pressed to her chest. Cavanaugh laughed.

"Michael seems impressed with your natural attributes, my love."

Michael suddenly pulled his hand away. Lola laughed and leapt to her feet.

"I'm going swimming. I don't care how cold the water is." She looked over at Michael, reaching out her hand and wiggling her outstretched fingers in his direction. "Wanna come?"

Michael let her pull him to his feet. He looked down at Cavanaugh as the old man pointed a bony finger at a bulge in the crotch of Michael's shorts. "I suggest a cold plunge. Might help reduce that swelling."

Michael stared down at himself, his face going red. He turned and strode toward the water.

Lola watched him go, then bent over Cavanaugh and whispered in his ear. "So how am I doin'?"

Cavanaugh mimed casting a fishing rod. Then he slowly reeled it in.

———

Lola and Michael, soaked from their cold-water swim, stood shivering beside the blanket, trying to dry themselves with Cavanaugh's paper-thin motel towels. Cavanaugh was snoring, his mouth open, his zinced lips quivering gently with each exhale.

"Let's walk," Lola whispered.

She took Michael's hand and suddenly she was running. Michael held on, trying to keep pace. He didn't run a lot but he knew for certain he did not want to let go of Lola's hand.

Once they had gained some distance from the blanket, Lola slowed to a walk. Across the beach road to the west, behind low, coquina-colored walls, a line of mansions was backed up to the Intracoastal.

Michael felt the need to fill the silence. He wanted to impress this girl, but he didn't have much experience talking to females other than his mother. He fell back on his standard topic – movies, and the genius of Mario Bava and his successor, Dario Argento, who wrote and directed *Suspiria* in 1977. If they were the father and son of modern horror, Michael had dreams of following in their footsteps, sort of a cinematic Holy Ghost. When he let himself go into that semi-religious reverie, he knew who would be his not-so-virgin Mary. She was making a movie in the Everglades, less than 100 miles from this beach.

If a resident of the mansions lining the Intracoastal had looked out their window, gazing over the wall and across the two-lane road toward the beach, they wouldn't have seen a future auteur and an American Dream entrepreneur but a gawky teenage boy talking intently to a curly haired girl in a skimpy pink bathing suit who didn't seem to be paying attention.

Michael eventually moved from Bava and Argento to their current imitators, the slasher movie makers of the 1980s. Oh how Michael hated them. He waved his arms as he illustrated points he regularly made to the men behind the counter at *Horror Time Video.*

"They are just such bad copies. Like somebody looked at a Picasso once, then went home and tried to recreate it with crayons. You know?"

Lola was eyeing the large houses along the Intracoastal and pretending to listen. Whenever Michael stopped for a few seconds to take a breath, she filled the silences with "Hmmm..."

That response was enough for Michael. He was happy to jump back to his point.

"I mean, Bava was the genius of the genre. He invented the modern horror movie in Italy in the '60s and early '70s. Ask anybody who really knows and they'll tell you. *Friday the 13th* − they literally copied the murders in *Bay of Blood*, but without any of his style." His voice rose as the monologue built to a conclusion. "And the guys making Dawn's movies − they're frauds. There's no art there. It's all commerce. Heck, they don't even know how to frame a shot. Dawn deserves better. I mean, the world deserves better, right?"

Lola stopped walking and turned to Michael. "Don't you love Tara?"

"What?"

"Those houses there." She pointed across the road at two identical plantation-like mansions buttressed by a series of ornate Corinthian columns, differing from real plantations only by the lack of slave quarters out back. "They remind me of Tara. Or what I think it would look like today."

"What?"

"*Gone With The Freakin' Wind*? Scarlett? The big house? I thought you were the movie expert."

"Oh yeah...Tara."

"I've seen the movie maybe 20 times," she said. "You know, in the end, it's all about that house. Through everything - the war, the blood, the fire, Ashley and Rhett − for Scarlett, it's all about that house."

"I guess so, but..." Michael stammered. He got uncomfortable when his train of thought was derailed. He liked sticking to a script.

"What's it like waking up in a house like that?" Lola asked.

The question conjured an image of his mother, all fluttery and beautiful, coming into his bedroom, yanking back the heavy curtains, tickling the bottom of his feet, hoping her son would wake up so they could spend the day together. Michael tried to hold that image, but it always gave way to the bloody memory of Crystal dead in the tub.

Michael crossed his arms over his chest and looked away.

"I don't know." Michael stammered. "Ah...lost, I guess."

"Come on."

"It's so big. My house. Sometimes you can feel lost in it," he said.

"Not in my mansion. I'll wake up and ring a little bell. The maid will bring breakfast on a white tray, with a flower. I'll eat right in my bed, with the pillows pushed up behind my back. The light from wide windows pouring in."

"You've thought about this."

"A lot. Later, I take the limo to Worth Avenue to find a new dress for that night's big gala at the Everglades Club. There's a band with those fancy music stands and everybody is there – the Kennedy nephews, the Kleenex cousins, the Kellogg daughters. All of 'em kissing your cheeks as you tell them – 'Such a pleasure to meet you!' And they take your hand and say – 'Why darling, the pleasure is all mine.'"

Michael laughed. Talking with this girl was surprisingly easy, he realized. Just roll with it. He offered a formal bow. "Such a pleasure to meet you," he said in his best Palm Beach accent.

"Why, darling, the pleasure is all mine," Lola replied, with equal formality.

They both laughed. Lola looked around and nodded back in the direction they had come. "Cavanaugh says if your family finds you, they're going to lock you up in someplace called Palmdale Heaven."

They started to walk back toward Cavanaugh and the picnic.

"I think it's actually Haven. But yeah, I guess I am a fugitive," Michael said.

"A very dangerous dude," Lola added.

Michael felt his confidence soaring. Maybe he *could* banter with a woman.

"Yes, very dangerous," he said. "And unpredictable."

Lola grabbed Michael's hand and pulled him to a stop. Turning to face him, she placed her palms on his shoulders, pulling him so close Michael could feel her breath on his lips. "Don't let them catch you," she whispered. "I don't know about the nut house, but jail is hell on wheels. I mean it. I hate it there."

"I've never been to jail."

"You're not really going to kill this girl, are you?"

Michael was shocked.

"I don't know why people have that idea. I want to save her!"

"That's good. They don't really look so hard for you if you haven't killed anybody."

She let her arms fall away but she kept her face close to his. Michael noticed her eyes were emerald green in the afternoon sun.

"Cavanaugh thinks you're trying to kill yourself," Michael said.

"Because I sniff a little? I don't want to die. I just want to dream. "

"Huh? I don't understand."

"The powder gives me beautiful dreams. I mean big Technicolor dreams. Tara dreams." Lola stepped back and started spinning, her arms outstretched, her head back. "Big, big dreams. Brass ring on the merry-go-round dreams."

She stopped her dance and struck a sudden pose, her hips pushing right, her head tilted left, her eyes locked on Michael's. She held the position for a brief moment, then danced a bit more, before leaning forward, raising her face in a pouty pose that could have been lifted from a fashion magazine.

Michael framed his hands around his eyes, forming a makeshift viewfinder. He focused on the dancing creature before him.

"Yes," he whispered, as Lola spun again, then froze, tilting her head and bringing a palm to her cheek. "That's it. That's it..."

Lola laughed, then dropped the pose, taking off toward their blanket. Michael let his hands drop to his sides. He didn't need a camera to help him remember the look of this thin, copper-skinned creature, her hips swaying, her hair tousled, as she jogged away from him.

"Darling," he whispered, "the pleasure is all mine."

The Nearness Of You

—

Cavanaugh, a full flask of bourbon in his belly, was sprawled in the passenger seat of the convertible, his head thrown back, the wind rustling his hair, as Lola piloted the big metal boat away from Palm Beach. Michael rode in back on the passenger side, which offered the best views of Lola as she drove.

"*If I should take a notion to jump into the ocean, 'taint nobody's bizness if I do,*" Cavanaugh bellowed at full volume. "*If some gal ain't got no money, and I say take all mine honey, 'taint nobody's –*"

Lola reached over and slapped her hand over his mouth.

"Ow!" Cavanaugh mumbled through her clamped hand.

"SILENCIO!! BASTA!" Lola shouted. "I can't stand that song."

When she finally took her hand away, Cavanaugh swiveled toward Michael.

"It's money," he said, conspiratorially. "She thinks I'm careless with it."

"He drives me crazy," Lola shouted.

"Because I refuse to labor ever again in the caverns of commerce," Cavanaugh said, his head shifting slowly from passenger to driver. "Twenty-five years of faithful service in the American absurdatorium was enough for me."

"What's more absurd than your life?" Lola snapped. "Panhandling. Complaining about everything. Hatching one crazy scheme after another."

"That's rich, coming from the Mary Kay of the mattresses."

Lola swung hard, the back of her hand catching Cavanaugh

on the cheek and jaw.

"SILENCIO!" she shouted.

"What?" Cavanaugh said, his hand pressing against a red spot on his cheek. "A little too close to home?"

"Don't you ever judge me!"

Michael felt the bread and cheese churning in his stomach. He hated confrontation. His parents had done enough of it to last him a lifetime. He leaned over the front seat, so his head was between Cavanaugh and Lola.

"Please don't fight," Michael pleaded, as he looked from Lola to Cavanaugh. "I really can't stand it. Please?"

———

By the time they parked at the motel and started unpacking the convertible, the tension had eased. As Lola came around the side of the car, folded towels in her arms, Cavanaugh slipped up behind her, pulled her into a bear hug. Lola squirmed to break free, but it was clear the fight was over.

"*It's not the pale moon that excites me*," Cavanaugh cooed in her ear. "*That thrills and delights me, oh no –*"

Lola managed to wriggle away, but gently. "Stop it. I'm still mad at you, remember?"

"*...It's just the nearness of you...*"

She let Cavanaugh catch her just outside the motel door. Standing with his back to the parking lot, his hands on Lola's bare shoulders, his lips against her neck, Cavanaugh couldn't see the station wagon pull into the parking space next to the Lincoln.

The station wagon's door opened and Colleen's head emerged, taking in the scene.

That man. His height. The shape of his shoulders. It was him! It had to be. Remain calm, she told herself. You can do this. Please Jesus, let me do this right.

Colleen clambered out of the station wagon. She brushed some wrinkles from her dress, then bent to check her makeup and hair in the side mirror. Smiling at her reflection, Colleen rubbed her index finger against her front teeth, where some extra peach-colored lipstick had lodged. Satisfied, she stood slowly and took a long breath.

"Daddy?"

Cavanaugh lifted his head, but continued to sing. "*It isn't your sweet conversation, that brings this sensation, oh no....it's just the nearness of you.*"

Michael stepped out of his room and saw the tableau – his two friends together outside their door, and a third figure, a large woman in a flowered dress, her hair teased and sprayed into place, staring at them from the parking lot.

"Daddy! It's me. Colleen."

Something in the voice reached Cavanaugh. He released Lola and turned slowly.

"Hi, Daddy. They said at the desk that you lived here," Colleen said, trying to keep her emotions in check, the Serenity Prayer on a loop deep in her head. "*God grant me the serenity...*"

Cavanaugh grabbed Lola and spun her around, putting her body between him and the woman, as if Colleen were a gunman and Lola his human shield.

"Who are you?" he stammered. "What do you want with me?"

"It's me, Daddy. Colleen." She felt tears welling. This man was her father, only so much older, so worn and wrinkled. Clearly, the years had been tough for him, too.

"Stop! How did? How? You?"

"I've searched for you for so long. So many places. Oh, Daddy..." She held out her arms to him. Tears gushed, spilling down both cheeks.

Lola jerked out of Cavanaugh's grip.

"Daddy? You're her father?"

Cavanaugh stepped back, his face red, his arms going up, his hands waving wildly. He looked around at Michael and Lola.

"I don't recognize this woman," he said, before looking back at Colleen. "Who are you?"

"Daddy, it's me, Colleen. Your little Sheba! Remember?"

"Do you have some form of ID?" Cavanaugh asked, and then words seemed to fail him. "I mean. Are you? Uh. I mean. Ah..."

His back was pressed against the door of his room, his head swiveling around, his eyes unfocused. His hands suddenly clutched at his chest.

"OH! OW!"

Cavanaugh's knees bent and he started to crumple as Lola and Michael rushed to catch him. Colleen stared, horrified, as her father sagged, a dead weight in Michael and Lola's arms.

"Daddy! Are you okay? What's the matter?"

Colleen rushed to Cavanaugh, her hands reaching out.

On his knees now, Cavanaugh looked desperately up at Michael.

"My pills," he whispered. "I need my pills. Please, in my room."

"Oh, Daddy. Let me help you!" Colleen cried.

Cavanaugh gasped like a dying man. He raised his arm toward Colleen, his palm a five-fingered STOP sign. "NO! No! Please! Just wait here. I need to get to my pills. Lola. Michael. Help me into my room."

Each taking an arm, Lola and Michael eased Cavanaugh back toward his open door. Colleen stood back, her arms still reaching out, fingers clutching at the air. This wasn't how it was supposed to go. She looked up toward heaven and folded her hands below her chin.

"Daddy, I'll be right here. Just know I'm praying for you."

Colleen bowed her head in prayer.

"Please God, help my daddy!" Her prayer was almost a shout.

"Bless you," Cavanaugh coughed out the words, his head rolling toward his daughter, a bit of his tongue emerging. As Michael and Lola helped him across the threshold, Colleen ended her prayer, taking a step toward the open door.

The dying man somehow found enough strength to kick the door closed in his daughter's stricken face.

Within seconds, Cavanaugh made a miraculous recovery. He brushed off Michael and sat heavily on his bed. Lola emerged from the bathroom with a small white pill and a plastic glass.

Cavanaugh took the pill but refused the water, he leaned across the bed where the silver flask was waiting. He chased the pill with a long pull.

"Are you okay?" Michael asked, leaning over him.

Cavanaugh's voice was strong again. "Better. Yes, much better. Just let me catch my breath." He pushed Michael back roughly. "Is she gone?"

Lola peeked through the curtain. "She's waiting outside. And I think she's still praying."

"Maybe she'll go away," Cavanaugh said, first to Michael, then to Lola. "Look outside again and see if she's gone. Please!"

Michael kept staring at Cavanaugh; Lola leaned against the door, her arms folded tight against her chest. "Is she really your daughter?"

"Of course she's my daughter. What difference does that make? Make her go away."

"She's come to see you and I don't think she's leaving until she does," Lola said. "I sure wouldn't."

Cavanaugh gathered himself for a moment. He swallowed hard. "Michael, my boy, will you please go out there and tell her...tell her..."

"To come back tomorrow?" Michael offered.

"Yes. Exactly. Tomorrow. Tell her to come back at noon tomorrow. We'll do lunch. Have coffee. Take a walk. Something. Tell her and send her off. Okay?"

———

"What time? Did he mention a time?"

Michael had led the woman back to her station wagon and opened the car door for her. But Colleen wasn't ready to drive away.

"Yes. He said...uh... noon," Michael told her. "He's so sorry, but he's feeling ill just now. The shock of seeing you after all these years I guess. And apparently his heart is not so good."

Colleen leaned back against the car, bringing her hands up

to cover her face. After a moment, she wiped at her eyes, then lowered her hands to her sides. She looked at Michael and shook her head.

"Sorry. A little emotional. It's been 25 years. He's not upset about my weight, is he? It's mostly water weight. I tend to store liquid. You understand?"

"No. I mean, um, when did you last see him?"

"That would be March 12, 1956, at 6:15 p.m. He said he was going to the store for cigarettes and I asked him to bring me back a box of animal crackers. I was 10."

"Oh, well, you'll have a lot to talk about then," Michael said, trying to sound optimistic about their reunion.

"I've been praying about this for a long time. My minister said I should forget him, but I feel I need some closure. Losing a parent — it really screws you up. You know?"

Now Michael was the one who felt tears welling. "I...Um...I do. Yeah."

"What's he like? Now, I mean?"

"He's good. I think he's a brilliant man. I really do. He's helped me a lot."

Colleen stared hard at Michael, her eyes narrowing. "And who are you? Are you his son? Please don't tell me he has another family?"

"No! No. I'm just a friend. I mean..." he pointed across the parking lot to the door next to Cavanaugh's. "I'm Michael Smith, the neighbor."

"Sorry. Okay. And I'm Colleen Reilly, the daughter."

"Yeah. Nice to meet you." Michael extended his hand. Colleen looked down at it, then reached out and took his hand with both of hers. She held on.

"Well," she said, her grip tightening. "Tomorrow then, I guess." She reluctantly let go of his hand, turning back to her car.

"Yeah. Great. Tomorrow." Michael watched as she folded herself into the station wagon. "He'll be here."

———

"She's gone?" Cavanaugh asked as Michael stepped through the door. The old man was stretched out on the bed with his head propped against a pillow, the flask in his hand.

Coming inside, Michael saw a different Cavanaugh than the man he had met a few days before. This version was unsettled, sweating, twitchy. Maybe he isn't the sage I imagined, Michael thought. There on the motel bed, panting, his face flushed, Cavanaugh Reilly looked like an aging alcoholic running from his past.

Lola stood at the window, peering through the thin curtain to the parking lot as Colleen's taillights disappeared into the night.

"She says she hasn't seen you since 1956," Michael said, surprised by the harshness in his voice.

"March 12. I know. She's gone?"

"She drove off. Yeah." Michael said, looking away.

Cavanaugh's body seemed to sink lower into the bed. He reached around and fluffed the pillow. "Why does this happen to me?"

Lola spun from the window, her voice sharp as a blade. "You have a daughter and you haven't seen her in 25 years? How could you?"

Cavanaugh waved her off and reached out in Michael's direction. "Son, come sit," he patted the bed. Michael slowly walked over and sat down but he still refused to look at Cavanaugh.

"Now listen carefully," Cavanaugh said, sitting up a little straighter. "When it comes to sex nothing beats a Bible-thumping, Holy Ghost-loving, Christian woman. In the sack, they become unhinged. They have visions. They speak in tongues. It's incredible. But getting through those pearly gates requires a ring and some very serious vows. I'm warning you now. There are consequences."

"That's not a consequence out there," Lola interrupted, her voice still hard-edged. "That's your daughter."

"Look, both of you, I need some time alone to sort this all out. Please? Michael, can you take her somewhere? Take the car. Just leave me."

Lola shot Cavanaugh a look.

"I think I need some time away from you, too."

Michael remembered something he'd been planning to do before he had to flee his own home so abruptly. He looked over at Lola.

"You wanna go to a movie?"

We're Connected

—

A single fluorescent bulb buzzes in a darkened chemistry lab, throwing slatted shafts of light and shadow across Formica-topped workstations crowded with Bunsen burners and racks of test tubes and beakers.

Dawn Karston, as Kimmy Marston, costumed in the plaid pleated skirt and white lace collar of a Catholic schoolgirl, steps warily through the lab.

"Bobby?" she says. "I know you're in here. Bobby?"

On one desk, a Bunsen burner ignites, as if by magic. Then, another and another, until the room is dotted with tiny golden flames. A vaporous fog rises from the test tubes and beakers. It gathers at the front of the classroom where the teacher's desktop is clear, except for a few books wedged between lion-head book-ends, and a single red apple.

Slowly, the vapor comes together into a shimmering, gaseous being. A square wooden box on a chem table next to the swirling figure opens with a snap, revealing dozens of neatly arranged dissection blades at the end of long silver handles.

Now, the gaseous figure forms into a teenage boy, in a football uniform, with full pads and a golden helmet. The football player reaches out and pulls a dissection knife from the box.

"Kimmy," he says, "You swore you'd wait for me, but you didn't..."

Kimmy turns. She is terrified.

"Bobby?"

Bobby lifts the blade over his head and begins to move in her direction.

"Bobby! Noooooooooooooooooo!"

The girl turns and struggles to escape the lab but chairs block her way and when she stumbles to the end of one aisle, Bobby is waiting, blade poised.

Bobby grabs her by the shoulder, his almost-solid hand still oozing small charcoal puffs of gas. Light glints off the dissection blade raised in his other hand.

The camera moves in close as Kimmy SCREAMS!

As she does, Bobby blows a thick river of swirling smoke from his mouth into hers. Kimmy is frozen in mid-scream, as the gas begins to fill her up. She expands, swelling like a human balloon, larger and larger. The blade in Bobby's gaseous hand is poised to strike. When Kimmy has fully expanded into a skin-stretching balloon girl, the blade comes slashing down.....

———

Inside the packed movie theater, dozens of teens recoiled in horror as Dawn/Kimmy exploded with a gut-spewing POP! Girls screamed. Their dates turned their heads or laughed nervously.

In the dead center of the theater, Lola buried her face in Michael's neck and shoulder. Michael couldn't decide where to keep his eyes. First the screen, then Lola, then back to the screen.

Twenty minutes later, Michael and Lola strolled toward the Lincoln waiting at the far end of a vast mall parking lot. Stepping through pale circles of security lights, Lola held her date's arm with both her hands. In the background a white plastic marquee glowed behind black letters spelling out: HIGH SCHOOL HORROR SHOW.

From a spot along the sidewalk outside JCPenney a stocky man in a leisure suit, partially hidden behind an old Ford Pinto, watched the young couple with interest. He snapped a flashlight on and looked down at a picture of Michael Donnelly and his mother, then looked back at the boy getting into the passenger side of a large white convertible.

Tomorrow morning, Jaime thought, you're mine.

——

Twenty minutes later, the young couple stood face to face outside a motel door, the boy's hands on the girl's waist, her hands clutching his shoulders.

"Well," Michael stammered, struggling again over what to say to the beautiful face looking up at him, with skin painted emerald and coral by the motel's neon sign. "I mean. It was..."

"Fun," Lola offered. "It was fun. She's pretty."

"Who?" Michael asked.

"Dawn," Lola said. "Pretty, you know, in a *gringa* sort of way."

"Oh, yeah. She is. Beautiful. If only they knew what they had. I mean she's..."

Lola put her fingers to his lips to stop him. She somehow moved even closer. "*Basta!* Okay then, I guess...*buenas noches.*" She squeezed his shoulders, then eased back slowly.

"OK. Yeah. Um. Good night." As she backed away, Michael smiled awkwardly and slowly turned to open his door, struggling to get the fish key out of his pocket and into his hand.

After unlocking the door, he looked back, but Lola had disappeared into Cavanaugh's room. Stepping inside his own room, Michael slammed an open palm against the wall. I should have kissed her, he thought. He pulled open the door to see if she might have thought the same thing, but the sidewalk was deserted.

"Going somewhere?" The voice from deep inside his room startled him. Michael swung around and saw Lola, the door that connected the two rooms open behind her.

"We're connected," Lola said, waving back at the open door. She moved toward Michael, who stood frozen. "I realized that was our first date and we didn't kiss goodnight."

Lola moved so close he could feel her breath on his face.

"Yeah, I wasn't sure," Michael said.

"Even though you already have a girlfriend, right?" she

teased, her index finger tracing a line on his lower lip. "And I have a boyfriend."

"Isn't he going to be jealous?" Michael asked.

"He's out cold," Lola whispered. "Come here."

Lola leaned closer. Slowly, their lips moved together. Michael felt the room spinning until all he knew was the warm, moist feeling of Lola's lips on his.

The kiss broke after a long beat, much quicker than Michael would have liked.

"*Hasta manana, mi novio,*" Lola whispered. She raised her finger again and painted an imaginary cross on Michael's forehead. Her fingers then drifted slowly down his cheek.

"See you tomorrow," she purred, backing through the connecting door.

"Tomorrow," Michael managed to say as the door clicked shut.

A Lover, Not A Loved One

—

Tomorrow arrived early for Cavanaugh.

The night before, while Michael and Lola were at the movies, he had packed the two hard-sided Samsonite suitcases he had carried for 25 years and took his framed portrait down and leaned it against the wall by the front door. He gathered Lola's things into her military-duffle bag and left them next to the portrait, alongside a dozen sample bottles of American Dream polish and cleansers.

At first light, while Lola slept, he carried the suitcases and Lola's duffle outside, setting them gingerly into the yawning trunk of the Lincoln. He was about to close the trunk, when something stopped him. He bent and snapped the clasps on one of the blue Samsonite bags. Flipping it open, he rummaged a bit, until he came out with a crumpled paper bag.

Opening it, Cavanaugh looked in at the small box inside. He lifted the box to his nose and sniffed.

"What are you doing?" Lola stood in the doorway in his terry cloth robe.

Cavanaugh quickly put the small box back inside the paper bag and sank the bag deep in his suitcase.

"What does it look like I'm doing? I'm fleeing. I'm taking my bow. I'm setting off for parts unknown."

"You can't do that. We're in the middle of something here." She stepped toward him.

"I don't care. We've got a car. I've cashed my social insecurity check. Let's just go. Now!"

Lola put her face close to his, staring up and standing on tip-toes. "That's how it's always gonna be with you, right? Half-assed. Never see anything through."

"You want me to follow through with something? I can do that." With his hands on her shoulders he eased her back two steps, then dropped to one knee. He looked up and smiled, hoping he looked gallant.

"Lola Fernandez Famosa – will you please come live with me in Savannah? We'll make love under the oak trees. Eat lobster with grits. Drink aged bourbon. Be happy. What do you say?"

"And what about your daughter?"

"Nothing about my daughter. Forget her. She'll be okay. Better really, without some brief, syrupy moment with her old dad. Let's go."

Cavanaugh grasped Lola's hand, offering another smile. Lola wrapped her fingers around his and yanked him to his feet.

"You can't do that to her again."

Cavanaugh tried to pull away but she wouldn't break the grip.

"Look," he pleaded. "I'm a lover, not a loved one. I tried. I really did. But fatherhood is not in my genetic code. Never was."

"She's spent years looking for you."

"That's not my fault. I haven't spent years looking for her. Go put on some clothes. We've got to get going."

Lola pushed Cavanaugh off the sidewalk and up against the grill of the Lincoln. She pointed a finger in his face.

"Listen to me now. I can't leave. Not like this. I've got customers and distributors. I'm building a business here."

"Please come with me. You won't regret it. Savannah is a very dirty city. They need cleaning supplies. And I need you."

She shook her head and started walking back to the room. At the motel door, she stopped and turned back. "Look, I love you, I think. I don't know. But I can't do this. Not now. You're on your own."

Just then Lola saw two muscular women in khaki slacks and polo shirts climbing out of a cream-colored *Palmdale Haven* van parked at the far side of the parking lot. Lola rushed back to Cavanaugh and spun him around, pointing at the van. "They gotta be here for Michael. Did you call them?"

"No, I swear."

———

Michael woke to find Lola standing over his bed, buttoning up her white blouse.

"Get dressed! Now!" She pointed to the open connecting door. "And come to Cavanaugh's through this door! Don't go outside!"

As Michael pulled on his T-shirt and shorts, someone began pounding on his door. He ran through the connector and locked it, joining Cavanaugh and Lola at the window where they peeked out.

"Jesus H. Christ, those are the two biggest women I've ever seen!" Cavanaugh said.

"They're here for you." Lola pulled Michael to the window so he could get a look at the women and the van.

"Look. I'll give myself up," Michael said, stepping back. "You two don't need to be involved in this."

"You can't do that. You don't want to get locked up." Lola stepped over and took his hand as Cavanaugh turned back from the window.

"She's right, son. Being locked up is like being married, but you can't go out for cigarettes and disappear. You're stuck. And the food is lousy."

Cavanaugh pulled Lola and Michael into a huddle.

"Michael, go back through the connector and grab your bag and get back here fast. Don't open your front door and don't forget the money and the plastic. If we're going on the lam we'll need lots of cabbage."

When Michael was gone, he turned to Lola. "Let's get him out of here and then we'll talk. Okay?"

Lola slowly shook her head.

"Please. I got a little crazy when my daughter... You know?"

Cavanaugh said. "But I'm back on it now. Let's stick with our plan. If we get the kid close to the movie set, his dad will pay a small fortune to get him back. We can do this."

"Suddenly, it's all a little too much. They really are going to lock him up."

"Now who is not following through?" Cavanaugh whispered sharply as Michael returned with his backpack.

"I think they're going to knock down my door!" Michael said.

"Here's the plan," Cavanaugh announced. "I'll go start the car and when it's going, you two come running. We'll make a break for it."

Lola nodded at Cavanaugh. He backed toward the door, then, like a brave celluloid hero, he brought his fingers to his lips and threw Lola and Michael a kiss.

When he was gone, Lola knelt next to an American Dream cardboard box and began to fill it with some loose bottles from the floor. "Go," she told Michael.

The boy stared down at her. "You are coming, right?"

She looked up and shook her head. "I can't."

"Please come. I want you to come."

"Tell Cavanaugh I said I was sorry. I can't follow through. He'll understand." She stood and moved close to Michael. "And don't trust anybody − especially him, okay?"

Michael felt himself starting to cry as Lola rose and gripped his arm.

"Good luck. Don't let them catch you − ever!" With her index finger, Lola drew another invisible cross on Michael's forehead, then kissed him on both cheeks. Across the sidewalk, the Lincoln's horn bleated. "Now − go!!"

Michael turned and eased open the door, but before he could move, a hard push rocked him back, his hand still gripping the doorknob. Suddenly, Jaime was inside the room, two meaty paws clamped on the boy's shoulders.

"Got you, you rich little nutcase!" Jaime shouted.

Michael squirmed but couldn't break the grip. He heard female voices calling his name from his own room next door.

He didn't notice Lola slipping up behind the big man. She swung a dark bottle of High-Gloss, All-Season, Furniture Magic against Jaime's head. The bottle shattered, spilling thick golden liquid down his neck and over his white guayabera. Jaime dropped like a dead man to the floor. Lola and Michael stared down at his limp body in horror.

"Is he dead?" Lola gasped.

"I don't know," Michael said, looking down. "Maybe."

The body on the ground was as still as a corpse.

"I killed him! I killed someone!" Lola whimpered.

"Are you sure?"

She reached down and shook Jaime. He didn't respond, only the tip of his tongue edging out of his mouth. She looked up wildly at Michael, her eyes darting around the room. "Look at him! Shit! Let's go! Now!" Lola grabbed Michael's hand and kicked open the door. The Lincoln was just steps away, its chrome nose pointing toward the apartment door, Cavanaugh still blasting the horn.

Sammi and Sheila had gotten Michael's door open but found his room empty. Rushing outside they saw a curly headed girl and a skinny kid, each carrying bags, leap into the front seat of the white Lincoln beside an old man. Before they could give chase, Cavanaugh gunned the Lincoln onto the sidewalk aiming for the two women standing outside Michael's door. Sammi and Sheila leapt back inside the room. Cavanaugh slammed the car into reverse. With tires screeching and throwing off smoke, the Lincoln careened back, back, back, back until it slammed hard into the *Blue 'Arlin* sign. The sign jolted, the big neon fish shook and then, in a graceful arc, dove onto the hood of the Lincoln.

For a brief moment, everything stopped. The driver and his passengers sat stunned, letting the hard impact settle around them. Sammi and Sheila were frozen in place, their figures framed in Michael's doorway. Cavanaugh recovered first, reaching for the gearshift as the two women started running toward the Lincoln.

Cavanaugh spun the steering wheel and pressed the accelerator. At the edge of the parking lot, he made a hard right onto Dixie Highway, and the marlin sailed off the hood and skidded across two lanes of traffic and into the path of a Fast Moves Inc. panel truck. The fish shattered under the front tires, the fin coming loose and wedging itself onto the back axle, leaving the truck with a jagged reptilian tail.

Cavanaugh checked the rear view and saw the Palmdale Haven van turning onto the road in their direction.

"Come and get me, coppers!" Cavanaugh yelled, raising his fist in the air and shaking it. Racing south toward Okeechobee Boulevard, the Lincoln weaved around slower cars, bounced twice over the curb and ran through a red light as the drivers in oncoming cars braked and honked.

A moment later, waiting at the same red light, Sammi looked from the driver's seat at Sheila.

"They don't pay us for car chases. How about a late breakfast?"

"Maybe we take an hour for a run on the beach instead?"

Sheila had been trying to lose a few pounds. Sammi nodded. The light changed and the Palmdale van, with its blinker on, made a slow left turn.

Cavanaugh continued to drive madly, a wide, devilish smile on his lips.

"Eat my dust, you assholes!" Cavanaugh shouted.

Lola, looking back through the window from her spot in the front seat, saw the van turn off. She leaned into Cavanaugh's ear and shouted: "It's over!"

"Not until I say it's over! They can't catch us." Cavanaugh pressed hard on the gas.

"Cavanaugh!" Lola yelled. "I mean it's over! They aren't chasing us!"

Cavanaugh slammed the brake. The car skidded and bounced onto the sidewalk, knocking over a tin trashcan, sending the lid rolling into an empty parking lot. The Lincoln eased slowly forward, two wheels on the sidewalk, the others on the road, until Cavanaugh saw a driveway and pulled into the parking lot of Corsica Jean's Tavern, a beer bar still hours from opening. Cavanaugh's face was bright red, his breath coming in gasps, like an athlete who had just finished a 100-meter dash.

"Damn. That was fun," he finally said, when his breathing eased. He looked over at Lola and Michael. "Did you feel it? Did you?"

"The crash?" Michael asked.

"No. The chase. We were alive! That's what it feels like. You're careening along – anything can happen. You don't know how it will end! That's the real thing, my boy. The absolute, one hundred percent real thing."

Michael looked back at the street, the excitement making him smile for no reason he could explain. He stared at Lola as she wrapped her arms across her chest and shivered. She leaned her head back into the upholstery, her eyelids pressed tight, shutting out the world.

This was getting good again, Michael thought. He was with his friends – including the beautiful young girl who had kissed him last night. And they were headed toward another girl who was waiting for him just an hour or so away.

He Looked Kind Of Dead

—

After a long time on the floor, the dead man stirred. His brain was electrified, a million sparking short circuits looking for a connection. Somewhere, there was a voice.

"Are you okay?"

Jaime tried to move. His hand, apparently unbidden by his brain, rose to touch the back of his head. Again, the voice: "How do you feel?"

With much effort, Jaime willed his eyes to open. Slowly, they did. The world was out of focus but there seemed to be a familiar female figure bending over him. He was a boy in his tiny bed, his mother leaning down to wake him, gently.

"*Mamá, eres tu? Mi Madre?*" Jaime managed to whisper. "*Hola mama!*"

He blinked once, twice, three times. Slowly, the female figure came into focus. Golden light poured in around her, giving the woman a heavenly aura. This wasn't his mother. It was a woman he knew from hundreds of stained glass windows and life-sized statues.

"You've got a really bad bump on your head, but I think you'll be okay. There's no blood."

The vision of a haloed female figure seemed to give Jaime strength.

"*Madre Immaculata, disculpame! Yo sene! Estoy un hombre muy malo. Immaculata...*"

His arms reached up. He struggled to stand.

"*Madre Immaculata*, please take me to heaven," he pleaded,

in English now, his arms reaching the figure, his hands gripping the back of her neck, trying to pull himself into a sitting position.

"I wouldn't stand up yet, if I were you." But Jaime couldn't be stopped.

Colleen rose with him. Halfway up, his legs gave way and Colleen pulled him close, her body pressed against his. When he raised his head, they were face to face. Jaime now saw a beautiful woman before him, sweating and breathing hard. Oh my God, he thought. It's been so long.

He kissed her roughly. "*Tenga mis hijos. Mi amor. Por favor, tenga mis hijos.*"

"I'm sorry," Colleen sputtered, still reeling from the kiss that, except for a hint of lemony furniture polish, was very sweet. "I don't speak Spanish. What are you...?"

Jaime, filled with passion now, pressed his body against her.

"Come to me. Let me suckle your dark nipples and taste your sweet nectar." His eyes twitched with desire, his fingers gripped and released Colleen's arms. Then, just as quickly as he had come to, Jaime passed out, his head sinking into the soft valley between her breasts.

"Oh...Don't try to talk," Colleen said, staring down at the top of the man's head, enjoying the feeling of his face pressing into her chest. "Let me just get you to the bed."

Jaime suddenly rallied, his head jerking up. "Yes," he shouted. "The bed!"

His head dropped again to her breasts. Colleen eased him back toward the motel bed, step by slow step. She was close enough to let him down, but she held on for a long moment, still savoring the feeling of a man pressed hard against her. When Jaime's head rolled back, she tried to lower him gently to the mattress, but he was too heavy and slipped from her hands, the bed springs screeching as the dead weight of him crash-landed.

Colleen reached down and lifted each of his tree-trunk legs onto the bed. She saw a knitted blanket on the bedside table. She stretched it over him, then slipped a pillow under his head.

"Well, okay then...Just rest a while," Colleen said to herself as much as to him. She stepped back, not sure what to do. "I'll be right over here."

She pulled a straight-backed chair to the edge of the bed. When she sat down, she felt her hands rising, almost involuntarily. She pressed her palms against the breasts where Jaime's head had been. She could feel her heart pounding inside her chest.

Realizing where her hands were, Colleen jerked them away, folding them tightly into her lap.

———

Even with the top down, Lola was hot. The cold front was a day old now, the sun bright at 4 p.m., the humidity creeping back. The wind whipping through the car was thickening, almost tropical.

But the pulsing heat she felt was something else, Lola thought. And what was this dull ache just behind her forehead and the persistent itch deep in her gut?

"Can't you get hooked on this stuff?"

That was her question a year ago, when Dio, her neighbor at the time, offered to trade Lola's cleaning supplies for the product he was peddling.

"Nah, man," Dio assured her. "Heroin's got a bad rap. You sniff a little, you be fine. Jus' no needles. Needle's the fuckin' slipp'ry slope."

So they traded. Dio's magic powder for Lola's American Dream Tile Magic, American Dream Toilet Magic and American Dream Laundry Magic.

It was a perfect trade. Dio liked things clean. The powder made Lola feel as if she were swimming a leisurely lap along the bottom of a heated pool, the thick water swaddling her. She liked that. And the dreams – oh how she loved the big, candy-coated dreams.

But her relationship with the baggie had intensified during the past six months, after she made what she considered a strategic decision to put herself on sale for a limited time only, planning to use the quick cash to make a major investment in American Dream products, buying in at the Patriot Level, about halfway up the pyramid, where annual sales could reach six figures. Currently a Junior Achiever, Lola had yet to make any real profit, plowing her earnings into more products and hustling to build her sales force, which at this point was a cocktail waitress with a drug habit, a stripper at Vegas Showgirls, and a motel maid named Clarita.

Lola discovered quickly that pushing expensive cleaning products to poor people and selling yourself to rich ones was difficult, often degrading work. The baggie was a good way to get your mind off all of it.

Lola had always been disciplined and determined. She set goals. She was sure she could be the boss of the baggie. But somehow, the baggie had become the alpha in their relationship. Racing along in the convertible, the wind roaring in her ears, she could hear it calling from inside her purse.

Fifteen minutes earlier, the Lincoln had slipped under the concrete canopy of the Florida Turnpike. In this part of Florida the toll road connecting Orlando to Miami was a border of sorts, dividing all the sprawling subdivisions, the car lots, 7-11s and hamburger joints east to the Atlantic from the sugar cane fields to the west, fields which eventually gave way to countless acres of pine forests and cypress swamps and beyond that the flat expanse of water, grass, mangroves, snakes, birds and gators known as the Everglades.

The three travelers hadn't spoken for a while. Lola swiveled to see Michael in back, wide awake and scratching notes on a large pad with a silver pen, clearly excited to be moving closer to his movie star. She watched Cavanaugh stuff a cigarette between his lips, leaning in close to the steering wheel to avoid the wind, as he sparked his lighter, the smoke flying back over his shoulders as he exhaled. Despite all his trash talk about families, at this moment Cavanaugh looked to her like a happy father − no, she thought, make that a happy grandfather − out for a Sunday drive with the grandkids.

Her traveling companions were clearly enjoying this adventure. It was her life that was coming apart. The struggle to start her business, the horrors of the street-corner sex trade, the days and nights lost to the baggie, and now, she had killed someone. They won't care that it was more like an accident, a brief moment of crazy. No, someone was dead.

Staring out the window at the flat expanse of Florida, she flashed on an image of her father, laid out in the Miami morgue, as the attendant pulled back the thin white sheet, uncovering what looked to Lola like a clay mask of her father's face.

Julio Famosa had dropped dead three years earlier waiting for a bus ride to his minimum wage job stocking shelves at a Hialeah grocery store. Lola was 16 then, living with him in a concrete block public housing unit just outside Little Haiti.

Her sweet, always smiling father, had owned a newsstand and cigar store in Havana before the revolution. Lola had no memory of her mother. Julio never said much except that Lola's mother had dreamed of becoming a film star. According to Lola's *abuela*, after giving birth to her only child, Chelo Famosa landed a small role in a propaganda flick called *Revolución del Corazón*. By the time production wrapped, Chelo had moved in with a burly key grip. Cleaning out her father's chest of drawers after his death, Lola found a glossy black and white publicity shot of a pouting woman in a form-fitting white gown, pin curls descending from a black bouffant, twisted into commas beside each of her almond eyes.

The loss of his young wife to the film business hadn't soured Lola's father on cinema. After fleeing Cuba with his daughter in the early '70s, Julio learned English by watching old movies on television. He and Lola spent most weekends in classic movie palaces, like the Miami Theater on Flagler. The day before the stroke killed him, he and Lola were at the Coral Theater on Aragon Avenue for a Sunday matinee of *Gone with the Wind*.

The next afternoon, after identifying her father's body, Lola climbed five flights of stairs to the hospital's tarpaper roof. From there, she could look out at the skyline of downtown Miami and across the wide, azure bay to Miami Beach.

She thought she had come up to cry, but instead, she felt Scarlett O'Hara moving inside her. She walked to the ledge and raised her fist to a vast blue sky.

"As God is my witness, Lola Fernandez Famosa is going to be super fucking rich!" she shouted to her adopted city, arms waving defiantly, her body angled out over the ledge.

She finally cried five days later, after a Greyhound ride to Tampa. She had come to spread her father's ashes in Jose Marti Park, a narrow strip of grass, wrapped by a tall iron fence, in the heart of the Ybor City immigrant district. While the deal had only ceremonial meaning, Cuba held the deed to the tiny park. As she emptied the chalky contents from the wooden box below a bronze bust of the Cuban patriot, she whispered: "You're back home, Daddy." Bitter tears, held for so long inside swollen clouds of grief, finally came pouring down.

"You okay?" It was Cavanaugh, looking over from the driver's seat.

"I don't know," Lola said, turning back to give him a wan smile.

She felt herself shudder. The pain in her head and the itch in her stomach were back, a grinding, focused pain, like a dentist drilling a molar without Novocain.

Cavanaugh looked over. "Come on, baby, cheer up. We're on a road trip."

"They're gonna put me under the jail," Lola whimpered. She straightened on the seat and started to rifle though her purse.

Cavanaugh slowed the car and eased off onto the shoulder. A canal ran alongside the road, the water flat and dark, tall stalks of Muhly grass sprouting along the water's edge like a thousand wind-swept parentheses.

"So do you think he's really dead?" Michael asked, after Cavanaugh turned off the engine.

"The gendarmes have very thick heads. It's a job requirement," Cavanaugh said. "I'm willing to bet he's alive, but I'm sure he's not happy."

Lola looked up from her purse.

"I don't know what came over me. He grabbed Michael and I just smacked him with a bottle of All Season Furniture Magic. I didn't want Michael to get locked up."

"I know, dear," Cavanaugh said, his hand going to her shoulder.

Lola quickly shrugged it off.

"But now I'm wanted. You kill somebody, they don't forget something like that. They find you."

Cavanaugh put his hand back on her shoulder, but this time he grabbed hold. "I told you. He's not dead."

"You don't know that! I saw him. He looked really, really dead. Jeezus!" Lola pulled out her own pack and lit up. Then she dug deeper into her purse.

"Michael, what did he look like?" Cavanaugh turned back to look into the backseat.

"He looked kind of dead," Michael said.

"Have you ever seen anybody really dead? Not Hollywood dead. But actual *mortum*?" Cavanaugh asked him.

Michael hesitated.

"Just once," he whispered.

Lola turned back. "You did?"

"His mother," Cavanaugh said quietly. "Sorry my boy, I forgot."

Michael nodded. "I really didn't see much. Blood and stuff. But then..." His voice trailed off.

"You need to get that image out of your head," Cavanaugh said. "It's toxic."

"You've seen a lot of dead people?" Michael asked.

"Ever heard of the Battle of the Bulge? So many dead, we had to stack them like fire logs. Men frozen just the way they fell. Some still gripping their rifles." Cavanaugh's voice quieted, he turned away from Lola and Michael, wiping a hand across his eyes. "But it's funny. A body – once the life leaves it – is just a sack of bones and blood. It resembles a living person, but, in a way, it looks kind of like a mannequin, a fake."

"Stop it! I saw this guy! He's dead!" Lola finally found what she was looking for – a tightly rolled plastic baggie, with a mound of white powder at the bottom. She unrolled it and scooped a bit of the powder onto her upturned fingernail.

Looking hard at Lola, Cavanaugh yanked the stub of his cigarette from the holder and tossed it out the car window. "What are you doing?" he demanded.

"Taking some medicine. For my nerves." Raising her fingernail to her nose with shaking hands, at least half the dose spilled onto Lola's lap.

"Damn," she whispered, digging into the bag again. This time, she consciously steadied her hand, but just before she reached her nose, Cavanaugh grabbed her wrist spilling all of it onto her lap.

"Dammit, Cav. What are you doing?"

"Don't do that! You're killing yourself."

"And you're not? Jeezus! Unfiltered cigarettes and cheap bourbon? You got no right to jump into my business."

"I'm dying slowly. Gracefully. The way God intended. Bourbon is a carriage ride to the undertaker. That stuff's the express train."

"I'm scared, okay? I don't want to go to jail again. I hate it there. And you can't run a business on one phone call a day." She tried to scoop up the white flakes on her pants, but Cavanaugh brushed them away.

"Dammit!" she screamed. Lola's head dropped forward and she began to sob.

"Come on. Put that away." Cavanaugh slid over. His index finger moved slowly up her cheek tracing the line of a single teardrop. She stopped shaking as her sobs eased. After a long moment, Lola looked over at Cavanaugh, then rolled the bag and dropped it into her purse. Close to her now, Cavanaugh pulled Lola's head against his shoulder.

"You know that I love you, right? I wouldn't let anything happen to you. You do know that?"

Lola didn't respond, but kept her head pressed to his shoulder.

"My Lady," Cavanaugh intoned, suddenly sounding *veddy* British and *uppa* crust. "Sir Michael and I will be your knights in shining armor. Your safety is our charge. Have no fear."

Then he dropped the accent. "Besides, if you're in jail for 40 years, I'll be extremely horny by the time you get out."

Lola raised her head now, dabbing at her eyes with her fingers. She almost smiled at Cavanaugh.

"Love me?" he asked.

She did – a little – she knew that. This was the second time he'd told her he loved her that day. Clearly, this thing between them meant more to him than it did to her. But looking at his face, suddenly boyish and insecure, awaiting her answer, she felt a wave of tenderness sweep over her. She also felt the cramp in her stomach easing, as the small dose of powder she had managed to get into her nose did its work.

Lola glanced briefly back at Michael, then took Cavanaugh's face in her hands. She leaned her forehead against his lips.

Putting his arms around her, Cavanaugh pulled her close and held on for a while. Lola felt the heat deep inside her easing up. When she was calm and still, Cavanaugh set her up straight in the seat, brushing some stray curls from her face.

Cavanaugh winked at Michael, then cranked the car. Yanking down the gearshift he gunned the Lincoln off the grassy shoulder and onto the gray band of concrete snaking along a narrow canal. Looking out the window, Lola saw clusters of snowy egrets wading bent-necked along the edges of the canal. Looking closer she thought she saw the ridged back of an alligator just below the water's gunmetal skin.

Closing her eyes, Lola felt the powder's familiar reverie drawing the curtains on her troubles. She drifted back to the park in Tampa; this time the powder she was spreading was her father's ashes. She was scooping them with her hands from a large plastic baggie. A baggie that stayed full no matter how much of its contents she spread. Smiling, Lola felt herself rising above the park, like an airplane moving from sunlight into a puffy castle of clouds.

Seeing her drift off, Cavanaugh turned and whispered to Michael: "Watch and learn, my boy. Women require very special treatment."

Michael smiled back at him.

"So I see," he said.

"OK. Hold on tight. We're following this concrete carpet straight into the heart of darkness."

I'm Not Bothered By Human Things

—

When she first found the big man passed out on the floor of her father's motel room, Colleen reverted to her training as a nursing assistant, wiping the goo off the man's head and neck with a towel from the tiny bathroom, then checking for a wound. But there was no blood, no gash, just a small knot where the bottle met his head.

She wasn't sure exactly what happened, but she felt certain the man was okay. She was even more confident of her diagnosis after she got the big man onto the bed. His eyes weren't glassy when she lifted the lids, his breathing was easy, and at one point, he began to snore.

Still flushed from their erotic dance as she helped get him on the bed, Colleen tried to distract herself. She threw away the broken glass and wiped up the goo on the carpet with the towel. Colleen thought the dark stain left behind blended well with the half-dozen other splotches on the matted gold carpet.

Once the cleanup was done, she wandered around her father's motel room, taking in the walls collaged with clipped magazine photos of Gandhi, Beethoven, Elizabeth Taylor and Einstein, along with a half-dozen Playboy centerfolds, airbrushed to perfection.

She found Cavanaugh's framed portrait leaning against the wall next to the door. She lifted it carefully, taking a long look at the handsome man in his business suit, posed on a curtained stage, a Georgia state flag furled on a gilded staff behind him.

This was the Daddy she knew.

She wasn't sure who the new version of Cavanaugh Reilly was.

Colleen sat in the wooden chair next to the bed, listening to the low snarl of the man's snores, her father's picture on her lap, the shadowy room holding the skunk of cigarette smoke and mold. A few shafts of sunlight shot through the opening in the curtains, each band illuminating a glittering constellation of dancing dust. She felt almost giddy. After months of frustration, sleeping some nights in her car to save money, her stomach in knots from greasy diner food, her spirit beaten down as promising leads turned into dead ends, it felt good to sit in a room her father had occupied just a few hours before – a room where an odd and exotic man lay stretched across the bed nearby.

Sitting quietly, with the man's soft snoring as a soundtrack, time turned tidal, ebbing and flowing until Colleen drifted off. She didn't know how long she'd been asleep when she heard the man snort and begin to stir.

Colleen snapped to her feet, looking down at the big man on the bed. She switched on the tiny metal lamp on the bedside table. The man blinked, then slowly rolled onto his side, groaning as his hand found the spot where the bottle had landed.

"You're coming around," she said.

The man struggled to sit up. Settling on the bed beside him, Colleen gripped his shoulders and tried to help him rise. Once he was sitting upright, he lolled there for a long moment, his eyes closed, his hand on the back of his head. Colleen watched as he blinked twice, then opened his eyes.

The man didn't seem able to focus on her or the room. She studied him. His skin was golden in the lamplight, a cluster of spidery tracks – tattoos from the wrinkled pillowcase – spread over one cheek. He had a prize-fighter's face – the nose fleshy and blunt, his lips thick, just a few centimeters separating the bristling black eyebrows atop his ridged brow.

He turned to look at her. "Who are you?"

"I'm so glad you're awake and sitting up." Colleen tried to brush a curl from his forehead. He reached up, pushing her hand away.

"What are you doing?"

He tried to slide away but the sagging bed and the crumpled bedding held him.

Colleen realized the man didn't remember what had happened after she found him on the floor; not the strange words in Spanish; certainly not his hands gripping her body or his face pressed hard against her breasts.

"Oh, sorry."

Colleen stood quickly and turned away from him, embarrassed, the blood rushing to her cheeks. She picked up Cavanaugh's portrait and sat back down in the chair, lowering the frame into her lap, the image facing up.

"Excuse me. I'm Colleen Reilly. I, uh, I found you. On the floor. Are you a friend of my dad?"

The man didn't answer, but struggled to stand. Setting down the portrait, Colleen rose again and grabbed his arm, in case he started to crumple. Jaime didn't push her away. He was busy looking around the room.

"Gotta go," he said, trying to take a shaky step.

"Really, you probably should stay put for a while longer," Colleen said.

"No, I really gotta go." He waved his arm in the direction of the bathroom.

"Oh," she laughed. "Sure."

Colleen stayed close, her grip tight on his arm as the man lumbered toward the bathroom like the Frankenstein monster, one arm extended in front of him, waving about for something to grab.

"I could come in," Colleen said, when he lingered shakily in the doorway. "I'm a certified nursing assistant. I'm not bothered by human things. Let me help you."

The man brushed off her grip and staggered into the bathroom, slamming the door behind him. Pressing her ear to the door, Colleen could hear his insistent pee echoing off the porcelain. Then she heard water running in the sink for a long time.

"Better?" she asked, as he stepped warily from the bathroom, water dripping from his face and hair, his four-pocketed shirt wet around the shoulders and across his chest where he had tried to wash out the remains of the furniture polish.

The man didn't acknowledge her. Instead, he lumbered to the middle of the tiny room. Stopping between the edge of the bed and the door he turned with some difficulty to face Colleen.

"The old guy?"

"That's my Dad. I was just coming for a visit. See, we haven't seen each other—"

He cut Colleen off with a slow-motion wave. She was quiet as she watched him gather his thoughts. He opened his mouth once and nothing came out. He shook his head, droplets of water flying off his wet hair. Closing his eyes and standing still for a few more seconds, he finally managed to produce a full sentence.

"What's...his...ah...relationship with...Michael Donnelly?"

"Who? Oh, Michael? The boy from next door? I don't know. See, I haven't seen my dad—"

He cut her off again with another wave of his arms. He started walking, or more accurately wobbling, toward the door.

"Is he coming back?" Colleen asked. "We're supposed to have coffee. Or maybe lunch."

The man stopped, his hand on the doorknob. He turned back. "Who?"

"My Dad. Cavanaugh."

He let go of the knob. He took a shaky step back toward Colleen.

"What...do you know...about the boy? Was he traveling...with the old man?"

"There was a convertible that I think was the boy's or maybe my father's. And a girl." Colleen was trying to think hard, her words coming slowly. "Young...her hair was dark, and curly, tight curls, and she might be Latin. No, she's definitely Latin."

"Latin? You mean like Puerto Rican or Cuban or Mexican or Dominican?" The man's voice was firmer now. "Latin doesn't tell me a lot. What about the car? What kind was it?"

"A big one! Yes, very big." Colleen was sure she was being helpful. "It's white...and big...yeah. Did I mention convertible?"

"That's it?"

"Ummm. Maybe. Look, could you tell me your name?"

"Why?"

"Because I'm asking?"

He reached into a front pocket and pulled out his business card.

"If you hear anything from your father that could help me find the boy, I'd appreciate a call."

Colleen looked down at the card: *Jaime Solano. Private Investigations.*

Turning to leave, the man opened the door, squinting as a harsh midday light hit the darkened room like a nuclear blast. He raised his hand, forming a visor over his eyes.

A Ford Pinto was parked by itself at the far edge of the parking lot. Framed in the motel doorway, Colleen watched the man stagger across the asphalt lot toward the car.

"Wait!" she called. "You should have that looked at. Your head, I mean. You know, just in case. I could drive you."

"It's okay." He kept walking.

She called out. "Could you take me to him? I'm so close. I don't want to lose him now."

Jaime didn't stop. Colleen watched as he put his hands into his pocket and drew out the car keys. He stopped and looked down at them, as though he was surprised to find them in his hand.

Colleen ran across the parking lot toward the Pinto. She didn't run a lot, she realized. Pausing a few feet from the man, she felt her breath coming in harsh gasps. Dozens of dark balloons blotted out her vision. She bent over, letting blood return to her head, hoping the spinning world would slow down.

"Do you have any idea where they might be going?" she heard him ask.

Still bent forward, Colleen raised her head, her eyes meeting his. She still couldn't speak but at least she could see again. She managed to shake her head "no."

"That's what I thought."

He turned back to his car.

Colleen wished she had a better answer. She wished she could catch her breath.

She watched the man reach for his door handle. He was a stranger now, but she felt close to him. They had shared something. And she knew if she was going to find her father again, this burly, gruff detective, climbing into a tiny car, was the one man who could help her.

The Pinto's engine gurgled to life. The man looked out his window at Colleen, then turned to look over his shoulder, as he put the car into reverse.

Colleen watched as the Pinto backed from the parking space and crossed the lot. She saw the taillights glimmer as it reached the street. The red flash of the brake lights seemed to flip a switch for her. The old Colleen would have given up at this point. But she didn't feel like the old Colleen, especially with this man. He had held her. He had whispered sweet things to her in an exotic language. And he was the only link now to her missing father.

It would not end here.

This man was going to help her whether he wanted to or not.

Colleen turned and ran like a mad woman toward her station wagon.

We Doubled
Our Security Team

—

Security was not in the budget for *Swamp Fiend* II, but Dawn's manager kept calling, and now Charlie Gray, the producer of Dawn's current blood and boobs epic, was looking across a wide cypress desk at Jake and Jerry Messer, his brand new security team.

Charlie kept his look stern, but inside he was pleased with himself. Shooting movies in Florida was a fucking bargain. His production office was a ramshackle fishing shack, his production trailers were second-hand, his crew was non-union, his actors mostly amateurs. These two smelly locals would fit right in.

The "job" interview was more cursory than official. The Messer Brothers worked cheap and they were big, scary-looking and available. Todd, Charlie's location guy, had provided the closest thing the brother's had to a resume: "They skipped out of Belle Glade High at sixteen and seventeen. By all accounts they spent the next decade taking graduate-level courses in Harely-riding, beer-drinking and reefer-smoking. You need 'em to kick some ass, they're willing."

"So you got any experience in the security arena?" Charlie asked the brothers, trying hard not to make eye contact.

"We been up close and personal with a lot of cops and security guards, if that's what you're asking," said one of the brothers.

Just then a sneeze that would have registered on the Richter scale pulled Charlie's focus to Jake, or was it Jerry? Charlie had no interest in knowing which was which. He looked away, but couldn't un-see one member of his new security team look down at the mucus slathering his hand, then rub it all away on the knee of his already greasy blue jeans. His brother, Jerry maybe, had both hands busy – one was digging into a molar with a toothpick, while the other vigorously stroked the stalks of stubble on a cheek slashed from ear to chin by a Pepto-pink scar.

If Charlie had been the kind of person to be bothered by such things, then hiring these two semi-literate chunks of gristle and fat might have caused him to rethink his life or at least his career choices, but Charlie wasn't that kind of person.

His Mega Watt Studios produced blood-soaked horror films headed directly for drive-ins and video stores, while Love Armor Ltd., working out of a warehouse in Chatsworth, churned out 15-minute full-penetration flicks aimed at middle-aged men sitting on stools in darkened video booths thoughtfully equipped with paper-towel racks for easy cleanup. The profit margins were slim, but enough to buy a split-level in the Pacific Palisades, with a fully restored 1968 Pontiac GTO in the garage. And there was Sandy, a curvy blonde in the late stages of her 30s, who had parlayed an overbite and a willingness to wrap her mouth around just about anything into a minor porn career. When she wasn't sipping a margarita by his pool, Sandy was a big earner for Love Armor Ltd.

The jangling phone made Charlie jump, but he let it ring three more times before picking up.

"Pam, I got it." Charlie spoke loudly so that Dawn's manager, at the other end of the line, would hear the conversation with his imaginary production assistant. The Messer brothers would know he was lying, but Charlie prided himself on not giving a shit what the help thought. "You get back to the set, sweetheart. Tell 'em I'll be right there. Ben, is that you?"

Charlie didn't wait for an answer. Years in the shallow end of the movie-making pool taught him not to leave too many gaps in business calls for investors and managers to fill with pesky questions.

"Look, I told you there's nothing to worry about," Charlie

continued. "First off, we're in the middle of East Bumfuck here. I got lost findin' this place and I knew where I was goin'. There's one dirt road in and out and it's blocked off. We got professional security at the gate 24-7."

At the other end of the line, in a dimly lit office above Hollywood Boulevard, Ben Hoffman was not in great shape. An old film crew buddy, fresh from a shoot in Hawaii, had shown up at 5 p.m. the day before with two Thai Sticks and a bottle of macadamia-flavored tequila. Ben had awakened in his office chair a few minutes before this scheduled call with a monkey banging on a pot lid in his brain.

"You told me you'd add extra security for this one," Ben muttered. "The kid is on the lam and we think he's headed her way."

Charlie laughed.

"And I'm telling you we doubled our security team. The supervisors are here in my office now." He looked over at Jake and Jerry. "Nothin' to worry about. We've spread a flier with the kid's picture around the 'glades. Not that's there much around – just miles of swamp, a million hungry mosquitoes the size of goddam hummingbirds and a small army of horny gators. These fuckin' gators! You can hear 'em doing the reptile nasty all night long. I'm thinkin' I could use it as a soundtrack for an outdoor porno series. If the kid manages to get anywhere near the set, either we'll get him or the gators will."

"Alright," Ben sighed. "Just make sure Dawn has somebody with her out there. She's got herself way too worked up about this kid."

"Ben, I'm tellin' ya, we're good here. Dawn's first couple of days have been stellar. We're on schedule. And I'm getting daily security updates from my team. As soon as I hang up with you, I'm meeting with them. So don't worry. Just let me know when they snatch up that kid."

Not waiting for Ben to respond, Charlie barked "gotta run" and slammed down the phone. He stood up and looked hard at the Messers.

"So what the fuck's up with you guys? You're hired. How

'bout you get to the gate and start guarding the shit out of this place, okay?"

Jake, the brother born exactly 12 months ahead of his sibling, raised the hand that had recently been covered in mucus.

"Todd said we got paid – in cash. Every day. And food, he promised food."

Todd, the location manager for *Swamp Fiend* 2, was Charlie's fixer. A skinny, whip-smart 30-year-old who never seemed to sleep, Todd got shit done. He had found this location, the former site of Captain Eddie's Lunkerland, and paid some locals minimum wage to shore up the old clapboard shack, nestled in a copse of twisting scrub oaks that was now Charlie's production office. Using the shack as an office saved Charlie the cost of another film trailer. And that's why Charlie loved Todd. He was fucking frugal, like his boss. Charlie Gray hadn't climbed to the middle rungs of the B-movie ladder by spending money he didn't need to spend.

The $250,000 budget for *Swamp Fiend* II was double the one for the original *Swamp Fiend*, and that meant a location shoot in an actual Florida cypress swamp and the screaming services of an up-and-coming starlet named Dawn Karston. He'd done the original *Swamp Fiend* by filling his porn studio with silk plants (rented and returned), a dozen Slip 'n Slide plastic sheets hooked to water hoses and, for authenticity, B-roll of the actual Everglades purchased cheap from a starving LA filmmaker who couldn't get financing to finish his *Vanishing River of Grass* documentary.

Todd had found that footage when Charlie needed it, just like he found the Messer Brothers when Charlie told him to track down some cheap security. Todd was currently in Moore Haven, the Glades county seat, passing out a few envelopes of petty cash, a move designed to head off any pesky visits from overzealous county inspectors.

Charlie looked from the Messer Brothers to the big desk calendar he had marked with black Xs for each completed shooting day. Just 15 more days, he thought. He could do this. He heard a low buzz, then felt a tiny pinprick as a mosquito dug into his neck just south of his left ear. He slapped hard. He couldn't do much about the mosquitoes, but he wasn't going to let these two rednecks get under his skin. Money? Food? Good luck, assholes.

Born in Secaucus, New Jersey, Charlie was using a fake Southern accent and channeling a down-market version of Jimmy Buffett on this set. The day he arrived in Florida, he wrapped his brawny, 50-year-old body in Hawaiian shirts and surfer jams, let his Ray-Bans hang from nylon strings around his neck, and stuffed his salt-and-pepper curls into a Miami Dolphins baseball cap. Just 5-foot-7, Charlie had the gritty, intimidating bark of a Marine drill sergeant.

"Goddammit!" Charlie leapt to his feet, bellowing in the direction of Jake and Jerry, as his fist came down hard on the desk. "You'll get what you're owed! Now get the fuck out there and earn it!"

The fury of Charlie's words lifted Jake and Jerry from their chairs, sending them scuffling and scrambling out the door. Charlie sat down and didn't look up until he heard the door slam behind his security team. That's when he leaned back, idly scratching his fresh mosquito bite, and allowed himself a brief smile. He knew from years of experience that shouting at employees, wives, girlfriends, and children was a good way to end stupid conversations about money or food or anything else he didn't feel like talking about.

It worked every time.

———

Heading toward his office, Jaime knew he needed to focus. But it wasn't easy. The part of his head that wasn't throbbing kept flashing on images of the woman from the motel room. Sure, he had given the woman his card, but he told himself it was just business. He didn't look at her in his rearview mirror as he drove away, though he had wanted to. No, absolutely not. Women were off the table. Too dangerous. So he left, cruising south in the Pinto toward Lake Worth, a city where office rents were even cheaper than the cheap rents around downtown West Palm.

He flicked on the car radio. It was tuned to a Miami station that played disco hits in Spanish – his ex-wife's favorite station. He didn't want to think about her either. So he flicked it off.

For a guy who earned his living pulling back the curtain on other people's secrets, Jaime had had no idea his wife had been plotting an escape until she was gone.

Laura had often complained about his hours, his attitude, his pessimism. Part of the job, he told her. Investigators work nights and see the world at its worst. Toward the end that he didn't know was the end, she called him at his office to say she wasn't happy and didn't want to raise their infant son alongside an absent and uninterested father.

"Who's happy?" Jaime told her. "Look at my folks."

His parents' imperfect union proved marriages don't have to be happy to last. Refugee families had to work hard, stay together and just keep going. Of all people, Jaime thought, Laura should have understood. Her parents had fled Cuba in 1960, a year before his. Like most of the other early refugees, they lost not only their possessions but their credentials. In Cuba, her father had been a doctor. His was a building contractor.

Jaime had learned from his father – who had hung drywall and smoothed concrete foundations for years before he got a Florida contractor's license – that refugee husbands were supposed to do whatever it took to support their families. Refugee wives were supposed to smile and be supportive and make sure the kids didn't starve and got to school on time. They certainly weren't supposed to pack up a 2-year-old boy, leave a 10-word note on the kitchen table, and move to Tampa with a professional jai alai player nicknamed El Coyote.

The anguish he felt after Laura's departure had surprised Jaime. The hurt was sharper and deeper than the time his appendix almost ruptured. He couldn't sleep. Couldn't concentrate on his cases. But he could eat. Laura's departure was part of him now – about 30 pounds of pain.

After the initial shock wore off, Jaime doubled down on his hours and his pessimism. She'd been gone two years and Jaime hadn't asked a woman out. Stay focused, he kept telling himself. So he'd ignored the warm feeling in his chest when he'd looked at the woman in the motel. Don't go there. Avoid it like a bad dog. Focus.

Climbing out of the Pinto, Jaime's legs went rubbery and he felt the world spinning. He grabbed an edge of the open car door to keep from falling, his other hand instinctively rubbing the spot on his head where the bottle had shattered. After a few seconds the Tilt-a-Whirl slowed and the asphalt parking lot came back into focus. He took another deep breath, then trudged stiffly to the glass door of his office and inserted the key.

Solano Investigations was located in a 1960s strip center at 719 South Dixie Highway, just beyond a concrete bunker of a beer bar with the oddly glamorous moniker in red neon over the door, The Club 717. Solano Investigations shared the strip center with Lake Worth News and Books, a store that sold cigarettes, periodicals and eight kinds of beef jerky, but was known mostly for the Adults-Only section tucked behind a beaded curtain in back. The building was also home to a one-seat salon called Judy's Hair-Um, and Bernie's Second Time Around Bookstore. Jaime had peered through Bernie's window just after he moved in. The glass was greasy, but he could make out rows of shelves stacked with books and filigreed with spider webs. Bernie, or whoever owned the place now, hadn't put a key in the front door in the two years Jaime had been a neighbor.

Once inside, Jaime settled heavily behind a metal desk cluttered with papers and notebooks, a black rotary phone, five empty Coke cans, two Almond Joy wrappers, and a long-lensed black Nikon. His table lamp was a bronze hula dancer, her breasts bare, her hips and legs covered by a stringy gold skirt that shook when the light was on. It was a gift from Laura, at least 10 birthdays ago. A few days after Jaime found Laura's goodbye note, the hula dancer froze, never to sway again.

In the pale light, Jaime could see that the Dawn Karston blow-up doll, its air slowly escaping, had folded into a yoga position his ex-wife used to practice called Downward Facing Dog.

He thought again about the woman at the motel. She was bigger than his ex but pretty in her way. She reminded him of the red-haired girl in his first grade class at Hialeah Elementary. He had always been too shy to talk with her, and his fresh-off-the-boat English was no good anyway. But thirty years later, he could remember every detail of her pale and beautiful face.

Jaime shook his head, then reached into a bottom drawer and pulled out a fresh guayabera.

In the office's tiny bathroom, he stood barechested, twisting around as he tried to get a look at the back of his head in the mirror. He gave up and stared instead at his face, suddenly noticing a cluster of stiff black hairs jutting from his nostrils. He opened the medicine cabinet, took out a small pair of scissors, and leaned close to the mirror. He somehow didn't notice the woman standing in the open doorway behind him.

"Excuse me..." Colleen said nervously.

Jaime jumped, jamming the blunted end of the scissors into his nostril.

"SHIT!" he shouted, turning to confront Colleen. "What the hell..."

"I'm sorry." Colleen took a step back. "Your front door was unlocked."

Jaime grabbed his shirt off the sink and tried to cover the soft expanse of his bare belly.

"You can't just come in on a man like that. This is my office. My bathroom. What's the matter with you, lady?"

"I said I was sorry."

Jaime pushed past her and walked toward his desk, shrugging into his shirt and wrestling with the buttons. When the shirt was finally buttoned up, he turned back to Colleen.

"And that's supposed to do it? Saying I'm sorry? Anglos always bustin' my ass and thinkin' all they gotta do is say 'I'm sorry.'

That ain't enough."

"Okay," Colleen said, remaining calm despite his anger. "I'm *really* sorry."

Jaime shook his head and walked around the desk, plopping down in his chair. He didn't look up at Colleen, now facing him from the other side of the desk. He shuffled papers, opened and closed drawers, feigning work.

Finally giving up his charade, Jaime slammed down a stack of papers and glared up at her.

"What do you want from me?"

Colleen looked around the office, then back at the big man behind the desk.

"You feel like getting something to eat?"

Standing Up For America

—

Forty-five minutes out of West Palm Beach, Cavanaugh eased the Continental onto U.S. 27, a two-lane highway that starts abruptly, just north of Miami, then slices northwest through sugar cane and cattle country; a glorified country road through Florida's quiet places, far from the cacophony of the coasts. Cavanaugh looked out at marshy cane fields and wide meadows rolling to the horizon, occasionally broken by stands of pine trees, a smattering of lone palms or a low-slung, drive-thru hamlet, offering gasoline or barbecue.

The sun, which had been glaring in his eyes moments before, now nestled on the horizon, painting the low, wispy clouds lavender and pale pink. Cavanaugh smiled. Florida could be beautiful once you got beyond the squalid cities and the carbon-copy subdivisions.

He glanced over his shoulder at Michael, asleep in the back seat, his head on Lola's duffle, his gangly limbs akimbo. He looked at Lola beside him, finally asleep, her tight curls mashed against the car window.

Cavanaugh always enjoyed a long drive on an open road, especially with friends around him, and most especially when they were asleep. Gave a man time to think. Although at the moment, his thoughts were not all happy ones.

He felt bad about his daughter. Maybe he should have spoken to her last night. Hugged her. Talked an hour or so, then sent her on her way. But after so much time, what was there to say? Where would he begin? Long before he declared war on the world of marriage, careers and mortgage payments, he'd felt the pressure building, especially when The Darks flooded through him, stealing his sleep and his hope. But for twelve years the love he felt for his daughter had held him. To him, Colleen had been the one thing in his life that made any sense. But after years of using alcohol to medicate his misery and beat back the depression, he decided his daughter would be better off without him.

That didn't make the actual leaving any easier.

On that March night in 1956, Delia O'Reilly was attending a meeting of her women's bible study at Alpharetta Baptist. Colleen was stretched out on the living room couch in front of the big walnut box that held the TV, watching *Father Knows Best*. Cavanaugh leaned down, kissing her reddish curls, his palm lingering on her back.

"I love you, Little Sheba."

"I love you, Daddy."

Cavanaugh let the moment linger, then he turned toward the door. Colleen's voice stopped him.

"Oh Daddy, are you going to the store?"

He turned back and nodded.

"Could you bring me a box of animal crackers? The good ones. With the circus wagons on the box and the white string?"

"Didn't you already have your dinner? You know your Mom doesn't like you sneaking snacks."

"We don't have to tell her. Do we? She's not here. And I really, really love those crackers."

"Sure, Little Sheba, I'll buy you a box," he said. "If that makes you happy."

The chubby, ten-year-old smiled up at him. She had a beautiful face, especially when she smiled. Looking at her from across the room, Cavanaugh took a mental picture of that smile and tried to file it somewhere he wouldn't lose it. His departure, he knew, had to be all or nothing. He had been a good soldier, but now he was deserting the battlefield, and everything, including his daughter, was about to become a casualty of war.

He was starting his new life in New Orleans. He'd figure it out from there. He had $500 in cash; the rest of the money he'd secretly saved over the past two years – almost $15,000 – was left for Delia and Colleen in the joint checking account. At the 7-11, he bought fresh cigarettes and some supplies for the drive. Passing an aisle with cookies and candies, he picked up the small, colorful box of animal crackers. He knew he wasn't going to take them home but he would buy them. He'd promised her that.

Snapping back to U.S. 27, Cavanaugh shook both the child and the grown-up Colleen from his head. Better that she gets on with her life, he was certain of that.

A few miles later, he thought about Michael, another child who lost a parent unexpectedly. He looked over his shoulder at the boy sleeping peacefully in the back seat. He had developed his own fatherly feelings toward the kid. The double-cross plan that seemed to make so much sense when he first met the boy was starting to unravel as he got to know him.

If Cavanaugh had learned anything living on the fringes of society, it was that you should always trust your gut. And his gut was telling him to be gentle with the boy. As the car followed the curving highway, Cavanaugh started gathering together the strings of a new plan. Michael had a wad of cash and a credit card. Maybe he didn't need to call the boy's father. If Cavanaugh could get Michael to the film set, the boy would certainly let he and Lola take off for Savannah in the Lincoln, with some cash for the trip. He'd propose it as "a finder's fee."

He felt the strings knotting together. Yes. It's a win-win for everybody. This could work.

A series of make shift road signs pulled his mind back to the highway. He saw them before he could actually read them. Lit by the last beams of daylight, they were bent and brown. As he got closer he realized they were actually cypress branches rising from single stalks, the wooden letters nailed to curving arms forming short sentences. Like the old Burma Shave signs, they were spaced fifty yards apart along the roadside.

Your kids are begging....
Your wife says please....
Dad, won't you stop....
So we can see the cypress knees???

Cavanaugh took in the signs, then slowed the car, turning in at a dirt road marked by a fifth sign:

Tom Hawkins's Cypress Knee Museum and Motel

The road wound around some trees and intersected another dirt road where an arrow carved from a cypress branch pointed the way. Cavanaugh followed it over some jolting bumps for a quarter mile into the swamp, before it opened up into a white gravel parking lot.

The place seemed like something you'd conjure in a dream. Surrounded by cypress swamp and nestled in a slow rising fog was a large barn and, across the lot, a clapboard motel – five rooms fronted by a plank sidewalk. Just beyond the rooms sat a single cabin with a red door, marked by a handmade cypress sign: OFFICE.

Stepping out of the car, feeling the blood rushing back to his legs, Cavanaugh looked around at the ramshackle motel and museum and smiled. Of course, there had to be a cypress knee museum somewhere in the world. And when you're living the vagabond life, places like that always turn up just when you need them.

———

Looking out the car window at the motel, Michael thought they had somehow ended up on the set of *Psycho*. He expected to see Norman Bates watching them through the office window.

"Where are we?"

"We're taking in some local culture," Cavanaugh told him. "Let's see if the natives are friendly."

"Aren't we going to the set?"

Michael was wide awake now, all the anticipation around this quest rushing back into his chest.

"We need a base of operations," Cavanaugh said. "We don't even know exactly where we're going yet. But we'll get you there. Just need to trust me on that."

Cavanaugh walked around the long convertible. He reached in and gripped Lola's shoulder gently. She turned, blinking sleep from her eyes.

"We're stopping for the night."

Lola's eyes fluttered open and she nodded at Cavanaugh.

The Lincoln was parked in front of the barn-like building. More hand-cut letters identified the place as *Tom Hawkins's World Renowned Cypress Knee Museum and Gift Shop*. The double doors were open and light from a dozen fluorescent fixtures spilled out.

Curious, Michael stepped quickly to the double doors, peering inside at a large room lined with cypress bookcases, the center of the room haphazard with card tables and rough-sawn, wooden pedestals. And on every shelf and tabletop sat shafts of polished honey-colored wood – cypress knees – each rising a foot or two from a flat base, each one identified by a hand-lettered sign.

Cavanaugh and Lola joined Michael, each stepping solemnly down the tight aisles, hands folded behind their backs, like visitors at an art gallery. On this table – *Joseph Stalin, Flipper, and Satchmo*. Over here – *Lady Hippo Wearing a Carmen Miranda Hat, Atom Bomb, Apollo 13 Rocket* and on a special table all by itself - a cypress knee *Marilyn Monroe*.

If you looked carefully enough, Michael thought, cypress knees pretty much resembled everything and everyone in the world. He heard Lola saying something to Cavanaugh and turned to see them snickering.

"What is it?" Michael asked, his question making Lola laugh even harder.

Cavanaugh picked up a knee from the display table. He ran his hand along the shaft of wood that tapered up to a knobby round top.

"Well, Lola said it another way, but let's just say this place appears to be a shrine to the erect male member."

"What?" Michael stared.

"It's a bunch of dicks!" Lola laughed, bringing both hands to cover her face.

Cavanaugh picked up the sign for one of the more majestic knees, holding it up so Michael could read the description: *Michelangelo's David*. "Remember when I said Florida was a total cultural wasteland? I take it all back."

"We're staying here?" Lola asked.

"I can think of no place I'd rather be just now," Cavanaugh said.

———

The Cypress Knee Museum's executive director, curator, security officer and custodian was at work in the motel office when Cavanaugh eased open the screen-door, raising his palm in a "ladies first" wave so Lola could make an entrance. He slipped in behind her.

When Michael arrived a few seconds later, he found his friends frozen side by side, staring as an odd little man lifted a stub of cypress to his lips, his gray tongue knifing out-and-in, spreading a coating of saliva over the wooden shaft.

Tom Hawkins was the size of a ten-year-old waiting for a growth spurt. His gray hair was shaved close to a head that seemed to come to a point atop his skull and under his chin. Decades of Florida sun had cut jagged canals into his bronzed face like the cracks in a shattered car windshield. His bony, mantis-like body was decorated with a *King of Beers* t-shirt and baggie shorts, no shoes. He worked standing up, behind a flat-topped podium, a thrift store find that still bore the round plastic logo of the *Belle Glade Chamber of Commerce*.

He glanced up at Lola, his tongue retracting, a sly smile spreading.

"Be with you in a just a sec," he said, his voice a Southern-tinged tenor. His tongue quickly went back to work.

"Wow," Lola said, struggling not to laugh. "Your museum is... well. I mean, how do you do...ah...these things?"

Tom stared over at the girl, his tongue still moist and darting, the knee obscuring the side of his face. After another few seconds, he lowered the shaft of wood.

"My knees? I boil 'em, then strip 'em to get this satin finish. Then I finish it off this way." Hawkins said, letting his tongue flick out again, snake-like, in Lola's direction.

"You have to lick them?" Cavanaugh asked, disgust in his voice.

"The final phase requires some of your own spit. But I'm 82 and still doing 100 pushups a day. I credit all the wood fiber I'm takin' in."

"People, like forests, can become petrified over time," Cavanaugh announced.

"Don't joke," Tom snapped back. "If it wasn't for wood fiber, you and me wouldn't be alive. In case times ever get real hard and there are plagues or famines across this earth, you'll know where to come to stay alive. It's all right here in the Florida swamp."

Cavanaugh snorted. "We're living in a country run by a television pitch man. Those plagues and famines could be coming sooner than you think."

Tom set the saliva-coated cypress knee on the counter and glared at Cavanaugh.

"That talk won't stand in here, my friend. You're speaking about the President of these United States. A man who managed to dodge the bullets of a deadly assassin only a few months ago."

Tom pointed over his shoulder to an 8-by-10 color photo of Reagan, autographed and hanging inside a cypress frame.

"Sent me that," Tom said. "After I wrote and told him the goddamn Army Corps of fuckineers and the Sugar Nazis up in Clewiston were killing the Everglades and he needed to put a stop to it."

"Good luck with that. Your president works for those guys," Cavanaugh snorted. "Reagan's nothing but a puppet wearing pancake makeup and holding a script."

Lola grabbed Cavanaugh's arm and pulled him back from the counter.

"Cav, stop it. Mr. Hawkins is right. You're talking about the man who is standing up for America."

Tom eagerly joined the chorus.

"You listen to her, mister. President Reagan is putting this country back on the right track after decades of unchecked socialism. This little gal is obviously a patriot. I respect that. Even in a wetback."

But Cavanaugh wasn't done.

"I guess illusion loves company. You two enjoy your fantasy president." He stepped close to the counter. "Listen, we need rooms and some information."

The old man ignored Cavanaugh. He looked only at Lola.

"Young lady, I'll answer any questions you have, but as for your grandfather, I'm not speaking to him."

"Grandfather. Dammit, you –" Cavanaugh lurched forward, but Lola reached up and slapped her hand over his mouth.

"Cavanaugh! *Silencio!* Go outside, get the bags."

Keeping one hand over his mouth, Lola used her other hand to yank Cavanaugh away from the counter. When he tried to turn back, Lola cut him off.

"*Ahora!* I mean it."

Cavanaugh sputtered but obeyed, pushing past Michael and slamming the door behind him. Turning back, Lola put on her street-corner walk, hips gyrating ever so slightly. Once she reached Tom, she leaned over, her hands gripping the edges of the podium, as she flashed the come-hither smile she normally aimed at cars cruising down Olive Avenue. Lola may have believed she lacked certain assets, but Hawkins seemed entranced by the view down the gaping V-neck of her T-shirt.

"We'd love to rent a couple of rooms for tonight."

Michael joined Lola at the counter. Tom kept his eyes focused on the girl.

"Can I ask you something?" Michael walked toward the

counter.

The old man reluctantly looked at Michael. "We're supposed to be working on that horror movie set but we can't find it. Do you know where they're filming?"

Tom nodded as his eyes swiveled back to Lola. Of course he knew about the movie. He was a man who made sure he knew everything going on in his part of the world. And he was sure this cute little Cuban girl would appreciate knowing such a man.

"The movie folks? Yeah, I know where they are."

He smiled at Lola.

"You do?" Michael asked.

Tom nodded but said no more. He seemed to be waiting for something. Michael pulled out his wad of bills and peeled off a $20. He slid it across the podium to Tom.

"You're close," the old man said, slipping the money into his shorts. "The turn-off's just seven miles up the road. Not marked though. Just a gravel road."

Michael plunked down a wrinkled map of South Florida. "Can you point it out?"

"I could." Tom smiled at Lola again, then paused.

Another $20 appeared in Michael's hand and then disappeared into the pocket of Tom's shorts. The old man again stared down at the map. A bony finger slid slowly, like a kid using an Ouija board, until it marked a spot.

"We're here." He let his finger slide less than a half-inch on the map. "And they are over here. Just the other side of the old fire tower. They're set up about a mile off the road. It's kinda the north end of the glades. Not really sawgrass. More of a cypress swamp, like what we got all around us right here."

"You a fan of horror movies?" Michael asked him, as he folded the map.

"I stopped with Frankenstein and Dracula – the originals. In the museum I got a Bela Lugosi and a Boris Karloff. Mummy, too. How many rooms you need?"

"Two...please?" Lola said.

Tom reached behind the desk to a cypress pegboard with

keys hanging. He lifted two off brass hooks. He offered the keys to Lola, then, as she reached out, he pulled his hand back.

"That old man," Tom said, looking off at the door Cavanaugh had left through. "A girl like you can do much better. Much better indeed. Take my word."

He dangled the keys over Lola's outstretched hand.

"Room incudes admission to the museum and the boardwalk that runs into the swamp. Museum closes in an hour but re-opens at eight tomorrow morning. That's sixty dollars for two rooms. Cash. In advance."

Lola looked at Michael. The roll reappeared. Michael pulled off three more twenties and passed them to the old man.

"Here's the keys," he said, letting them drop into Lola's palm. "And keep the noise down after eight. I turn in early. Unless you'd like a private, moonlight swamp tour, little girl. You just knock. I live in the back."

Lola flashed another sexy smile. "Thanks. I'll keep that in mind. You've been so kind."

The boy left first. Tom kept his eyes on the girl, who turned back and waved, offering a silent "thank you" before slipping through the screened door. Watching her swaying hips as she left the office, Tom felt a surge of wood fiber moving through him. But at 82, he knew it was mostly just a feeling.

When he could no longer see her, Tom returned his attention to his latest museum piece. The round peak of the knee looked to him like a man's bald head, so he had decided to name this one for Reagan's wounded aide – James Brady.

This knee was a natural find, which made it even more special. The cypress knee scientific community may have consisted of only one man, but he was very imaginative and persistent. Tom liked to help nature's creative process by wrapping young cypress stalks in wire or taking the base off a glass bottle and forcing the knee to grow through it. To Tom, knees were like Florida clouds in the summer, morphing and shifting into the shape of humans, dogs, cats, dragons, rocket ships, almost anything. No two ever exactly alike.

Tom didn't mind that the old man had laughed and made fun of him. It wasn't the first time. Hell, Johnny Carson had once sent him a first class plane ticket so millions of people could laugh at Tom Hawkins on national television, as he licked a cypress knee and drank a glass of liquefied wood fiber. The hour he spent in the green room, and his seven minutes on Carson's couch, were the longest stretch in more than 30 years when his feet were clad in shoe leather.

What do people know, anyway? Tom thought. They don't actually take the time to see what's really going on around them. Living alone in his swamp over 50 years, doing his experiments, building his shrine to these living creatures, Tom had taken all the time he needed. Time to see the bulbous buds peeking out of the rust-colored water during the rainy season. Time to wade through the muck during the dry season, when the water receded, exposing nations of knees, some clustered like parents and children, others in military battalions, like so many silent sentinels, their knotty faces focused on something only they could see. Some rose into Gaudi-like cathedrals, the rippling towers set apart by the gray trunks of cypress trees, and all of them – the families, the sentinels, the cathedrals, even the trees themselves – leaning imperceptibly but urgently toward the receding water, the elixir that suckled them, that gave life to Hawkins's' magic kingdom.

Tom set James Brady carefully on the podium. He walked over to a small cypress desk in the corner, extracting a single sheet of paper from the center drawer.

He looked down at a picture of the boy who was just in his office. Below his face were the words: "*Escapee from a mental institution. Dangerous. If you see this young man, call 310 777-6688 immediately.* CASH REWARD!"

Tom didn't make a lot of money from his motel or museum. He was a fan of cash rewards. Setting the paper carefully on the desk, he lifted his phone and dialed the number.

Frick-Frackin'-Fiddle-Sticks

—

"My minister thinks it all goes back to the box of animal crackers," Colleen said between bites of a cheeseburger. She and Jaime were sharing a booth at The Clock, a 24-hour diner set along the five-block strip of mostly empty buildings that passed for Lake Worth's downtown.

"He never came back with those crackers and since then, I've just had this hunger, you know? For food or booze or daytime TV. Anything. But I keep thinking all I really want is that one box of animal crackers. *Barnum's Animals*? You know, the kind with the string handle?"

Jaime stopped in mid-bite. "Why didn't you just buy some?"

"I did. I ate every box they had within 100 miles of Atlanta. But I always felt hungry afterwards. So look at me now." Colleen popped a handful of pencil-thin French fries in her mouth.

"Maybe you're just a fat person. Me, I'm a fat person. I know it. I don't fight it." Jaime took another big bite of his burger. "See," he said, his mouth still full of food. "I am what I am."

Colleen finished chewing her fries, dabbing at her mouth with a napkin before continuing.

"I'm not a fat person. I'm a troubled person. There's a difference. That's why I need to talk to him. There was no closure. One minute he's my dad and the next minute he's gone. I really think when I get some closure, I can lose this weight and get on with the life I was meant to have."

Colleen stopped. It suddenly felt like she was telling her tale of woe at an AA meeting, not sitting across from a man on some semblance of a date. She picked up the burger and took a large bite.

Jaime wiped his mouth with the back of his hand and smirked at her.

"Maybe you should just *closure* mouth."

Colleen swallowed hard. Then brought the napkin to her lips again, letting Jaime's rude comment hang there a while.

"Go ahead. Mock me all you want," she finally said. "I thought you were a loving person. Guess I was wrong. Could you pass the ketchup?"

Jaime passed the Heinz bottle.

"What gave you that idea?"

"What?" Colleen twisted off the top, flipping the bottle above her plate and shaking it over a clear space next to her fries.

"What gave you the idea that I'm a loving person?" Jaime asked.

Colleen looked up at Jaime as thick blobs of ketchup puddled on her plate. "When you...back in the motel room." She offered Jaime her best impression of a sexy smile.

Jaime ignored the look and went back to his burger. Looking down at her plate, Colleen saw her fries were buried under an avalanche of ketchup, the red goo oozing over onto the Formica table.

"Oh, frick-frackin'-fiddle-sticks!" The words came out in a high-pitched wail that seemed to surprise Colleen.

"Sorry about that," she whispered. Colleen put the bottle down and began wiping the ketchup off the table with a napkin.

"Fiddle sticks?" Jaime asked, the slightest hint of a smile on his face.

"Just help me find him." Colleen didn't look up at Jaime, so he wouldn't see she was crying.

"That's not my job."

"Then I'll hire you."

Jaime shook his head.

"I'm already hired."

"So, you get paid twice. And you only have to do one job. They're traveling together. Find the kid, you find my dad."

"Look." Jaime said, his stern face returning. "That happy family thing is just bullshit sold on sitcoms and Disney movies. I don't do family reunions. I do disunion, disloyalty, discord. That's the real world. My advice is to go home and forget it. Your old man obviously doesn't want to be found."

They were staring at each other now, the food forgotten on their plates. Tears had left snail tracks down Colleen's cheeks.

"I'm sorry." Jaime let his grimace ease.

Colleen didn't know why she was telling this man so much about herself. She had never really done that before outside of a meeting. Maybe it was desperation or lack of sleep, or maybe it was something else. Whatever it was, she couldn't stop.

"Look at me," she said. "I've tried everything else. Booze. Pills. Food. Nothing works. I *have* to find him and you're the one who can help me do that."

"And I said no."

Jaime's hand was on the table, next to his plate. Colleen thought it looked more like a paw, with short, thick fingers, jagged nails, as if Jaime had clawed his way up a particularly rocky cliff. Bitten down, more likely, Colleen realized. But she could also see the skin on the back of his hand was chamois soft, and the color of coffee with cream. She felt her heart beating. He's like a dog without an owner. He needs care. Love, maybe. She reached out and took the big hand in both of hers and lifted it off the table. Jaime's grimace returned, but he didn't pull his hand away.

Colleen offered a tiny smile.

"Please..."

She watched the grimace leave his face. His dour mood seemed to brighten. Maybe she was reaching him, Colleen thought. Just then the waitress appeared with a coffee pot and she watched the light in his eyes switch off. He snatched his hand away from hers.

"Look, I'm sorry." Jaime stood up, dropping a twenty on the

table. "But the answer is still no."

———

Sitting on a white plastic chair in her shabby cave of a trailer, sipping from a lukewarm can of Tab, Dawn plotted an escape. Not so much from the teenage maniac who was stalking her, or this God-forsaken film set, but from the whole slasher film *thing*.

Five movies, she thought. Weren't they supposed to take her somewhere? Up the ladder? Onto real features with big-name stars, luxury trailers and good catering? Scripts with dialogue a human might actually speak?

She had visited sets for films like those, where craft services was a table covered with treats – cashews, bananas, candy bars and packets of pretzels and chips. Where coolers brimmed with name-brand sodas and exotic juices, and tables held urns of fresh coffee and boxes of tea, with honey in a squeezable plastic bear. For *Swamp Fiend*, Craft Services was a tannin-stained Mr. Coffee, a can of Chock full o'Nuts, a loaf of Wonder Bread, a jar of off-brand peanut butter and an industrial-sized plastic bucket of cheese puffs.

Dawn looked at the cardboard taped over the windows of her trailer. Real film trailers were clean, well-lighted places, with glass windows, working bathrooms, and comfortable chairs. They weren't ripe with the musky aroma of cigarette smoke and sickly sweet smell of pee.

DAMMIT! My movies make money! I'm the face on the posters! There's even a Dawn Karston blow-up doll!

But here she was, sitting in a swamp, doing another low-budget feature about a group of horny teenagers in the woods, out for what they believe is a wild weekend of beer and sex, except slowly, one by one, they start to die. Dawn, as usual, would survive the early carnage, only to be the slasher's final horrifying kill.

At the end of each shooting day, Dawn and the other vic-

tims — she refused to call this cast of junior college drama students *actors* — were driven into Clewiston, the nearest town,
in a late-model minivan with a broken A/C. So much for the
limo Ben Hoffman swore was in her contract. Charlie Gray, the
producer, was housing his cast and crew at The Sugar Palm, a
decrepit, '50s-era motel on Highway 27.

Ben had promised her the Swamp Fiend would be played by
a "major star" but Todd Fishman — yes, Fishman was his real
name — had last appeared as a singing waiter at the Burt Reyn-
olds Dinner Theater just north of West Palm.

In a plotline lifted from *King Kong*, the Swamp Fiend sees
Dawn's character swimming off a boat dock and, poleaxed with
desire, decides to take her back to his lair and explore the intri-
cacies of inter-species lovemaking. To keep things appropriately
gory, before making off with Dawn, the Swamp Fiend drowns a
few of her friends and uses the razor-sharp claws on his flippers to slash the face of her boyfriend. Then, the creature drags
Dawn through the swamp to his cypress tree-encircled lair,
which features a limestone cave for a honeymoon suite. After
some failed attempts at intimacy, the love-struck amphibian
accidentally kills the object of his desire while trying to give
her a hickey. In the movie's most touching scene, the fish man
secretes a single tear as Dawn, her bikini barely hanging on,
gasps her last breath, cradled in his slimy, webbed flippers.

Her character dies just before two Seminole Indians, who
have joined forces with Dawn's badly scarred boyfriend, find
the hidden lair and harpoon the monster, stringing him upside
down on a tall wooden scaffold fishermen use to display their
big catch. THE END.

Dawn had felt her heart sink when she read the script. Here
we go again. This was the glamorous life that had lured her
to L.A. four years earlier? Just 15, Dawn had fled Dayton in a
1971 Mustang with an 18-year-old boyfriend who dreamed of a
career as a Hollywood stunt driver. She wished she knew what
happened to Bobby. He was sweet and she had dumped him
for a production assistant who promised her a tiny part in a

horror film being shot at an old campground in the Angeles National Forest.

While that walk-on had proven to be the first step in her bloody hike to the peak of B-movie stardom, Dawn also discovered that what passed for love and relationships in Los Angeles was as phony and shallow as most of the products the studios and production companies churned out.

Maybe it would be better if this Michael kid did kill her.

Dawn shook the dark thoughts from her head. This would be over soon. Ben always told her – once you're famous, *Swamp Fiend* is the kind of movie you'll talk about with Carson or Letterman while perched on their couch in something sexy and short.

At the moment, Dawn's outfit wasn't sexy, just a pair of sweatpants and an Ohio State sweatshirt to ward off the dampness of the swamp. It was early evening, a magical time when the sun faded, and the first stars dotted the wide sky above the swamp – reminding Dawn of the electric stars twinkling from the roof of Dayton's Classic Theater, where she had gone as a girl. It was also the hour when the mosquitos went back to wherever they go and a million cicadas, gathering like some arachnoid tabernacle choir, began their skittering hum, a sound so intense the film crew had to stop work until it stopped, always as abruptly as it started.

Time for a walk, she thought. A chance to relax before spending the next five or six hours up to her knees in murky water, her feet sinking into the spongy muck below. She came down the three front steps of the trailer onto the shell-covered parking lot, feeling the crunch beneath her slippers as she headed to a spot where a break in the trees revealed the night sky.

So far only one star. A lot like this picture, Dawn thought, allowing herself a smile.

You're supposed to make wishes on the first star of the night, but what would a realistic wish be? A film role that didn't involve her being eaten, stabbed, sawed in half, or worse? That was something worth wishing for.

Dawn heard angry voices from the direction of Charlie's production shack. She added that to her wish list — how about I work on a movie where the production office isn't a fucking falling-down shack!

She saw Charlie Gray on the porch waving his arms and shouting at one of the two morons that constituted the *Swamp Fiend* security team. Dawn knew one of them was Jake and one was Jerry, but they were pretty much interchangeable. She called them Jethro One and Jethro Two.

Both had hit on her as soon as they were on set. In separate visits Dawn had opened her trailer door to find a beer-bellied, greasy-haired redneck, smelling like reefer and cheap cigars, standing on the landing offering her a snaggle-toothed smile.

"How about I show you the 'glades on a Harley Davidson?" they had pretty much both told her.

How about you lose 50 pounds and get your teeth fixed?

She had wanted to say that, but instead, Dawn just shook her head and slammed the door in their faces. This was the crack security team Ben had promised her? Like everything else on this set, the two Jethros were a cheap joke.

Charlie's production shack was about 100 feet from the cluster of trailers that wrapped the parking lot. Strolling toward the commotion, she saw that Charlie was yelling at Jerry Messer. She knew it was Jerry because of the scar that curved across his stubbly cheek from ear to chin. It was at least a quarter-inch wide and sickly pink, like the color of bologna when you take it out of the refrigerator and realize it has gone bad.

"Go grab his ass and don't fuck it up!" Charlie yelled down from the porch at Jerry.

From his back pocket, Jerry pulled a silver set of handcuffs, likely ones that had shackled his own wrists at some point, and waved them at Charlie.

"He's as good as caught," Jerry said.

Dawn spotted Jake approaching from the gate, as Jerry waddled ten steps to his Harley, climbed on and cranked it up. The raw rumble of those 750 horses was deafening. Jake got close to the chopper and Dawn watched Jerry lean down and shout something in his brother's ear. Stepping back, Jake offered a "thumbs up" as Jerry twisted the accelerator. Man and bike roared off down the dirt road in a cloud of gray smoke, leaving Dawn's ears ringing and the smell of exhaust fumes in her nostrils.

When Dawn turned back, she saw Jake staring in her direction, offering a leering smile. He started to wave but was rocked by a sudden sneeze. Dawn knew what was coming next but she couldn't look away. It was like watching a car wreck. Jake gathered the goo from his nose and his chin with his open palm, gave it a quick, meaningful glance, then drew the wet hand across his thigh, adding another layer of scum to his filthy blue jeans. When he was done, he leered again at Dawn and, using the just-wiped hand, now balled into a fist, he made a series of short jerking motions near his crotch.

Dawn spun around and stomped back to her trailer. She sucked hard on her straw, but the Tab was almost empty and all she got was the low gurgling of liquid and air.

A Need For Knees

—

Now that rush hour was over, the drive from the Donnelly Avionics compound to Palm Beach wouldn't take more than twenty-five minutes. Dick could have called, but some news was better delivered in person. He knew Alex would be home. It was Tuesday, the night of his weekly blues jam. At least Alex considered it a jam. Dick thought of it as an opportunity for Alex's musician buddies to eat and drink for free.

Dick wouldn't admit it, but the drive was also an excuse to spend more time behind the wheel of his new 1982 Lincoln Town Car. Sure, the black luxury liner didn't corner like his old BMW but, when he was settled into the leather cockpit, the air conditioner whispering from the dash and Sinatra and the Basie band blowing from the speakers in back, Dick felt like an astronaut tucked inside a NASA capsule. The outside world couldn't touch him.

He hadn't made this drive much since Jack Donnelly had died and his son had stepped into the business. He drove the route when Jack's widow, Frances, was felled by a wicked stroke. And the day Crystal did the horrible business in the bathtub.

Dick liked Alex and felt a grandfatherly affection for Michael but he didn't like Palm Beach. Never had. A bunch of rich phonies, he thought. Spoiled. And not bothered by pesky things like morals or scruples. But it had made sense for Jack and now Alex to live there. If you're a fisherman, Jack had been fond of saying, you really should wet your hook where the big ones are biting.

Though Jack had been dead almost 20 years, Dick still missed his partner. Dick Adams and Jack Donnelly had been Delta Tau's at the University of Florida. Jack the gregarious good old boy with a head full of business ideas, Dick the behind-the-scenes fixer who could bring Jack's brainstorms to life – like Jack's idea for a keg delivery business. Frats needed kegs for their parties, but most of the brothers were under twenty-one. Let's bring the beer to them, Jack said, before heading out to make the sales calls. While Jack was getting orders, Dick lined up graduate students, all legal drinking age, to make the purchases and deliver the kegs.

The profits were plowed into Jack's next idea. Tennis shoes were a hot item and Jack thought UF students would buy tennis shoes adorned with a Florida Gator logo. Dick found a Dominican manufacturer to produce the shoes and a design student who came up with something close to the UF logo, but not close enough to get them in trouble with the school. Pretty soon fraternities and sororities were bulk-ordering tennis shoes emblazoned with gators and their own Greek logos.

During a round of golf just before graduation, Jack met an alum who had become a defense contractor. Jack came back to Dick with his biggest idea yet. It was 1952. The Cold War was ramping up and the tax dollars were gushing from the Pentagon.

"We just got to get in front of the spigot," Jack had told him.

It took ten years and two presidents to get the spigot flowing, but when the avionics business took off, thanks to a briefcase full of defense contracts, Jack bought a Gatsby-like mansion near the Breakers and its finely manicured golf course. Dick built a two-story, rock and cypress retreat in the beach community of Hobe Sound. Let Jack live the Palm Beach whirl. Dick and Judy, his college sweetheart, liked the quiet.

Sailing up and over the Intracoastal on the Flagler Bridge, with its 1920s Florida Fantasy turrets, and a string of golden lamps glowing like landing lights on a runway, Dick shook Jack Donnelly from his thoughts. Alex was his partner now, and while he wasn't his father, he was okay. He could close his share of deals and he listened to Dick when it counted. So what if he never met a guitar he didn't want to buy? Business was good. And with this new president reigniting the Cold War, it was only going to get better. Alex Donnelly could afford his indulgences.

Dick got no answer when he rang the bell, so he let himself in with the key he kept for visits like this one. Dick found Alex and Randy Stewart jamming in the music room. Randy was a subject on which Alex and Dick had agreed to disagree.

"I'm not sure I trust him," Dick told Alex when he found out Randy was living in the pool house.

"What's wrong with Randy? I think he's fun."

"Call it an instinct. I just get a bad feeling."

But Dick hadn't pushed it. The thing with Randy was personal, nothing to do with the business. Let Alex have his musician pals and his jam sessions. At least that's what he thought until today.

Alex and Randy had their backs to the door and were hammering out a song that Dick was happy he didn't recognize. He flicked the light switch a few times until Alex spun around, smiling at him. Alex took his hands off the strings and a few seconds later, realizing he was playing alone, Randy put down his bass. But a hard, metallic thumping continued. Dick remained in the doorway until Randy walked over and switched off the drum machine.

"Drummer didn't show tonight," Alex announced as he gingerly set his Stratocaster on the stand. "It's gotta be big news to bring Dick Adams to the island. Is it Michael?"

Dick, still wearing his tailored suit and rep tie, took two steps into the room. He wanted to make this quick. "He's been spotted. At a motel on Highway 27. Just a couple of miles from the set."

"That's my boy!" Alex beamed, looking over at Randy. "Man, did you think the kid would ever get that far? My son is a fucking great fugitive!"

Alex looked back at Dick who was giving him a "Don't joke" look.

"But I mean, they've caught him?" Alex quickly added. "Right?"

Dick shook his head. "I talked to the producer, Charlie Somethingorother, kind of an LA asshole, but he's sending his head of security to pick up Michael. They'll keep him overnight in a local lockup. He says it's an Andy of Mayberry sort of jail."

"Should we alert the detective?"

"I called him. He'll pick up Michael early tomorrow in Moore Haven. He's going to arrange for the van from Palmdale to meet him there."

Dick nodded at Randy, who was bent over, pulling a beer from the mini-fridge. "Oh, and the detective said something else. He told me he spoke to the owner of the motel where Michael was staying in West Palm. Low-rent joint on Dixie Highway. Seems Michael was dropped off by a guy with salt-and-pepper hair driving a two-door white pickup truck."

He looked hard at Randy, who had set the beer down on his amp. "You know anybody around here who matches that description?" Dick asked, loud enough so Randy wouldn't miss it.

Alex looked at Randy, then back at Dick. He shook his head. "Randy?"

Randy snapped open the beer, then walked over to his amp.

"Look, I owed him a favor. I mean, he's a good kid. He's not going to hurt anybody, right?"

Alex walked over to his bass player. He reached down and snapped off his amp, then put on his adult voice. "Take the beer and be out of here before morning."

Randy nodded slowly. Alex turned back in Dick's direction.

"So what do you think? They're not going to mistreat Michael out there?"

"Producer said they'd be gentle. Maybe Aunt Bee will bring in some fried chicken. Let's just hope this security guy knows what he's doing."

———

A full moon was rising over the scrub oaks and palm trees as Jerry coiled the chopper in slow arcs back and forth across the double yellow lines of Highway 27.

What can go wrong on a night like this, Jerry thought? The

road was deserted. The joint he and Jake had huffed down just before Charlie called him over was Myakka Gold, grown by farm boys in the swamps near Bradenton. Awesome shit.

He liked the way the wind felt on his face, and when he looked at the fat yellow moon the whole night seemed to shimmer.

Sure, things had been shitty for a while, what with that stint in county and Delores kicking his ass out, but now he and Jake were working together for the FUCKIN' MOVIES! The set was crawling with cute babes with no chaperones. And there would be a bonus involved when he came back with the nutcase kid handcuffed to the back of the Harley. Not that Charlie had mentioned a bonus. But he'll pay, Jerry decided. No bonus. No kid. THANK YEW VERY FUCKIN' MUCH!

He and Jake had been to Tom Hawkins's place once, showing up drunk and shouting something like "We got a need for knees!" but the old man had shooed them away with the business end of a sawed-off shotgun. Hawkins was a complete nut job, with his wood pulp and his homemade signs and those fuckin' celebrity cypress knees that looked like a bunch of dicks, but his place was located just off Jerry's favorite nighttime cruising spot − Highway 27.

Jerry grinned and goosed the bike, the front tire rising just off the pavement.

Don't fight it kid, he thought, your ass is mine!

A Room Service Kind Of Place

—

Colleen had never thought of herself as determined. She had spent her life feeling guilty about giving up too easily on just about everything.

She had stopped telling people when she was starting a new diet (the secret shame was too much when she weakened and found herself ordering a Whopper and large fries at the Burger King drive-thru). She changed bars if the bartender gave even the slightest hint that she might be drinking too much. She had abandoned her nursing assistant job after a medical resident, probably working his eighteenth straight hour, yelled at her for forgetting to update a chart.

After she got sober, Colleen moved in with her mother and joined her at church three times a week, but she had never felt more timid, more fearful about taking the wrong step. Better to just give up than risk falling back into her alcoholic malaise.

That's why she had let go of Bart, the drywall subcontractor who told her she was beautiful, just before he held her hand in the church parking lot following a Wednesday night prayer meeting. After three chaste dates, Bart asked her if she'd consider getting married and moving with him to Alaska where he had an offer to work in the oil fields.

Too scary, Colleen thought. She told him as much in a note she slipped to him at church. She didn't stick around for him to read it. Eventually Bart's letters from Alaska – post cards actually – dwindled, then stopped altogether.

"Honey, you need to commit to something," her mother had

told her the morning after Colleen had quit her part-time job in the church office. The pastor's wife had said something snippy about her filing skills.

"I'm committed to Jesus Christ as my Lord and Savior," Colleen told her mother, as she spooned some peanut butter onto a slice of toasted Wonder Bread. "I'm committed to staying sober. That's two biggies."

"And I love you for that," her mother said. "But we're living in this world at the moment. You need to commit to something here."

"Maybe I'm like Daddy."

"No," her mother said. "You are not at all like your daddy."

But maybe she was. Sure, her father was often drunk and erratic, but he wasn't afraid of anything. And when he decided to do something – like flee his family – he saw it through. Once she decided to find her father, Colleen discovered an inner well brimming with courage and determination. All the rejections from scowling motel owners, or the government workers at Social Security and the VA who dismissed her with a bored wave, didn't deter her. Neither did her father's abrupt disappearance the day they were finally supposed to meet for coffee, or Jaime's insistence he wouldn't help her. Things that would have normally sent her home in tears had only solidified her resolve.

She would see this through, no matter what happened.

Jaime had been almost tender at one point during their dinner. She could feel it. But she could also see the well-tended battlements he erected around his feelings. As they stood outside his office door after dinner, their hands almost touching, she watched the gates behind his eyes close and lock into place.

"I can't help you," he said, before disappearing into his office. "Go home."

But Colleen wasn't going home. She was going to do whatever it took. Like sleeping in her car outside his office after he said goodnight. She knew he was spending the night on a cot near his desk, waiting for word about the boy. He might not agree to help her, but he was going to be on the road at some point heading toward her father, and she'd be with him.

Well, maybe a few car lengths back, but she'd be there.

———

During their getaway, Cavanaugh had sent Michael in to buy a box of fried chicken at a roadside store on the outskirts of West Palm Beach.

"I guarantee there's nothing to eat for miles around in that God-forsaken Florida wilderness."

It was sunset when the three fugitives passed around the bucket and a roll of paper towels, sitting silently at an oak-shaded picnic table behind the Cypress Knee Museum.

The cypress swamp started just a few yards from the table. Tom Hawkins had erected a ramshackle boardwalk so museum guests could go deeper into the marshy woods without getting their feet wet or meeting any stray gators or snakes.

After dinner, Cavanaugh announced that he and Lola were going to their room for a "private meeting." Lola, who had fallen back into a silent funk, stood absently when Cavanaugh took her hand. As he led her away, Cavanaugh turned back and gave Michael a "guess what's about to happen" wink.

Michael felt his insides contract. Lola had been Cavanaugh's girl since they met. Why were his guts churning now as he watched them go?

Still holding the chicken bucket, Michael walked to the edge of the boardwalk, but didn't go farther. He needed to do something but he wasn't sure what it was. His nervous energy led him on a hike around the perimeter of the motel in the gathering dark. There was a cypress rocking chair on the wooden landing outside his room and Michael rocked up and back for a minute, his head resting gently against the wooden slats. But he couldn't relax.

Inside his room moments later, Michael took out his pad and pens. For the first time in months, he wasn't creating a movie idea for Dawn. It was a sketch of Lola posing on the beach.

He was working on Lola's nose when he heard the distant buzz of a motorcycle growing louder, like a mosquito slowly circling near his ear. He tried to put it out of his mind, but moments later, the bike was snorting and growling right outside his door, a guttural yawp that could have issued from the throat of a monster from Mordor.

Then, all was quiet.

Peering through a crease in the curtain, Michael watched a hulking Ork of a man swing off a Harley. The parking lot was lit only by the bare bulbs hanging above five motel doors, leaving the figure cross-hatched in light and shadow. Michael could clearly see a long, sallow-looking scar slashed across one stubbly cheek. The man's dirty jeans were cinched below a roll of blubber, poking from the bottom of a smudged white T-shirt. The biker unfurled a square of paper from his hip pocket, looking from the paper to the row of five rooms that ran along a low, wooden landing.

A small tingle of electricity shot up Michael's spine, raising the hair on the back of his neck. Maybe he isn't looking for me, Michael told himself, but he knew better.

Grabbing the doorknob to make sure it was locked, Michael felt the handle being jiggled from the other side. He took two involuntary steps back as a fist pounded on the door, the hard echoes going deep into his chest.

"Yes?" Michael asked, speaking loud enough for whoever was outside to hear him. The pounding stopped.

"Uh...um...rume service."

For such a big man, the voice was high, almost feminine, phlegmy from too many cigarettes and joints, the sharp edges of his voice whittled down into a slow, Southern drawl.

"Rum service?"

"No. Rume service. For your rume. I got a tray out here. Open up."

The absurdity of it made Michael laugh despite his hammering heart.

"You mean room service? This doesn't seem like a room service kind of place," Michael said.

The pounding started again.

"Rume service. Open up."

Michael looked around his tiny room. There was no connecting door. No back door either. The biker pounded again.

"Is this going to cost me anything?" Michael asked, his face now close to the door. "I've got no cash."

"Nope," the biker barked. "It's...it's a damn freebie."

"Okay," Michael said. "Just a sec. I was in the shower. I'll unlock the door and you can just leave whatever it is inside. Okay?"

"That'll work," the biker said.

———

Outside on the landing, Jerry pressed his ear against the motel door. He didn't hear the lock turn, but when he spun the handle, the door opened. Inside, he scanned the room. A single lamp glowed on the cypress table, illuminating a red and white bucket adorned with the silhouette of a crowing rooster. The bed was made. There was a drawing of a woman and some pens on a small desk. A band of light seeped from the space below the closed bathroom door. Jerry could hear water pounding on porcelain.

This was going to be easy. He was proud of himself for coming up with the room service scam. Not that he'd ever ordered room service, but he'd seen plenty of people do it in the movies.

Wait'll I tell Jake about this one, he thought.

Jerry's boots left muddy footprints on the matted carpet as he crossed the room. Yanking the bathroom door open, he could see through the clear plastic curtain that the shower was empty.

He heard the front door slam. "What the fuck," he shouted, turning toward the door.

Stomping back across the room, Jerry snatched open the door and rushed outside. In his haste, he didn't see the wooden rocking chair now tossed on its side on the sidewalk in front of the door. With a loud "Goddammit!" Jerry tumbled over the chair, sprawling face first onto the gravel parking lot, the slip of paper with Michael's picture flying from his fingers.

Raising his head, Jerry pulled a pebble from his chin and felt something wet on his fingers. Looking around, he saw the thin figure of a teenage boy slip through two double doors into a large, dark barn.

"Aw shit!" Jerry uttered, as he struggled to his feet, wiped his bloody hand on his pants, and gave chase.

———

Michael wasn't sure why he was running toward the museum, except it was right in front of him and he thought he might be able to hide inside. He heard the splintering sound of the rocking chair as the biker tumbled over it, just as he twisted the rusting knob on the museum door.

The door was locked, but when Michael rattled the cheap knob, both doors swung open.

The museum was dark; two tiny night-lights plugged into wall sockets didn't do much to penetrate the shadows. Stepping inside, hoping his eyes would adjust, Michael immediately slammed into a table, and a cluster of cypress knees clattered to the floor like so many displaced bowling pins.

Michael knew the noise had carried across the parking lot.

He dropped to his own knees. Crawling around the tables and pedestals in the dark made more sense. There had to be a back door. He could slip out and disappear into the swamp.

Looking back, he saw the biker poised in the double doors, the distant glow of the motel lights turning him into a bulky silhouette. Michael hunkered under a card table as the biker strode in like some kind of movie monster, tossing tables and pedestals out of his path. The hollow "thock" of the cypress knees bouncing off the concrete floor reminded Michael of when his dad taught him how to keep the beat during jam sessions by knocking two blocks of wood together.

"Come out, ya little shit. I just need to talk to ya," the biker bellowed, in a voice that could have been lifted from another of Michael's favorite movies – Deliverance.

This would be a great scene, Michael found himself thinking. A brawny villain recklessly advancing in a darkened museum. The young victim scampering just out of reach, amid works of art all eerie and garish in the dim light. Very Bava.

As he framed the shots in his mind, Michael crawled until his hand found the back wall. He patted the wall to the left, then right, finding a door handle just above eye level. Michael crab-walked over and reached up, feeling a coiled chain and a padlock.

Of course it's locked, Michael thought. Exactly what Hitchcock would do. The only way out was to get around the biker, who was lumbering in his direction, tossing knees aside as he advanced.

Michael reached up, grabbing a knee off a table above his head. He threw it against the far wall, where it bounced back and took out another cluster of cypress knees. Michael couldn't see it but his throw had spun Julius Caesar, Robert E. Lee, and Mao Tse Tung into each other before they tick-tocked to the floor.

The biker moved toward the noise.

Leaping to his feet, Michael sprinted toward the front door. Hearing footfalls, the biker whipped around, his arm outstretched. His gloved hand snagged a piece of Michael's shirt, spinning him around. Michael shrugged off his grip, but now the biker was between him and the door.

Michael's eyes were adjusting to the dark. But, he realized, the biker's eyes were likely doing the same thing.

The man charged toward Michael, who pushed a pedestal down in front of him and scampered back. Now the man and boy were only a few feet apart, spinning and crashing against tables and display cases, the shadowed barn suddenly as loud as a busy bowling alley.

After one determined spin, Michael and the biker switched places. Seeing the open doors, Michael raced out into the night, the biker right behind him.

"Goddammit!" the biker shouted. "Stop!"

Pausing to get his bearings, Michael saw a light above the office door snap on. He looked left. The swamp loomed in the distance, thick and primeval in the pale moonlight, a gray mist rising off the water. He could hear the twitchy whine of the cicadas humming their post-sunset symphony.

In the movie version, the young victim would run toward the fetid swamp.

It had to happen.

So that's what Michael did.

———

Jerry was good in short bursts, but years of smoking, drinking and living off barbeque and Happy Meals hadn't helped his stamina. Winded after the chase through the museum, he was bent over outside the double doors, his breath coming in short, painful gasps as he watched the kid sprint toward the swamp. That's when Jerry made a strategic decision. He wouldn't have to catch this kid on foot. Hell, he had a bike.

He hobbled to his Harley and cranked it up, aiming his headlight into the darkness. Rumbling across the parking lot, he saw the kid's leg sink knee deep in the swamp. Jerry knew swamps. I got you now, the biker thought, as he twisted the accelerator in neutral, the metal machine growling like a grizzly. Kicking it into gear, the Harley's front wheel lifted off the ground, then slammed down as the motorcycle gained traction, gravel skittering away behind the smoking tires.

———

Michael's idea was to sprint into the swamp and find a hiding place. But as he stepped across the muddy bank into the water, where clusters of cypress knees jutted up alongside the trees that had spawned them, his tennis shoe sank ankle deep in thick muck. When he stepped back to free himself, the tennis shoe stayed behind. His other shoe slammed against a pair of rigid cypress knees and Michael fell with a loud splash.

When he got his feet back on the scrub grass at the edge of the swamp, he could hear the Harley roaring toward him.

After yanking out his muddy shoe, Michael looked for another escape and saw the boardwalk.

I could take that into the swamp, Michael thought, and then maybe climb over and hide. He didn't have a better plan.

The boardwalk was a handmade affair, about four feet wide at the mouth, and heading mostly straight into the swamp. Tom Hawkins had cut his own boards, sunk four-by-fours in the muck and nailed it all together. To enhance the boardwalk experience, Hawkins had littered the railings on both sides of the walkway with polished knees that didn't belong in the museum because they didn't resemble any famous people, places or things. In the moonlight, Michael thought the pointed knees rising from their shaved and sandpapered base looked like phantasmagorical billy clubs.

Michael grabbed knees as he ran down the boardwalk, clasping about a dozen in his folded arms. Hawkins was not a meticulous carpenter and Michael had to be careful not to let his feet slip into gaps between the floorboards. Stopping to look back, he saw the bike's headlight ricocheting off the trees. The Harley slowed as it eased onto the boardwalk, then it picked up speed.

Still running, Michael could feel the rickety walkway begin to sway. The end of the boardwalk arrived sooner than Michael thought it would. Tom Hawkins's ramshackle pathway widened at the end into a viewing platform, wrapped by a sagging, four-foot high rail.

Michael was panting as he looked over the rail at the black water below. The bog seemed to be steaming, the rising vapor lit by the full moon. He saw two unblinking yellow eyes staring up from the surface.

Spinning around, Michael saw the bouncing headlight coming closer. The boardwalk was shaking so hard Michael thought it might fall into pieces. Looking down, he noticed a break in the planks where the boardwalk widened into the viewing area. A gap just wide enough to hold a cypress knee, Michael thought, or maybe a dozen cypress knees.

Rocking each of them point-first into the gap with both hands, Michael was surprised at how these odd roots reconnected with the rough sawn cypress beams, like an estranged family coming back together in a crisis. The knees formed a barrier almost two-feet high. Michael looked up, the roar of the bike deafening now, the headlight ricocheting off the boards at the end of the viewing platform.

Another fine movie moment, Michael thought, as he bent low behind his makeshift barrier and closed his eyes.

—

Jerry was sure the boardwalk would go on a lot farther. He was loving the bouncing ride into a swamp bathed in pale moonlight, knowing his prey would be trapped at the end. This was a story he couldn't wait to tell Jake. Then his headlight caught the thin boards that framed out the viewing platform. He couldn't see the kid anywhere.

What the hell? Jerry thought. That was the moment he realized he was going too fast.

The searing metal against metal screech of the bike's brakes added a high harmony above the low growl of the Harley. Jerry shut his eyes as the bike's front wheel slammed into a wall of some kind, the rear tire rising, as the bike began a long flip.

This isn't going to be good, Jerry thought.

—

Crouching behind his ad-libbed barricade, Michael looked up into a suddenly slow-motion scene. He saw man and bike execute a long circle above his head spinning deep into the swamp, the bike's RPMs maxing out, the engine screaming and throwing off clouds of smoke. He heard trees snapping and finally, far away, a cannonball splash. And then, silence.

Michael stood slowly, his ears still ringing, the sudden quiet gathering around him like a cloak. Seconds later, as if nothing had happened, choirs of cicadas restarted their insistent whine. Michael leaned over the railing, staring hard, but all he saw were a few snapped trees, a million twinkling diamonds of moonlight dancing on the water and that same pair of stoic yellow eyes, now rising from a ribbed, reptilian snout. The eyes stayed focused on Michael for a long moment before the creature slipped below the shimmering surface of the swamp.

A Poet, A Runaway
And A Serial
Entrepreneur

—

No one spoke as the Lincoln turned off Highway 27 onto a dark, two-lane road, aiming south toward Alligator Alley, the rod-straight roadway that bisects the Everglades. Cavanaugh, in the driver's seat, thought it was a good idea to put some distance between the trio and the chaos at the Cypress Knee Museum and Motel.

The roar of the Harley outside the motel room hadn't disturbed him. Living in the Blue 'Arlin and other low-rent motels, Cavanaugh had learned to ignore the late-night noises. But two fists pounding on his door had gotten him out of bed. He found Michael on the landing holding up a mud-caked flyer with the boy's picture on it. Michael's words came in short bursts as he struggled to catch his breath.

Hawkins was turning circles in the parking lot, his crusty shell wrapped in a pair of cut-off shorts, waving a sawed-off shotgun around at some invisible intruder, shouting "Come out, ya' bastard!" Keeping the barrel aimed into the night, the old man backed into the double doors of the museum and flipped on a light switch, flooding the room with a harsh fluorescence. Behind him, Cavanaugh could now see tables and pedestals akimbo on the floor and hundreds of celebrity cypress knees tossed about like so much kindling.

He watched as Hawkins discovered the chaos that had been

made of his life's work. The shotgun dropped to his side, then slipped from his hands, landing with a clatter on the concrete floor. The tiny old man was frozen for a moment, then he seemed to fold in on himself from dozens of joints, his bony knees pivoting forward, his shoulders snapping down, his waist clicking back, his head bending as if in prayer.

The noise coming from inside the museum was soft at first, but grew in volume and rose in pitch. It wasn't a scream but something more primeval, sounding to Cavanaugh's ear like the screech of some tree-born bug furiously rubbing arachnoid arms together to produce a tinny, arpeggioing "eeeeeeeeeeeeEEEEEEEEEEEEEEE!"

Tom's quivering wail seemed to go on and on, filling the night. Then, as suddenly as it started, his wailing stopped. A jolt of energy seemed to pass through Hawkins. He skittered around the museum on all fours, gathering his precious children one by one and standing them upright on their polished bases.

Michael's more human voice snapped Cavanaugh back to the porch. The boy was stammering about a biker, the boardwalk, but he couldn't get much out. Pulling him into a hug, Cavanaugh could feel the furious thump of Michael's heart.

Lola, wearing only a white slip, eased around Cavanaugh, who handed the boy off to her. She pulled Michael close and held on while Cavanaugh emptied both rooms and stuffed suitcases and backpacks into the trunk. With Hawkins still skittering furiously around the museum, the Lincoln convertible was on the move, tossing gravel in its wake as it sped down the driveway.

Cavanaugh sat Michael in the backseat and Lola crawled in beside him, her arms wrapping his shoulders, her lips to his ear, her hair brushing his cheek.

"It's okay," she whispered. "It's okay."

Making the left turn, heading south into the darkness, Cavanaugh gunned the Continental.

"Where are we going?" Lola asked from the back.

"I'm putting some distance between us and the Gestapo. And Lola, find some makeup or something. We're going to need to disguise our young friend here. Apparently, we're traveling with a wanted man."

———

When Bobby Osceola marched through a rear door into the office of the cinder-block motel office, Cavanaugh thought he had seen him somewhere before. Bobby was a robust bantam of a man with stalks of ebony hair jutting from beneath a white cowboy hat. His broad chest and shoulders were wrapped in a loose, blousy shirt, decorated with jagged horizontal bands of aqua, crimson and gold. His blue jeans clung to a pair of short, bowed legs, the waist cinched with a beaded belt, the hems stuffed inside a pair of lizard-skin cowboy boots.

Cavanaugh realized he had just admired the man's life-sized, cardboard doppelganger on the porch outside. The smiling imitation man, one cardboard arm raised in a wave, was posed next to a stuffed alligator, jaws open and teeth gleaming. On the wall above this exotic pair hung a hand-painted wooden sign reading: *Welcome To Bobby's!*

Now here was the real thing, Cavanaugh thought. Maybe a little shorter than the cardboard figure, but the real Bobby still managed to cut an impressive figure.

"Welcome. Welcome!" Bobby said.

The motel office was maybe 12-by-12, with walls of rough-sawn cypress planks and three doors, each painted a pastel green. An easel by the front door held an architectural rendering of a sleekly modern hotel and casino. Tiny spotlights on the ceiling lit the rendering and the white ribbon on the top right corner that read: CHIEF BOBBY'S SEMINOLE INDIAN RESORT AND CASINO. COMING - WINTER 1984.

Bobby apparently wasn't waiting two years for the games to begin. Through the open door behind the check-in desk, Cavanaugh could see a round poker table, covered in green felt, surrounded by four rolling office chairs, two of them occupied by middle-aged men in overalls and plaid Western shirts, staring down at hands of cards. The third chair, with a spray of cards face down on the felt in front of it, had likely been Bobby's. Drinks in highball glasses and some plastic snack baskets littered the table. A fourth spot – without drinks or chips – appeared to be waiting for a player to be named later.

Cavanaugh's mouth watered. His flask had been empty for several hours.

"Welcome to Bobby's," the chief said, extending a large hand in Cavanaugh's direction.

"Are you?" Cavanaugh tilted his head toward the front door as he took Bobby's hand.

"You got him. Bobby Osceola. Chief Bobby or just plain Bobby – however you like it," he said. The man's voice was deep and oaky; his salesman's smile revealing a mouthful of polished white teeth.

Cavanaugh beamed. After all the chaos of this day, he felt like he'd finally found a friend. He continued to pump Bobby's outstretched hand well beyond the normal duration of a greeting.

"A pleasure to meet a real Floridian. Reilly is my name. Cavanaugh Reilly the third. A citizen of the sovereign state of Georgia. Trying to find my way home."

He nodded in the direction of Lola, in a black stripe of a dress, who was staring at the rendering of the casino, and a wild-haired young man in blue jeans and a black T-shirt standing near the single folding table that constituted Bobby's "gift shop," a pencil-thin moustache apparently drawn with eyeliner on the boy's upper lip.

"This is my lovely assistant, Lola Famosa, and that gentleman is..uh...Jerome...Jerome Smith. We are a band of gypsies in search of a traveler's teepee and some liquid libation."

Bobby's Southern-inflected English shifted into a dialect direct from a 1950s western. "White man want'um fire water?"

"On the rocks, if you please." Cavanaugh intoned.

Bobby shifted back to his normal voice, as he slipped behind the long counter. "I reckon we can handle that. How many rooms?"

"Just two," Cavanaugh winked at Bobby. "She and I..."

"Say no more," Bobby said, reaching under the desk and coming back with two keys. "Will that be cash or—"

Cavanaugh raised his hand, his fingers splaying out in a STOP sign.

"My friend over there will take care of the tariff."

Cavanaugh pointed in the corner. Michael was looking at Seminole tchotchkes that included a bowl of rubber alligators, a rack of beaded belts, some Florida ashtrays and oddly, a handful of snow globes.

Michael lifted a snail-shaped snow globe. He shook it and brought it up to his eyes, staring through the clear shell at a tiny, underwater replica of Bobby's future casino, looking like the Emerald City in the Wizard of Oz. The silver "snowflakes" swirling around the glittering edifice were tiny dollar signs.

"Gonna be a collector's item," Bobby said.

Michael walked over and set the globe on the counter.

"I'll take it."

"That and two rooms will set you back sixty-eight dollars." Bobby said, slipping the globe into a tiny shopping bag and handing it to Michael. The boy passed over a gold credit card.

Bobby looked at the name on the card, then pushed a desk register across the counter. "Okay. So, for the rooms, I just need a name, home address and phone number. And it would be great if it matched the name on the card."

Michael looked quickly over his shoulder at Cavanaugh, not sure what to write.

"We're not much for home addresses," Cavanaugh said, stepping to the counter and taking the card back from Bobby. "Always found them too constricting. I'm a man of the streets, mostly."

"You've come to the right place, then," Bobby said. "Seminoles were the first homeless people. They wanted us on a reservation in Oklahoma. We chose the swamps instead."

"I can't argue with that," Cavanaugh said. "I spent a year in Oklahoma once. No wait, I spent one day in Oklahoma, it just seemed like a year."

"When the Seminoles took to the swamps," Bobby continued, "we had an open door policy: convicts, runaway slaves, anybody too wild for the white man's so-called society. The name Seminole means *Free People*. So, whoever y'all are, you're welcome here."

"Much appreciated," Cavanaugh said. "Our little band has slipped the dark tentacles of the American capitalist nightmare. I'm a poet. He's a runaway. And she's a serial entrepreneur."

"If you paid in cash we wouldn't need any names or addresses," Bobby leaned across the counter and eyed Cavanaugh conspiratorially. "How's that suit you?"

Cavanaugh turned and whispered to Michael, who yanked out the wad of cash. Cavanaugh quickly swiveled, hoping to keep Bobby from seeing the money. With his back to the proprietor, Cavanaugh peeled off a C-note and slipped the rest of the wad into his pants pocket. Bobby, who had spotted the flash of green, now politely averted his eyes. He was looking over at Lola when Cavanaugh passed him the bill.

"So what are you building?" Lola asked, looking back at Bobby from a spot near the easel.

"Good-looking, right?" Bobby, still holding the bill, walked around the counter to join Lola in front of the casino rendering. "Two years from now you'll need a reservation to stay on the reservation. Bingo, slots, low-stakes poker and off-track betting all brought to you by the Seminole Nation."

Lola nodded in approval. "A casino. There could be big money in that."

"Yes, ma'am."

"You're going to need a lot of cleaning supplies."

"I suppose we will."

"I'm currently in the cleaning supply business. May I leave a brochure with you?"

"A beautiful gal like you can leave anything she wants at Bobby's."

Bobby returned to his spot behind the desk. He pulled out a

drawer and slipped the bill inside, then counted out the change into Cavanaugh's outstretched palm.

"Your rooms are just down that way." Bobby handed the keys to Cavanaugh, then waved in the direction of a side door that opened to the row of motel rooms. "Make yourselves at home. I'll be right back here if you need anything."

Cavanaugh looked hungrily at the card game paused in the room behind the office. Bobby noticed and winked at him.

"I got a full bar – plenty of ice – and an extra seat at the table, if you happen to be feeling thirsty or lucky. Or both."

Cavanaugh rounded up Lola and Michael and herded them toward the side door. Once they were outside, he turned back to Bobby.

"Save that last seat for me. I'll be back."

Some Kind Of Character Flaw

—

"I've got cigarettes," the old man said, as he settled beside Lola on a downtown bus bench. She wasn't waiting for a bus on that still October night. She had flopped down minutes before, too exhausted to take another step, especially in red high heels.

"Honestly, I don't recommend any of the buses that stop here. They just take you places you don't want to go."

Lola stared ahead, trying to decipher from the man's Southern-tinged baritone if he might be friend or foe. She picked up a hint of her dad's Old Spice, mixed with the standard Dixie Highway bouquet of carbon monoxide, salty sea air and day-old garbage.

The man lit a cigarette and passed it to Lola.

"I can offer some companionship and conversation. I have a place I'd like to show you. It's not far from here. The name is Cavanaugh Reilly and you would be?"

Lola still didn't answer. Instead, she sucked on the cigarette, turning her head just enough to get a peek at her companion. Old, like seriously old, she thought. Maybe 60. Maybe more. But nothing about him scared her. That was something.

"So what do you say? The view from this bench will not get any better, I promise."

Lola turned again, a "don't fuck with me" look on her face. Cavanaugh responded with a wink and a four-star smile.

"Don't worry. My friends will tell you I don't bite," he said. "At least not on the first date."

Despite herself, Lola's grimace relaxed into something almost resembling a smile.

"So I'd be honored if you'd come join me for supper," he continued. "It's truly not far."

He stood and Lola did the same, following him down the sidewalk in her bare feet, the red heels dangling from her fingers by their narrow straps.

Lola was a few months into her American Dream fund-raising campaign – which meant selling herself on street corners near downtown in a uniform of cheap high heels and form-fitting polyester dresses. What she thought was a casual flirtation with the white powder her neighbor was peddling had gotten serious. And to put a bow on it, a sweet-faced guy had pulled up in a Jeep Wagoneer one afternoon in late September and Lola got in. Moments later she was under the unforgiving fluorescents at Central Booking, one more minnow caught up in a prostitution cast net. She met the old man on the bus bench two weeks later, at the bottom of another rough cycle.

The walk to Twin Palms, a motel much like the ones Lola often called home, lasted as long as her cigarette. Turning the key, the old man stepped back, executing a crisp bow, while waving his upturned palm toward the threshold.

"I insist. Ladies first," he intoned.

Lola's instincts said run, but she had already decided to see where this was leading. She took a single step into the dark room.

Easing in behind her, the man flipped a light switch. The place wasn't the bare hovel Lola expected; instead it appeared to be a clubhouse for an organization with just one member. There were posters and magazine covers push-pinned to the walls – she didn't recognize all the faces but she knew Martin Luther King, and the smiling Einstein and his electric-shock hair. Languid Playboy centerfolds – backs arched, lips pouting, flat stomachs sliced by a crease in the paper – hung alongside the famous faces; a child's record player rested on a table; knitted quilts in rainbow colors covered the bed and the back of two chairs; a makeshift kitchen was set up in one corner. A small chalkboard leaned against a wall with white, hand-written letters: PEOPLE I'M NOT SPEAKING TO TODAY. There were five names on the list including the current District Attorney of Palm Beach County.

The man stepped around Lola, moving swiftly through the room, lighting squat, scented candles, putting a disc on the turntable. As Fred Astaire sang "I've Got You Under My Skin," the man returned to the front door, where Lola waited, flicking off the overhead light.

"Welcome to Chez Reilly."

Lola couldn't explain it, but somehow, this narrow box of a room, lit by flickering candles and littered with odd treasures, reminded her of a sacristy of a particularly bizarre Cuban cathedral. She felt safe here. She hadn't felt that in a long time.

"Make yourself comfortable. Nothing to worry about here," the man told her.

Cavanaugh Reilly turned out to be a man of his word. Directing Lola to an aging leather club chair, he quickly brewed a cup of tea, loaded with honey. As she sipped, he drew a bubble bath, leaving her to bathe privately, behind a closed door. When she emerged, wearing the terry cloth robe he'd hung on the back of the door, Lola found the old man in the club chair, reading a book. The last man she knew who read books was her high school English teacher.

"Are you hungry?" he asked, closing the book. Lola shook her head.

"Tired."

Rising gingerly, he pulled back the covers on the bed, and encouraged her to lie down. Lola balked.

"Oh, I insist you take the bed. I'm an old combat soldier. I'll make a pallet on the floor."

Lola sat stiffly, the mattress sagging beneath her, as the man fluffed the lace-trimmed pillows, their white satin cases yellowed with age.

"Go on, then," he said. Lola slowly eased under the sheet, as the man tucked her in, settling the quilt over her, pulling it up below her chin. "Comfortable?"

Too tired to answer, Lola closed her eyes, letting herself sink into a deep pit of sleep as Astaire sang a tune from a musical she had watched with her dad.

"'S wonderful. 'S marvelous. You should care for me."

When she awoke, daylight was seeping through the thin curtains; the room was quiet. The man was still in the club chair, book in his lap, smiling in her direction.

"Ah, Sleeping Beauty awakens."

"How long," Lola stammered. "How long have I..."

"A day, okay, two days. I believe you must have been quite spent. Now, maybe you're hungry?"

"Starving."

The sex part didn't start for another few days. First, he courted her with flowers and ice cream and candle-lit dinners. He reached out to a lawyer and got her charges dismissed. He even tracked down the four cases of American Dream products she'd stashed in the closet of an abandoned house in Lake Worth. When he did join her in bed, the sex was frequent but quite tender, without any of the kinky demands of her regular clients.

"Was that alright?" Cavanaugh asked her in a moment of afterglow. "I can't really believe someone as beautiful as you is sharing my sagging old bed."

Lola pushed her nose into his neck, her fingers rifling through his thick, salt and pepper hair. He smelled of cigarettes and yes, Old Spice aftershave. She liked that.

"It was perfect."

"You know you can stay here as long as you like."

"Okay," she whispered. "Maybe I will."

Truth was, since the death of her father, Lola had missed having an older man in her life. Maybe spending time with Cavanaugh Reilly would give her some stability. She planned to use the time to put a new life together, the kind of prosperous life people enjoyed on the Palm Beach side of the Flagler Bridge.

But now, just four months later, she was deep in the Everglades with the longing for the white powder roiling her gut, making her skin crawl. She had likely killed a man that morning. And this crazy plot to take money from the kid was spinning out of control. Maybe it made sense a few days ago, but she knew Michael now. He was confused, but sweet, and, while she was pretending to be attracted to him, she found herself starting to have real feelings for this odd teenager, who was only a year younger than she was.

Trailing behind Michael and Cavanaugh as they left Bobby's office, Lola could hear the baggie calling. The throbbing behind her eyebrows was back, along with an itch deep in her belly and a sizzle of electric current pulsing just below her skin. The white powder always made her feel like she had wings, but after each flight, she always crashed landed onto the concrete runway of reality.

She needed a few minutes – maybe a few hours – alone with the baggie, so she could sort all this out. Cavanaugh wasn't going to be the problem. She knew he couldn't resist the drinks and the card game. But Michael was showing no signs of leaving her alone.

"I think Michael should stay out of sight," Cavanaugh said to her. "I'll hang with the Chief and keep an eye out for stray bikers."

Michael came out of his room and joined them on the sidewalk.

"Michael, I'm going to hang onto the cash for safekeeping," Cavanaugh told him. "If they snatch you, I might need to bail you out or bribe somebody."

"Um. I guess so," Michael said, though he didn't sound certain. "I mean, are you sure?"

"Don't worry son, I'm on your side." Cavanaugh's hand settled on Michael's shoulder, as the old man flashed his most sincere smile, marred only by the missing incisor.

"You do know I'm on your side, right?"

"Sure. Absolutely." Michael said. "I trust you."

Lola shot Cavanaugh a look. She didn't like the sound of this.

"Now can you two entertain yourselves for a while?" Cavanaugh asked. "I've got to consult with the locals. Figure out how we approach Michael's rendezvous with destiny tomorrow."

Grabbing his arm, Lola yanked Cavanaugh into their room, leaving Michael on the sidewalk.

"What are you doing?" she asked, after shutting the door behind them.

"Just let me handle this, okay? I'm working on a new plan. Maybe we don't need the Dad's money, especially if I can take those rubes for some cash at the card table."

"Maybe you should leave some of Michael's cash with him. In case you're not as lucky as you think." Lola said, her eyes locked on his.

"Don't worry your pretty little head about that. You take care of the kid. I'll take care of everything else," Cavanaugh said.

Lola was about to raise several objections, when Michael began knocking gently. Cavanaugh put his index finger to Lola's lips.

"Yes, my boy?" Cavanaugh asked, as he opened the door.

"Everything okay?"

"Everything, as they say, is beautiful. "

Cavanaugh pulled a handkerchief from his back pocket and rubbed Lola's eyeliner moustache off Michael's lip. He took a few steps down the walkway in the direction of Bobby's card game before turning back and smiling at Michael and Lola.

"You kids get some rest. I think tomorrow's going to be a very big day."

———

Raising a plastic lighter with a shaking hand, Lola struggled to connect the quivering flame to the bobbing tip of the cigarette.

"Dammit," she said, yanking the unlit cigarette from her mouth.

Standing on the sidewalk outside their rooms, she and Michael watched Cavanaugh almost dance back to the card game, whistling the sing-song chorus of "*Heigh Ho*" from Disney's *Snow White.*

"I think he's happy," Michael said.

As she tried a second time to light the cigarette, Michael saw goose bumps bristling on Lola's bare arms. "You want a sweater or something?"

A Canadian cold front was riding a fast train to South Florida, bringing wind, rain and temperatures in the 60s, but the train wouldn't arrive until the following day. At the moment, Bobby's Indian Village was a tropical oasis, the air stirred ever-so-slightly by a languid Caribbean breeze.

"No sweater," she mumbled, raising the lighter again.

This time she managed to ignite the Marlboro 100. As she sucked hard on the filter, her eyes danced around the parking lot. With her free hand, Lola rubbed the backs of her arms, then her neck, looking to Michael like someone with an itch they couldn't quite scratch.

With her eyes wandering everywhere but his direction, Michael lovingly – or more accurately lustfully – gave her a long, slow look: the crest of her cheekbones, the slight hook of her nose, the bee-stung lips pouted around the cigarette, the ridged ledges of her collarbones visible in the scoop of the black dress, the muscled thighs above tapering calves, and her tiny feet, the red lacquer on the toenails mostly chipped away.

Michael felt his own itch buzzing deep inside.

"You want to go in and watch TV?" he asked.

Lola tilted her head back, releasing a dusty cloud of smoke into the night. "I'm really tired. I think I'll go to bed."

As she turned away, Michael tried desperately to think of something that would keep her here with him.

"I've been thinking a lot about it – today, I mean. And that guy in the motel room, I don't think he's dead. Really! You shouldn't worry about that."

"You're sweet. Thanks." Lola took one more long drag, before flicking the butt toward the parking lot. "Sorry I'm so tired. Been a very strange day. I'll see you tomorrow."

After Lola closed the door, Michael lingered on the landing, alone in a circle of light thrown by the bare bulb above his head. Looking down at his hand, Michael saw he was still holding Bobby's snow globe. He gave it a shake, lifting the tchotchke to his face, the swirling silver dollar signs schooling in the water around Bobby's mini-casino.

Stepping into his room, he set the globe on a wooden table. Bobby's motel was a long way from Bobby's future resort, Michael thought. His room was Spartan - just the table, a metal-framed double bed and a walnut chest of drawers, the wood faded and chipped, one drawer missing a knob, and a TV bolted high on the wall facing the bed. There was one non-generic feature: when you flipped on the light switch, a tiny spotlight revealed a framed photo of a smiling Chief Bobby hanging just inside the front door.

Like his room at the Blue 'Arlin, Bobby's motel had connecting doors, so large families could move easily between two rooms. Michael knocked softly and after a minute, Lola turned the lock, cracking the door open just two inches.

"Michael?"

"I was gonna get a Coke. Want anything?"

"That's okay. I'm fine. Going to bed."

She closed the door, leaving Michael alone. He turned slowly, not sure what he would do next. The whole plan was suddenly not making sense. He was alone inside another low-rent motel room, his face was on a wanted poster, multiple people were trying to capture him and now, when he thought about what he really wanted, he saw Lola's face instead of Dawn's.

He wished he could call his mom. She'd know what to do. Or maybe she wouldn't, but she'd be on the other end of the line and that would make everything a lot better. Raising the phone receiver to his ear, Michael let his mother ride in on the drone of the dial tone.

"Come on! You can do it!"

The day was cloudless and sunny. Late summer. Waist-deep

in the family pool, the Intracoastal flat and calm behind her, Crystal Donnelly raised long, lovely arms as her tearful, eight-year-old son hovered above her on the marble pool edge, a flowered swimsuit hanging to his knees. The suit was a gift from Alex — "the surfers call 'em jams. You'll be the coolest kid at the pool."

Michael, as usual, was the only kid at the pool. It was just he and Crystal, happily filling the hours between his dad's departure and his return from Donnelly Avionics. There were bad days when Crystal could barely leave her room, and Michael would sit reading to her, or rubbing her bitten-down fingertips with Vaseline. But on good days like this one, Crystal lit up the mansion, often racing from room to room, creating instant games for her and her timid son to play.

The family's Olympic-sized pool was one of Crystal's favorite summer spots.

Moments before Michael had watched his mother — trim and athletic in a white one-piece swimsuit — dive gracefully into the aqua-blue pool, kick along the bottom, then break the surface, beads of water rushing off her tanned skin, her hair flattened back from her forehead, wet strands falling to her shoulders.

Now here she was right in front of him, waving her beautiful arms in his direction. He could fall right into her smile.

"I'm right here, baby!" Crystal called. "Nothing can happen. Just jump!"

He wanted desperately to do as she asked. To cannonball into the pool, letting Crystal lift him up, pressing him to her chest. But the first plunge was always the coldest. And Michael wasn't a kid who jumped at things, even when he wanted them. Something bad might happen.

"Michael, don't think about it so much. It's better if you just take a leap!"

Michael looked over his shoulder at the back of his family's hulking wedding cake of a house. Through the tall, first-floor windows he saw Anabella, in her black, lace-collared uniform, pushing the vacuum across the living room's maroon and black

Oriental. He quickly toggled back to Crystal, her arms outstretched, her fingers wiggling in his direction.

"Come on baby. Take a leap!"

Closing his eyes and summoning his courage, the boy sprang
from the pool's edge toward his smiling mother. He never hit
the water. When he opened his eyes, he was 17, and alone in a
low-rent motel room, a smudged white phone receiver pressed
to his ear, the dial tone droning on.

Hanging up, Michael walked quickly out the front door. He
didn't know where he was going, but he needed to be somewhere besides this motel room with the ghost of his mother
and the glowing portrait of Chief Bobby.

———

A few moments later, with a can of Coke from a vending
machine, Michael peered through the office window at the card
game in progress. He watched a beaming Cavanaugh pull a pile
of chips from the center of the table toward his own stack, as
Bobby tossed down his cards, shaking his head.

It didn't surprise Michael that his pal was a good poker player. Cavanaugh Reilly was a master at so many things. No matter
what happened now, at least this crazy excursion had provided
him with his first real friend since his mother died.

Looking away from the office, across a dark meadow, Michael
could see the shapes of a few oak trees and sparkles of moonlight dancing on open water. In the other direction, the road
that left the parking lot ended in wide track of open ground,
bordered by a cluster of squat dinosaurs. Looking closer, Michael realized the creatures were bulldozers likely there to
scrape an earthen pad for Bobby's hotel and casino.

Though Bobby's place wasn't that many miles from the oak
and cypress swamps around Tom Hawkins' Museum, this terrain
was different. Bobby was the ruler of a patch of high ground, a
tiny peninsula in a vast expanse of waving grasses, mangrove
thickets and shallow sheets of water in the heart of the Ever-

glades.

The motel was a horseshoe of wooden rooms and a stand-alone office at the edge of a parking lot, fed by a dirt road meandering in from Alligator Alley. Michael thought if he explored a little, he might chase the twin images of Lola and Crystal from his mind.

He followed the sidewalk to a postage-stamp playground with a swing set, a shiny metal slide, and a teeter-totter. Two picnic tables were nearby, so parents could keep an eye on their kids games. Guarding the playground was a stuffed black bear rising on its hind legs, its paws outstretched like the Frankenstein monster. The bear was at least a foot taller than Michael and lit by the vaporous glow from a security light bolted to a telephone pole.

Sitting on a wooden swing, one hand gripping the heavy chain, Michael leaned back, letting his heels push against the ground to gain momentum. He'd loved his backyard swing set as a kid. Swinging then was all soaring and no thinking. But tonight, no matter how high he swung, his mind wouldn't settle. He leapt off during an upswing, landing on his feet, the Coke can slipping from his fingers, the dark liquid pooling atop the hard-packed dirt. Michael left the can where it fell and walked back to his room.

He lingered briefly outside the door of the room Lola shared with Cavanaugh. There was a light on inside, but the curtains blocked his view. Pressing his ear to the locked door, Michael couldn't hear any sound. No water running. No TV. He raised his fist to knock, but thought better of it. She didn't want to be bothered. She had made that very clear. He pulled out his key and let himself into his room.

He stopped just inside, his eyes finding the connecting door. He'd try one more thing. His fingers settled gently on the handle. He wished hard and when he turned the handle, his wish was granted – the door wasn't locked. Easing inside slowly, just his head and neck at first, Michael could see a lamp glowing on the bedside table. The room was empty.

"Lola?" he called softly. A band of light seeped from beneath the bathroom door. Stepping into the room, Michael called a bit louder this time, "Lola?"

After two gentle knocks, Michael eased open the bathroom door, just as he had opened his mother's bathroom door six months before. He flashed on the image of his mother, dead in the tub, the knife sunk up to the hilt in goo on the tile floor, crimson tracks threading through the grout lines. He blinked away the memory and returned to the motel bathroom. Lola's bare legs and feet protruded from the narrow space between the toilet and the wall.

"Lola?" he called her name softly, kneeling quickly beside the prone body. She was on her back, the black dress bunched up around her thighs, the edge of a plastic baggie visible where her leg pressed against the wall.

"LOLA!"

Michael lifted her head. Lola's neck seemed to be made of rubber. Looking her over furiously, he found no trace of blood. Leaning close to her lips, the edge of the toilet tight against his shoulder, Michael could hear the shallow rattle of her breath.

He slid her away from the toilet, raising her into a sitting position, one hand clutching her shoulder to keep her upright. Lola's head nodded into his chest. Easing her head back, Michael slapped her cheek, softly at first, then harder. The flat snap of the blows echoed off the tiled walls.

"Lola! Wake up. Lola! Come on...wake up – please!"

Another slap and Lola's dark lashes fluttered. Michael reached under her armpits and lifted her to her feet. She seemed to weigh nothing, but then, as her feet gave way, Michael thought he wouldn't be able to hold her up. "Come on. You've got to walk. Lola!"

Her feet and knees gained some traction.

"Please. We gotta walk."

"No. Don't. Fine," she muttered.

With his arm around her waist and her arm thrown over his shoulder, Michael managed to get Lola across the room and out the front door.

"Where'r we goin'?" she asked, her words slurred and slow.

"I'm going to get some help."

Lola's eyes rolled fully open as she put on the brakes, planting her feet so Michael couldn't move her. Despite her resistance, she was smiling. It was a big, tooth-baring grin, the kind of smile a student might flash as she crossed a stage to pick up a diploma.

"Whoa. Easy now..." she mumbled. "Not so fast. Please. Pretty please..."

"I gotta get Cavanaugh. You might need a doctor."

"No!...No doctor. I'm good right now. Just like this."

"You were white like a ghost. I thought you were..."

Lola's head rotated in super-slow-motion toward Michael.

"Dead? Silly boy. I was dreaming. Golden houses. Brass tubs. Tara..." She switched to a Southern accent with just a hint of Cuba in it. "Lawdy Miss Scarlett, ah don't know nothing about birthin' no babies..."

Then, her voice deepened into something in the vicinity of Rhett Butler. "Frankly, Scarlett, you can go fuck yourself!"

Her variation on Rhett's classic line put Lola in stitches. Michael couldn't help himself and he laughed too. She pulled her arm off his shoulder and punched him softly in the jaw.

"Just lighten up, willya pleeese? I'm fine. I'm really, really fine. Just need some air."

"Come on. I know a place."

Michael led her on a wobbly walk along the horseshoe of rooms and out to where the life-sized bear guarded the playground.

"If you'll just bear with me..." Lola whispered, waving a hand at the stuffed animal, her own joke cracking her up again.

Michael got her to a picnic table and settled her gingerly on the top, her feet on the seat below. Michael sat next to her, his arm wrapping Lola's waist for support. After a moment, Lola's head settled on his shoulder. He liked being this close to her, her hair brushing his face, her taut skin beneath his fingers. They remained like that for a long time before Lola raised her head.

"You still like me?"

"I like you," Michael said.

"But what about her? You're so close to her now, I bet you can smell her."

"Who?"

"She's out there in the swamp waiting for her poor little rich boy to show her what he's got."

"I just want to meet her. Share some of my ideas...Just talk to her."

"Just talk, my ass!" Lola looked over at him, her marshy green eyes shimmering in the security light, the whites cross-hatched with red spider webs, her pupils shrunk to pinpricks.

"It's okay," Lola said. "You're a guy. Just like all the rest of them. You got the world right in front of you. But you're looking off toward some balcony, some beach, chasing a dream you had one night with your hand on your cock. I make my living knowing how men think."

"Right now I don't know what I think. About anything."

They were silent another moment before Lola spoke again. "I know I don't love him anymore."

"Cavanaugh?"

"I did. I really did. I think so anyway. But he's got no real plan. He just makes it up one day at a time."

"He's a brilliant man. He knows everything."

"But what's he doing with all those brains? Living in cheap rooms. Panhandling. And running from his own daughter. I can't live like that."

"He loves you. He told me. I can see it when he looks at you."

"Maybe so. He says a lot of things. But I refuse to spend my life wondering where I'll be sleeping or what I'll do for money. I lived that life already."

"Bad things can happen to anyone. Money can't save you."

Lola eased herself off the table. On wobbly legs, she started to spin, very slowly at first, her arms outstretched, her head back, taking in the vast, moonlit sky.

"I disagree," she said, her circling dance growing faster as the strength returned to her legs. "If you're rich, bad things can happen and you don't mind it so much."

"I don't know about that. Having money is not all it's cracked up to be," Michael said. "Just ask my dad."

Lola stopped, facing Michael.

"Well, poverty is all it's cracked up to be. My dad could have told you that. None of it is good. Waiting for a handout from a relative. Afraid to answer the telephone 'cause maybe it's the bank or the bill collector. Afraid the phone won't ring 'cause they turned it off. Seeing your beautiful daddy laid off first — 'cause he's the Cuban guy. Watching him get old and scared and sick."

"I'm sorry."

Lola started spinning again, her arms spread, her neck arching back.

"That's why I'm not going to put myself in that position. I'm gonna be the boss! I'm gonna make my own success. And I'll do whatever it takes to get there."

"Like work the streets?"

Lola froze again, this time glaring at Michael, anger flushing her face.

"Look — in America you get rich using your talents, your brains or your body. I need to raise some cash fast to build the business. Don't judge me, rich boy."

"Yes, but what you're doing, it doesn't seem—"

Lola waved away Michael's words.

"You do what you have to do to reach your goal. I have one. He doesn't. And I don't think you do either. Not a real one anyway."

"I do know that I'm very glad I met you," Michael said. "I mean, really, very glad."

Lola's angry thunderstorm cleared as quickly as it had arrived. She moved close to Michael, still perched atop the table.

"Well, that's good, because I think I really like you." She leaned closer to him. He could feel her breath on his face. "I mean, this sounds crazy but I know I really like you."

Michael wanted to speak but couldn't get a word to actually appear. Lola giggled.

"Tell me something. Why am I always falling for the wrong men? You think I got some kind of character flaw?"

Michael thought he could feel Lola's heart beating but she was still a few inches away from him. It must have been his own heart he was hearing.

"You seem, ah, perfectly fine to me," Michael said. "No flaws. At all. I've looked pretty closely."

"I've seen you looking. Don't think I haven't. And don't think I don't know what's running in your head while you look."

Michael didn't have an answer for that.

"But never mind. It's okay. This is about my flaws, not yours."

She stepped back, so Michael could take her all in.

"See any flaws here?"

"Not a single one," Michael whispered.

"You could be right, but what if I have a serous character flaw. Hidden. Really deep. You haven't really checked me closely." She pulled him off the table and pressed herself against him, her lips brushing his. "Have you?"

"No," Michael stammered. "I guess I haven't. But...um..."

"And I haven't been with a virgin in a very long time."

Michael pulled back. "What makes you think?"

Lola put her index finger to his lips. "*Silencio*. And don't worry. I don't consider it a character flaw. Do you?"

Lola climbed onto the table again. Michael quickly joined her there.

She pulled him close, her lips finding his. Lola's lips were incredibly moist and warm. Except for their brief kiss the night before outside his Blue 'Arlin room, Michael hadn't kissed a girl before, though he'd seen plenty of big-screen kissing. He always thought the part with your tongue would take a lot of practice, but it seemed to come naturally to him. For a few seconds his tongue sparred with hers, then pushed past it into her mouth. Lola brushed her fingers across the front of Michael's jeans. His erection was throbbing and almost painful.

Breaking the kiss, Lola leaned back so she could see his face.

"Listen to me now," Lola whispered. "I don't think I'm very good at the love part. But the sex part is how it starts. Then you gotta see if it goes anywhere from there. So how about we start with sex? Is that okay with you?"

Michael nodded, then pulled her back into a deep kiss. Taking her wrist, he moved her hand back to the lump in his jeans.

After a minute, the kiss broke. Michael struggled to breathe. He leaned in to kiss her again, but Lola leapt off the table.

"Come on," she whispered.

Taking his hand, Lola led him back to his room. Inside, under the glowing eyes of Chief Bobby, Lola helped him out of his clothes, except for his tight white briefs. She guided him onto the bed.

"Be right back," she murmured in his ear, before disappearing through the connecting door.

Leaning back against the pillow, Michael closed his eyes, reliving the blockbuster moments on the picnic table, and how the electricity shot through him when her fingers brushed his jeans.

Hearing the door handle click, he looked up to see Lola, wrapped in a motel blanket, holding a burning candle and a tiny foil packet. She settled the candle on the side table as she sat on the bed. Lifting the packet to her mouth, Lola bit down, tearing open the foil. She waved the tight roll of rubber at Michael. "I'll show you how this works."

Lola reached over and switched off the lamp.

"Are you sure this is a good idea?" Michael whispered. "I mean, what about Cavanaugh?"

"I told you. I don't love him."

"But I think I do," Michael said.

"Don't trust him."

"Why?"

Lola shook her head.

"Shh..." she whispered.

Lola stood slowly, turning to face him. Covered in the white blanket, lit by the flickering candle and a pale glow filtering in from the parking lot, she could have been a visiting spirit, a sexy ghost. She shrugged off the blanket, letting it crumple at her feet. Lola held that pose, as Michael took in the curving bones of her ribs, her dark nipples, a tuft of black curls below her flat belly.

Lola slipped into bed, pressing her naked body against his.

"Don't worry about Cavanaugh. Not right now."

Michael felt her fingers tracing his chin, his cheeks. Taking his face in her hands, she pulled his head toward hers.

"Let's do this before I change my mind."

Read 'Em And Weep

—

Cavanaugh wasn't sure when his luck turned. Was it after Bobby poured him the third Scotch? After he doubled down on a pair of jacks? When he tried to snub out his cigarette in the ashtray and ended up knocking it off the table? It was all a blur at this point.

Cavanaugh was only certain of one thing: After losing the first few hands, Bobby had suddenly become a much better poker player. Bobby's winning streak started around the time Cavanaugh decided to convert Michael's cash – around $900 at this point – into chips.

Over the next two hours, Cavanaugh won a few hands, but watched nervously as his skyscrapers of chips dwindled into two- and three-story tenements.

Looking down at his latest hand, he could feel his luck turning. These were the cards he'd been waiting for. He pushed the last of his chips into the pile.

Now if only the room would stop spinning.

When the two other players tossed their cards facedown, Cavanagh shot a glance at Bobby. Seminoles must have invented the poker face, he thought. Bobby never offered a tell. Good hand. Bad hand. Those dark eyes. That sly grin. They gave nothing away.

But Cavanaugh was confident. He shook his head and looked again just to make sure. Yes, he held the king of diamonds and the king of clubs, plus a pair of eights.

"I guess I'll raise it say...five hundred," Bobby announced casually, pushing across a stack of chips.

Cavanaugh winced. He held a winning hand, but what good

was that if he couldn't call.

"That would be five hundred to you, my friend," Bobby said, when Cavanaugh continued to stare at his cards.

"So it would," Cavanaugh took a long breath and looked up at Bobby. "I'm afraid I find myself temporarily short of funds. Would you accept an alternate form of collateral?"

"What do you have in mind?"

Cavanaugh laid his cards face down on the felt and reached into his pants pocket. Out came the keys to the Lincoln. He waved them in Bobby's direction and Bobby nodded "Yes." Cavanaugh tossed the keys in the middle of the table, knocking over a pile of chips.

"I'll call," Cavanaugh spread out his cards face up, his lips spreading into a victorious smile. "Read 'em and weep, Chief."

Bobby abandoned his poker face for the first time all night, allowing a painful grimace to contort his features. He slowly laid his cards on the table. "Well, my friend, I'm afraid you've..." Cavanaugh looked down at a straight flush, ace-high. "...got to find some other means of transportation."

Bobby raked the keys and the chips toward him. Cavanaugh looked around the room. The overhead light, set in a slowing turning ceiling fan, was glaring in his eyes. Cigarette smoke clouded near the ceiling. The two other card players were smirking, like they'd seen this coming all night. Pressing both hands on the table, Cavanaugh rose slowly, waiting for his leg muscles to remember they needed to support him. He hoped his own poker face was intact, but he was afraid it wasn't.

"Well, gentlemen," he said, summoning up his best TV announcer's voice, "I suppose it is time for me to retire and live to fight another day."

"A pleasure doing business with you, Mr. Reilly," Bobby said.

"And with you...Chief...Big Chief.. Uh..."

"Just Bobby."

Cavanaugh wiped his palm across his face. It came back wet. He blinked a few times, hoping this was all a dream but every time he looked he saw Bobby sitting with all his chips and his car keys.

"Chief...I mean, Bobby, I believe you are going to do very well in the casino business."

"Thanks for that vote of confidence." Bobby smiled.

Cavanaugh finished his drink in one long swallow. He saluted Bobby and the two men still at the table, with a wave of his empty glass.

"Very well, gentlemen. Adieu."

Walking over, Bobby opened the side door and tipped his cowboy hat as Cavanaugh approached.

"We'll be back here tomorrow night if you're feeling lucky."

Cavanaugh shook his head. He stumbled as he stepped from the landing to the sidewalk that connected the office to the horseshoe of motel rooms. He heard the door closing behind him, the lock turning. Stopping, he collapsed back against the office door. The motel was ten steps away. He waited for the world to stop spinning, then stepped forward slowly, willing himself to stay upright.

Reaching the motel, he pressed his palm against the wall for support. The Lincoln was parked at the far end of the horseshoe of rooms. He had a long way to go. He needed help. It was clearly time for some Sinatra.

"It's a quarter to three," he whispered, taking the first few steps, his right hand sliding along the wall for balance. "No one in the place except you and me."

By the time he reached the room, he felt more sure-footed and he switched to his singing voice:

"We're drinking my friend, to the end, of a brief episode."

Cavanaugh stumbled over to the white convertible, running his fingers along the hood. A full moon, glowing behind a thin slipcover of clouds, lit the chrome grill. Staring up, Cavanaugh pondered the bright ball a little too long; the slowly spinning world suddenly picking up speed. Closing his eyes, he leaned back against the car until the crazy ride geared down.

"So make it one for my baby and one more for the road."

A few staggering steps forward and Cavanaugh grabbed the

door handle of his room.

"Shit," he whispered. Locked.

He didn't want Lola to see him this drunk. Didn't want to answer any questions about the money and the car he'd just lost. Cavanaugh turned around, leaning against the motel wall for support as he dug in his pocket, finally finding the key.

"Easy does it..." he whispered, stabbing the key toward the lock, missing widely. Wrapping his left hand around his right, and breathing deeply, the key found the slot.

Stepping inside the dark room, the tilt-a-whirl cranked up again. He lost his balance and began backpedaling, his arms reaching out for support, until he felt the doorknob pressing into his back.

There was a hint of light seeping from the crack under the bathroom door. Cavanaugh lurched in that direction. He eased the door open, the tin handle cold in his hand. A night-light glowed behind the sink. He could see the bathroom was empty. Noticing the toilet, Cavanaugh also realized his bladder was sending him an urgent message. Closing the door, Cavanaugh felt along the wall for the light switch.

The explosion of wattage was like a nuclear blast. Cavanaugh slapped his palms over his eyes. When he thought it was safe, he splayed his fingers just enough to sneak a peek. Keeping his eyes at half-staff, he moved to the toilet, his hand on the wall for balance, desperately trying to direct an errant stream toward the bowl.

Afterwards, he eased open the bathroom door, letting the light spill out. He could see the bedroom was as empty as his bladder.

"Lola...?" he whispered.

No answer.

"Alright, Private Reilly, attention!"

Cavanaugh's whispered order was not so easily followed. Still leaning against the bathroom doorframe, he shook his head vigorously, hoping to shake loose even a sliver of sobriety. Eventually, he felt the room righting itself.

He took two firm steps into the bedroom before the floor tilted away and he found himself stumbling into the wall dividing his room from Michael's. His fingers brushed the knob of the connecting door.

"Of course," he whispered. "She's keeping an eye on the prize."

With the same care a jeweler might employ when splitting a precious stone, Cavanaugh silently spun the knob, easing the door open.

A candle flickering on a bedside table illuminated two sleeping figures. A spike of hair on one pillow, tight curls across the other and the torn square of foil tossed on the carpet told Cavanaugh all he needed to know.

Pulling the door closed, he stumbled backwards, flopping hard on his own bed. His hand returned to his face, this time wiping away tears.

In his suitcase he kept a journal to record his most profound insights, his angry letters to politicians or journalists, and snippets of new poems. He rustled in the bag until he found it. There was a Palm Beach phone number scrawled on the inside back cover.

Opening the journal, he tore out an empty page. The handwritten note he left on his pillow was simple; the words slightly misshapen, but the message clear:

When final battle is lost, the old general must do his duty. Therefore, I shall fall, honorably, upon my sword.

— The late Cavanaugh Reilly III

Moments later, Cavanaugh was fumbling with the dial on the pay phone outside Bobby's office, his eyes shifting from the phone to a torn scrap of paper in his hand.

"Is this the Donnelly residence?" Cavanaugh asked when he heard a sleepy hello. "Are you looking for your son? I'm with the little bastard right now..."

A Focused, Goal-Oriented Adult

—

Cavanagh's suicide plan was vague at best. Behind the motel, Bobby had an airboat business that sped tourists around the 'glades, the flat tin tub pushed by a box fan on steroids. A launch led down to a wide expanse of water, framed on three sides by twisting walls of mangroves.

Stumbling toward the boat launch, Cavanaugh conjured the death scene from A *Star Is Born*, when a very drunk James Mason waded into the sea and didn't come out. That storyline seemed just about right for this moment. And it gave him the opportunity to do a last bit of poetry before his big final scene.

Pausing at the top of the concrete ramp, Cavanaugh called up a bit of Keats:

"*And such too is the grandeur of the dooms/We have imagined for the mighty dead,*" he purred, letting the moment build slowly into something truly theatrical. "*An endless fountain of immortal drink/Pouring unto us from the heaven's brink.*"

His eyes took a slow hike across a vast ebony sky awash with stars. Cavanaugh recalled a snippet of Dickinson worthy of the moment: "*Because I could not stop for Death/He kindly stopped for me/The Carriage held but just Ourselves/And Immortality.*"

The poet offered a tipsy bow then walked solemnly down the concrete corridor to the lake, as if cameras were recording each step. The black water was cool, the concrete giving way to a squishy river bottom. Taking slow steps, he felt the water soaking his knees, his waist, and finally, his neck.

Maybe it was the poetry or the rustle of his legs in the water but something roused a local lounging nearby. Cavanaugh didn't notice the squat reptilian creature, its knobby tail at least five feet long, rising from the scrub grass and padding silently into the dark water.

The silky liquid lapping just below Cavanaugh's jaw felt comforting, almost alluring. Go a little further he told himself, but another voice suggested he linger in the world of the living a bit longer. The scene begged for more poetry, so Cavanaugh raised his head, keeping his mouth just above the surface.

"*Good night, sweet prince, goodnight!*"

———

Lola woke to the sizzle of the candle drowning in its own wax. She had not meant to fall asleep. But the sweet sex, the afterglow of the baggie, and a day that started with a murder and ended with a betrayal had taken its toll.

She heard Michael's steady breathing, saw the covers bunched around his shoulders, as she quietly eased out of bed. Slipping through the connecting door, she walked carefully, feeling her way in the dark, until she stood beside the bed. In the dim glow of the bathroom nightlight she could see the bed was empty. She let herself relax. He was still at the card game. Maybe he wouldn't find out what had just happened in Michael's room.

Lola slipped under the covers and was asleep almost immediately, never noticing the yellow sheet of paper resting on the pillow next to hers.

———

For a person who is very tired or very drunk, a good splash of cold water can wake them up or sober them up, at least a little. And the chilly liquid engulfing Cavanaugh from the soles of his scuffed brogans to the frayed collar of his blue button down had that effect. The water's smell also got his attention – something like sardines packed in lemongrass. Somewhere in the back of his brain, lit matches were being pressed against wicks, putting the entire suicide scenario in a different light.

Every time a message from his brain urged him to "push forward and let's get "on with the show," another missive sizzled through his mental wiring commanding him to "wave your arms and kick your feet!" As a result, his head continued to float atop the rippled surface, like a plastic bobber laced to a fishing line, awaiting the downward pull of a hungry lunker.

He hadn't completely changed his mind about the suicide. All the reasons came rushing back if he summoned them. I'll tire soon and that will be that, Cavanaugh thought, but until then, I'll just float here a while, besides there was a Cole Porter song that desperately needed to be sung.

"Miss Otis regrets she's unable to lunch today, Madam. Miss Otis regrets she's unable to lunch today."

Moving deeper into the verse, Cavanaugh got the impression he might not be the only one taking a post-midnight swim. "She's sorry to be delayed, but this evening down on lover's lane she strayed, Madam."

Kicking sideways, Cavanagh's body spun left and he found himself starting directly into the primordial orbs of a curious bull gator, floating about three feet away. "Miss Otis regrets..." he offered, his voice a choked whisper.

Cavanaugh started to kick a little harder, using his arms as paddles to ease himself back from the creature's knuckled snout. Cavanaugh's new poetry matched his stroking motions – which became stronger as he retreated toward the boat launch and the shore. He kept his suddenly sober eyes locked on the stoic creature rotating in his direction. Even as he pushed back, the beast edged closer.

"Do...not go...gentle...into that...good night." His breath rushed in and out around the words. "Rage...rage...against the dying of the light. Do not...go gentle...into that...good night."

He found a new well of strength and a fresh love of life as he tried to put some distance between himself and his reptilian companion.

"*Rage...rage...rage...rage...rage...rage. ...rage...against the dying of the light!*" He was shouting now and splashing furiously.

When his feet caught the bottom Cavanaugh turned and lurched toward the shore. He did not look back until he was at the top of the boat launch. Stepping off the concrete, he stumbled, dropping face first to the grass. The shock of the landing took a moment to absorb, then Cavanaugh rolled over and sat up, shaking a raised fist at his amphibious adversary.

"Come on...We're on my turf now, you oversized handbag!" he bellowed, his voice deep and Shakespearean. "Do I look frightened now? Well? Do I?"

Looking out at the dark water, Cavanaugh watched the ridged shadow sink silently, leaving not a ripple.

A deep breath of drowsiness filled his chest. He settled onto his back – gently this time – the thick grass buoying his head like a soft satin pillow in a top-of-the-line casket. With his chin skyward and his palms folded across his chest, Cavanaugh ascended into a heavenly vastness, as the stars around him blinked out one by one.

———

It was the smell that woke him first. The sticky sweet aroma of pine logs catching fire. As the flames seared off the layers of bark, the sharp snaps and crackles pierced the cobwebby crevices of Cavanaugh's brain. He opened his eyes warily, taking an inventory of himself. He was on his back, his head tilted to the left, a campfire flickering a foot or so away. Clearly, he was dreaming.

"Am I in hell?" Cavanaugh asked, his voice a hoarse whisper.

"Nope, you're in Florida."

"Same difference."

Cavanaugh wondered where this dream was taking him. The

voice was familiar but dreams can bring voices from deep in the past. What he knew for sure was that in this dream he was soaking wet and stretched out on something soft. He could feel the fire warming his face. It seemed almost real. He jiggled his legs and then his arms, and when all his extremities responded, he decided to try and sit up. Rising to his elbows, Cavanaugh recognized the figure leaning in with a long stick to stir the kindling – Chief Bobby.

"I guess this means I'm not dead."

"I don't think so," Bobby said. "Though you just about scared a bull gator to death. They don't hear much poetry."

Cavanaugh sat up completely, pressing both hands on the grass to keep from tipping over. Once he was settled, Bobby passed him a steaming mug of coffee.

"A pity," Cavanaugh said, as he took the cup. "Perhaps I could secure a position here as poet laureate?"

Bobby laughed and sipped his own coffee. "I'm afraid that would make you just another endangered species."

"My species isn't endangered, it's as good as gone. I'm the last of the breed." Cavanaugh gulped the hot coffee, then quickly spit it onto the grass. "Wow. I think your Scotch went down smoother."

Bobby laughed. "So, your little dip there – were you aiming for extinction?"

Cavanaugh didn't answer. Bobby sipped his coffee and waited for the old man to pick up the conversation.

"Well, alright then," Cavanaugh finally said, looking across the fire at Bobby. "I just lost our money and our car. My lover is bedded down with my best friend. And I'm being stalked by my own daughter. Suicide seemed the logical next step."

Cavanaugh blew into the mug and took a tentative sip. This time, the coffee stayed down.

"That makes a certain amount of sense," Bobby said. "But the girl – she's way too young for you anyway."

Cavanaugh snorted.

"For a moment there, Chief, I thought you might be some

kind of wise man. But you're dead wrong. The lovely Lola is much too old for me. She's the focused, goal-oriented adult in this relationship. I'm the pimply-faced teenager who fell in love with the Avon Lady."

"And the boy?"

"He's a nut. But a harmless one. We're two frustrated romantics in search of the undefinable, the unknowable, and, along the way, maybe a little nookie."

Bobby held a piece of paper toward the firelight. It was the flyer with Michael's picture on it.

"Seems he is pretty well-known and apparently not so harmless."

"You didn't call that number, did you?" Cavanaugh felt his back stiffen, remembering his own phone call.

"That's not how we Seminoles roll."

"And how do you roll? Let's see: card shark, Indian chief, casino baron. What happened to the noble savages, living off the land?"

"Mr. Reilly, for a moment there, I thought *you* were a wise man."

"I know the history. You got screwed. But the Great Spirit Casino? The Trail of Tears Lounge?"

"Don't forget the cultural center. Seminole heritage and history."

"There's money in that?"

"If you throw in a little alligator wrestling, to keep the tourists interested."

"You wrestle gators?"

"I've been known to."

"I could have used you out there."

"You did just fine."

Looking up from the fire, Cavanaugh saw the first spires of sunlight spiking on the horizon. He looked back at Bobby.

"I guess you're not here to give me the car keys and my money back?"

"That wouldn't be sporting, would it?"

"No. I suppose not. Can't hurt to ask, though."

Bobby leaned toward Cavanaugh, his face golden in the fire-light.

"I am curious. Since suicide is out, what are you going to do now? Got a plan?"

"You know, you're starting to sound a lot like my ex-girl-friend."

Jesus Take
The Wheel

—

Colleen couldn't call what she was doing sleeping. Actual sleep is hard to achieve when you're sitting up in the front seat of a station wagon in the parking lot of a strip center. Dozing was more like it, nodding off and snapping back every few minutes as her head fell forward. Raising a hand to her face at one point, she found a crusty circle of drool coating her chin.

In the twilight between sleep and waking, some specifics of the dream were dimming, but Colleen recalled staring out the open passenger window of a moving car. She had felt the wind buffeting her face as she passed a parade of government offices, old motels, homeless shelters and dive bars – all landmarks on her search for her father.

The dream came with a soundtrack, her favorite Christian pop tune – "Jesus, Take the Wheel". She didn't have to look over to know the Son of God was driving and she was going wherever He wanted to take her.

When the light inside Jaime's office switched on, she could feel it before she actually opened her eyes. When she did rouse herself, sitting up straighter, the view through the office window was as vivid as Edward Hopper's diner painting: Jaime half-awake behind his desk, a thicket of black hair bristling around the yoke of his Stanley Kowalski undershirt, a telephone receiver pressed to his ear.

She knew the call was about the boy. And the boy was traveling with her father. The chase was about to resume.

"Thank you, Lord," Colleen whispered, her head bowed, her hands folded in prayer. "Thank you, Jesus!"

———

When his phone rang, Jaime wasn't sure if he'd been asleep or just drifting around the fringes of it.

Jaime could sleep on the military surplus cot he kept in his office, but not well. Since his wife left, the office had been his home and the narrow, sagging cot his bed. The rest of his life wasn't comfortable, why should sleeping be any different?

Alex Donnelly told him that Michael had eluded the film security team, but he'd just answered a 4 a.m. call from a very articulate drunk guy asking about a reward. The caller provided an address just off Alligator Alley.

"It's some kind of motel run by a Indian," Alex said.

"By Indian, you mean – "

"I mean a real American Indian. A Seminole. Chief Billy or Chief Bobby. Something like that," Alex said.

The kid was resourceful, Jaime thought; he had to give him that.

"On my way," Jaime told him.

Fifteen minutes later, he stepped out his front door in a clean shirt and a plaid sport coat, carrying a small zippered gym bag. Inside was a Colt .38 snapped into a black leather holster. The boy's friends had put his lights out before. Jaime was not going to be caught unaware and unarmed this time around.

He spotted the familiar station wagon parked beside his Pinto with Colleen asleep inside. Moving to the window, he saw she was curled slightly, so her head was on the top ridge of the seat, her face aimed toward the car window where Jaime lingered. It was 6 a.m., and a reluctant sun was starting to rim the night sky with a thick stripe of pale pink. Some of that almost holy light brushed Colleen's sleeping face, reminding Jaime of the stained-glass Madonna inside the tiny parish chapel he attended as a child.

He raised his fist to tap on the window, but changed his mind. He had a job to do and he didn't need any complications. It had taken two years to construct this brick wall around his heart. He wasn't going to tear it down now.

Inside the Pinto, Jaime backed up slowly. Pulling onto Dixie Highway, he didn't look back. He didn't see Colleen's eyes snap open or hear her station wagon's big V-8 roaring to life.

———

When you follow people for a living it's pretty obvious when someone is following you. Jaime first noticed Colleen's station wagon behind him as he headed west on Lake Worth Road toward 441.

He didn't try to shake this tail. He caught himself slowing down if she fell too far behind. If he beat a light and she didn't, he pulled to the side until he saw the wide grill of the Ford in his rear view again.

He wasn't going to take her with him, but if she came on her own, how bad could that be?

Jaime knew a cold front was approaching, but for now, the morning was cool and cloudless, the cane fields and scrubland along the highway vivid. It was the kind of morning where a man can convince himself something good is coming his way. Jaime allowed himself to smile. After he finished the business with the boy, maybe he'd take some time off. Ask Colleen out to dinner. Call his son on a day that wasn't a birthday or national holiday. Talk to the boy like a normal dad who just happens to be 400 miles away.

Heading south on State Road 29 toward Alligator Alley, he checked his mirror. Colleen's car was there. He kept staring at the cloudy mirror, hoping her face might come into focus.

It was a lovely stretch of road, with a canal running along the north side, bordered by tall grasses topped with fuzzy gold bristles. Beyond the canal, spindly scrub oaks and skinny pine trees spouted from clustered carpets of palmettos, like so many roadside question marks and exclamation points. Maybe Jaime was distracted by the view, or perhaps he let his eyes linger on Colleen, in his mirror, for too long. Whatever it was, the gopher was seconds from becoming road kill when Jaime registered what looked like a squat green footstool lumbering across his lane, the gopher's taut neck and pointy face stretching forward like a green arrow.

Slamming the brake and jerking the wheel, Jaime was quickly reminded that a Pinto is not a high-performance car. Sure enough, the car wobbled as it spun around the gopher, then careened onto the road's edge, which turned out to be softer than he had expected. He could feel the ground giving way and the nose of the car jerking to the right just before the grill hit the water with a cannonball splash, sending a flock of egrets skittering into the sky.

It had all happened too fast for Jaime to even curse his luck. Looking through the windshield at the water lapping at his grill, he did an internal check of bones and skin. All seemed intact. Glancing over his shoulder, he watched the gopher complete its slow trek across the asphalt.

He heard a car door slam.

"Are you okay?" Colleen shouted, from the edge of the road.

Jaime didn't answer, just gave a single wave out his open window. It was bad enough he had crash-landed in a canal, but it was worse luck that this woman was there to witness his folly.

He remembered his brief flirtation with happiness only a few moments before. It never lasts, Jaime thought. Never.

He got his door open and tried to gauge the depth of the water. He thought he could see the bottom. His first step put him in ankle deep water, but his second step was into a hole that sucked him in up to his waist, prompting a string of Cuban curses the detective had forgotten he knew.

Grabbing the Pinto's door handle, he was able to free his feet and get back into shallow water. Reaching over to the passenger seat Jaime picked up the canvas bag that held his gun and holster. He held it over his head as he clambered out of the canal, trying not to make eye contact with the red-headed woman who was standing on the bank, her hands on her hips.

"Are you okay?"

Waving away her comment, Jaime climbed the bank. He leaned over the hood of her car, head lowered, palms soaking up the heat rising off the metal. His pants and shoes were soaked, but so was his shirt and sport coat, not from the canal, but from his own sweat. Dark circles spread across his chest and under his arms.

My whole life, he thought, is measured in degrees of perspiration. In the air-conditioned chapel on his wedding day – a day he remembered as almost entirely happy - his tuxedo shirt had soaked through. Give him a real crisis, like his car in a ditch in the middle of nowhere, and the dam just broke.

———

"Are you hurt?" she asked.

Jaime didn't answer.

"I could drive you the rest of the way. If you want. We could get your car later."

Instead of answering, Jaime stomped both feet onto the highway, trying to shake the mud and moisture off his shoes and pants. He picked up the canvas bag and climbed into her car.

They rode together in silence for the next few minutes before Jaime barked: "Can't you drive any faster?"

His angry comment made Colleen smile.

"Oh, yes sir. Anything you say, sir." She offered a brisk salute, then pressed a little harder on the accelerator.

The two-lane road dead-ended into Alligator Alley. At the stop sign, Jaime didn't speak, just pointed to the right. Colleen made the turn.

"This is kind of exciting," she said, after another few minutes of stony silence.

"No, it's not."

"Come on," she said, keeping her eyes forward, but giving his shoulder a light punch. "Admit it. It's kind of exciting. Chasing people. Sneaking around. Being Mr. Private Eye."

Jaime didn't look in her direction. "Couldn't you just drive and not talk?"

"Are you really this grumpy all the time? Doesn't your wife get tired of it?"

"Don't have a wife," he snapped back, still staring forward.

"But you did, I bet. And I'll bet she got tired of it."

Now Jaime turned her way, putting on his best scowl and narrowing his eyes.

"Don't start with me," he said. "We're riding together but we don't have to be talking."

Colleen let a few seconds of silence hang there in the space between driver and passenger, but she wasn't finished.

"She left, didn't she?" She gave Jaime another playful punch in the shoulder.

"I said - don't start..."

"Didn't she?"

Jaime slammed both open palms on the flat top of the dashboard.

"YES GODDAMMIT!" He shouted, his face going red.

"Did she take the kids, too?"

Jaime didn't answer, but when Colleen looked over, she could see his anger was gone.

"Why are you doing this to me?" he whispered.

"I'm just asking, did she take the kids?"

"Yes, if you have to know. She took our son to Tampa and I see him twice a year in December and July, but only if I drive up there and get him." Jaime's head rolled back onto the top of the seat. He stared up at the taut, camel-colored fabric pressed against the car's ceiling.

Colleen waited thirty seconds and then whispered, "I'm so sorry."

"Just...fucking...drive...Please?" Looking over at him, she saw a man who had given up on being happy. She wanted to touch him - not a punch, but a hug or a soft hand on his shoulder.

But she kept her fingers wrapped around the steering wheel.

Another five miles of silence and a small roadside sign for Bobby's Seminole Village and Motel appeared.

"Turn there," he barked.

The Ford made a slow turn onto the dirt road, throwing up clouds of chalky dust as the tires stirred the dirt.

"They're down here?" Colleen asked.

"That what the tipster said."

Jaime pulled the small bag onto his lap and inched back the sluggish zipper before drawing out the .38, cinched into a black shoulder holster. Reaching deeper into the bag, he came out with a clip. He unsnapped the holster and removed the gun, slamming the clip into the butt of the revolver.

Colleen glanced from the road to the gun and back again. When she heard the clip snap into place, she slammed hard on the brakes. The gun and holster flew from Jaime's hands onto the floor as the wagon wobbled a bit on the dirt, then shuddered to a stop, a shower of dust rising higher than the roof.

"What the hell!" Jaime shouted.

But Colleen wasn't waiting for his comments. She was quickly out of the car, taking the keys with her. Jaime climbed out slowly. He found Colleen staring off into the scrubland.

"What are you doing?" he asked.

"That gun. This trip. You're not going to shoot him, are you?" Colleen turned to face him now, tears starting to fall. "I mean, he's a kid."

"Look. Somebody put my lights out last time I met this crowd. I need some leverage."

"But a gun?"

"Just part of the business."

Colleen turned abruptly. She started walking toward the main road.

"What am I doing?" Her words weren't aimed at Jaime, but herself. "This is nuts. He doesn't want to see me. I know it. I mean. I've always known it."

———

Watching her walk away, Jaime wasn't sure what he should do next. He told himself he needed to get her back into the car. He had a job to do. But somehow what was happening between him and this woman had become more important than any job.

Alto, a voice inside his head was saying. Stop right here. You know exactly where this will lead. Right? Nothing but heartache and trouble.

Jaime set the gun and holster on the hood of the car and started after her, the voice in his head louder now. Turn around right now, the voice said. *Ahora!* Jaime shook the voice from his head. It was probably a bad decision, but he had no intention of turning around, instead he walked faster.

"Wait!" He said. "Wait, please."

Colleen stopped but didn't turn back. When he reached her, Jaime carefully placed his hands on Colleen's shoulders. He could feel her body shaking. He tightened his grip and felt the shaking stop, but she still didn't turn to look at him.

"Why am I doing this?" she muttered.

Jaime pulled her backwards, wrapping his arms around her, enjoying the feeling of this woman pressed against him.

"Maybe because you love him," he whispered, his mouth close to her ear.

"What do you know about love? You don't do happy stories. Remember? You can't even keep your own family together." She eased out of his grip and turned to face him.

"I'm sorry." Colleen reached out, her hands on each of his arms. "I'm sorry. I didn't mean that."

Looking into her eyes, he could feel the wall he'd worked so hard to build begin to crumble. A sob caught in his throat. "I've made a lot of mistakes," he said.

"My whole life is a mistake," Colleen whispered.

Jaime pulled her into a hug, breathing in hints of lavender and vanilla. The crispness of her hair against his cheek made him say a silent prayer of thanks to a God he hadn't spoken to in years.

"Shhh," he whispered, his lips at her ear. "Don't say that."

"But it's true. I'm a fool! A stupid, stupid fool!"

"No, you're not."

Colleen stepped back just enough so she could see his face.

"I only know one thing for sure," Colleen said, as Jaime raised a thick finger to her cheek, tracing the line of a single tear. "I have a lot of love to give, but no one seems to want it."

"I see that," Jaime whispered. He leaned in, gently kissing each of her cheeks. "It's going to be okay. I promise."

Then with more tenderness than he thought he possessed, Jaime lifted her chin and pressed his lips against hers; it was the kind of kiss a couple might exchange seconds after a priest pronounced them man and wife.

Who Am I Going To Kill Today?

—

A woman's scream jolted Michael awake. It was the real thing. Or as real as any scream he'd heard in a horror movie. It was a scream worthy of Dawn Karston – screeching and sudden, sharp with terror, and definitely bad for the vocal chords.

Michael jerked upright. The other side of the bed was empty. Maybe it was a dream? No, he was sure it happened. There was a lump of red candle wax on the side table and he was naked. Michael never slept naked. When he rubbed his eyes, he could smell the musk of her on his fingers.

It *had* happened.

He leapt from the bed and ran to the connecting door. Pulling it open he saw Lola, wearing Cavanaugh's plaid flannel bathrobe, staring down at a piece of paper in apparent disbelief.

"What?" Michael asked. "Where's Cavanaugh?"

Lola didn't look up. Instead, she thrust out her arm, as if the note in her hand had just caught fire.

"He's dead. Just like that other guy. Two-in-one-day. Fuck me!"

She tossed the note to the floor then turned to look at Michael, standing naked in the doorway. "Who am I going to kill today?"

——

When Michael stepped out of his motel door onto the sidewalk a few minutes later, wearing jeans and a T-shirt, the harsh morning light seemed to white-out the world. He brought a hand up to shade his eyes. After a moment, the chrome grill of the Lincoln came into focus, along with the prone figure of Cavanaugh splayed across the hood, his head and back resting against the windshield.

Breathing in, Michael could taste the thickening air. A storm was coming. He squinted off through the scrub and pine trees to the open water. An unruly mob of gray clouds was massing on the horizon. Michael had seen enough Florida winters to know that the cold front barreling down from Canada had sent an advance team of rain, thunder and lightning.

Just then Lola stepped from her room, her feet bare, a blue cotton sundress clinging like cellophane, a pair of pink sunglasses on her nose. In the morning light, she looked young and fresh, like she had somehow hit a reset button. Michael felt almost giddy. It had happened. Last night was not a dream.

"Ah, the lovebirds." Cavanaugh said, slipping off the hood onto his feet. "Did we sleep well?"

Michael turned to see Cavanaugh scowling in his direction as Lola rushed toward the car.

"Baby, you're okay!"

Standing now, Cavanaugh pushed her away. "Yes, Lazarus rises from the grave. A little moldy but none the worse for wear. Physically, that is."

"Cav," Lola stammered. "I'm so sorry..."

Michael felt a knot forming in his gut. This was all suddenly very wrong.

The old man pushed past Lola without a second look, stopping in front of Michael, who remained frozen in place on the sidewalk. Cavanaugh leaned forward so their faces were inches apart, his voice frighteningly calm.

"Michael, I am most disappointed in you. I mean, the girl is a whore. We both know that, so her actions shouldn't surprise us. But you? I thought you were a fellow traveler. A friend."

"I'm...I mean...I -" Michael stammered.

Cavanaugh cut him off with a wave of his hand. Then, sifted into the accent of a Southern hayseed.

"Why offasuh, she jus' looked so dahmn guhd I cudden't he'p myse'f. Is that your story?"

Michael swallowed hard, but offered no answer. Cavanaugh backed up a few inches.

"If you think a love affair with this sexual entrepreneur will have a happy ending, I suggest you think again," he said, dropping his Southern accent. "She starts with acquisitions and ends with layoffs."

Lola didn't wait for more. She moved quickly, inserting herself into the narrow space between Cavanaugh and Michael. She stared up at Cavanaugh, her eyes ablaze.

"So did you do it?"

"Quiet," Cavanaugh said, trying to avoid her gaze. "I'm not ready to talk with you at this juncture."

"Did you? Did you call the kid's family, so you could play both sides of your little con game?"

"I said – BE QUIET!" Cavanaugh grabbed Lola's shoulders with both hands and moved her to the side.

Michael finally found his voice. "What's she talking about? What con game?"

Letting go of Lola, Cavanaugh backed toward the parking lot. "She is a professional liar and a drug addict. Mendacity is her middle name!"

"Sir Cavanaugh, the gallant defender of the downtrodden," Lola said, hands on her hips, her chin thrust out in his direction. "Tell him. Tell him your plan. How you get the kid to buy you a car and hand over his cash and you turn him over to his daddy for a nice reward."

Cavanaugh turned back to face her.

"Don't put this back on me. You were supposed to keep the kid interested, not give him a complete anatomy lesson."

"Keep the kid interested?" Michael looked from Lola to Cavanaugh.

"She is a businesswoman and you, my friend, are an opportunity. I admit my complicity, but at least I did not make you fall in love with me."

Michael felt the world closing in around him. These were his friends. They were in this together. Suddenly, this whole trip was a lie? Anger or pain or some even more toxic cocktail of bitterness fizzed up through his chest, clotting in his throat. He felt sweat soaking his shirt.

"So...both of you?"

Lola stepped toward him, her hand on Michael's shoulder.

"It's not like that," Lola said. "I mean it was. But last night wasn't like that. You need to believe me."

"I do?" Michael yanked her hand off his shoulder. "Even when this whole thing turns out to be a con job?"

Michael heard a distant door slam and turned to see Chief Bobby striding bowlegged from his office in his jeans and cowboy boots, another multi-colored Seminole blouse covering his barrel chest. A single set of keys dangled from his fingers.

"Sorry to break up this love fest, but I thought I'd take my new car for a spin."

As the trio watched from the motel sidewalk, Bobby tipped his white Stetson and climbed inside the Lincoln. The V-8 roared to life and Bobby eased the car into reverse.

"Pleasure doing business with you all." He raised his voice so he could be heard over the metallic thrum of the engine. "Stay another night, if you like, I'm compin' the rooms."

Looking very much at home in the white convertible, Bobby lifted his hat again and waved it in the direction of the trio before stomping on the gas and fishtailing out of the parking lot, the white wall tires – grasping for traction – tossing up a shower of shells.

"That's our car..." Michael said, as much to himself as the others.

"What happened to the money?" Lola turned to Cavanaugh, getting back in his face. "You didn't lose the money too, did you?"

Cavanaugh backed away from Lola, stepping deeper into the

parking space where the Lincoln had been. His eyes followed the white convertible as it turned onto the dirt road and sped away.

"Just a temporary setback, I assure you. Michael, I can work this all out."

Cavanaugh stood silently for a moment, apparently pondering his next move. Looking every bit of his age, he walked wearily to the sidewalk. Pulling a handkerchief from his back pocket, he leaned down to wipe away some dust, then seated himself on the slab with more than a little ceremony.

"It's all kind of funny, if you think about it," he said, as much to himself as his companions.

No one answered him.

Lola hadn't moved from the spot where the Lincoln's grill had been only a moment before. She didn't look at Michael or Cavanaugh. Instead, she raised her eyes to the bright sky, now going gray at the corners.

Leaning against the door of his room, Michael pressed his eyes closed, hoping for a moment of calm so he could sort out this whole crazy thing – the slasher queen, the flight from home, the low-rent motels, the biker on the boardwalk, the magic hour of sweet, sweet sex, and now, the ugly betrayal by his friends. In the harsh light of the Florida morning, it all seemed pretty foolish.

Weren't filmmakers supposed to be intuitive people who understood human nature and how the world worked? He was just as clueless about these so-called friends and this ridiculous quest as he had been on those last days his mother was alive. Crystal had been trying to tell him something with her eyes, her touch, maybe even the tone of her voice as she asked him about normal stuff – salad or sandwiches for lunch? How about a fashion show of the new dresses I bought on Worth Avenue yesterday? Please tell me you loved Goldie Hawn in *Private Benjamin!*

She had left him in the movie room that afternoon after sliding in a VHS version of Eisenstein's 1925 classic *Battleship Potemkin.* Michael's home schooling mostly consisted of watch-

ing classic films on historic topics in the movie room with his
mother, a bucket of popcorn on the seat between them. On the
day she left him her final note, Crystal was sure her son would
be occupied until long after the maids found her in the bathtub,
but the videotape went haywire just as the baby carriage came
bouncing down the staircase and Michael left the darkened
room to look for his mother.

He realized now if Crystal had been trying to tell him something in those final days and hours, he had missed every signal.

He'd gone over all the moments in his head for six months
– the grief and second guessing running on a loop, along with
the image of his dead mother in the tub, her arm outstretched,
her blood soaking the tile floor.

Only his stories and drawings and his belief in the unap-
preciated talents of Dawn Karston had given him some peace.
Now he was sure he'd soon be replaying every moment with
Cavanaugh and Lola, regretting every missed marker signaling
another looming disaster.

Michael's hand pushed deep in the pocket of his jeans and
came out with a quarter. It was over. That much he knew for
sure. Time to call Dad.

He heard something in the distance, a soft whirring, growing
slowly into a mechanical hum. It couldn't be Bobby coming back
so soon, Michael thought. He saw dust rising from the dirt road
and a wood-paneled station wagon turning into the parking lot.

He recognized the car. It was Cavanaugh's daughter. But
there was someone else with her. The car eased into the space
where the Lincoln had been.

Looking over, Michael saw Lola frozen outside the closed
door of her room, her body facing the door, her hand gripping
the knob. A few feet away, Cavanaugh remained seated on the
sidewalk, looking down at the bed of white shell that covered
the parking lot. If either of them heard the car approaching,
they gave no sign of it.

The passenger door opened and Michael finally recognized
Colleen's passenger as the big man who had grabbed him in the

motel, the man Lola thought she had killed. He was soaking wet from the waist down, his black shoes covered in mud, but he was very much alive.

The man strode toward Michael, the gray pistol in his right hand pointed at the center of the boy's T-shirt.

"Freeze, kid!" Jaime shouted. "I mean it. Don't fucking move!"

Involuntarily, remembering similar scenes from dozens of film noir caper flicks, Michael took a backward step, raising his hands over his head in surrender.

"Sorry," Michael stammered, his eyes focused on the gun barrel. "I mean, I did move, but I didn't mean to. I give up. It's okay."

He heard Lola scream again – but this time it sounded joyful.

"LOOK! He's not dead! He's not dead!" She rushed to Michael and only then noticed his arms were above his head.

"He's not dead! I'm not a murderer!"

Keeping his hands high, Michael stepped away from her.

"I believed you. I believed both of you. And it was just an act."

"Michael..." Lola reached for him but Michael shook her off.

Cavanaugh was quickly on his feet, putting himself between the man with the gun and Michael.

"Now hold on," he told the detective, his voice gentle but firm. "This boy isn't going to hurt anyone."

Jaime stopped a few feet from them, but didn't lower the gun. The driver's door opened and Colleen stepped out, leaning quickly toward the side mirror. She applied a smear of pink lipstick, then patted her helmet of hair back into place. Looking up, she smiled at her father. Her smile vanished when she noticed Jaime and his gun.

"Don't do that!" she shouted at Jaime. "You promised you wouldn't do that!"

Cavanaugh nodded, pointing in the direction of the pistol. "Believe me, sidearms are not necessary here."

Jaime kept the gun aimed at Cavanaugh, who held his ground in front of Michael. "I'll be the judge of that."

Jaime's eyes swiveled between Cavanaugh and Lola. With his free hand, he rubbed the back of his head. "You guys play hardball. You need to know – so do I."

His eyes settled on Cavanaugh. "Are you Reilly?"

Cavanaugh nodded solemnly.

"Mr. Donnelly says thanks."

"You really did it!" Lola shouted.

"Look, son," Cavanaugh said, turning away from Jaime to face the boy. "I'm truly sorry."

"I thought you were my friend," Michael could hear the emotion in his own voice. "I looked up to you. I ... I loved you."

"My boy, life can be very complicated."

Michael turned to Lola. "And I thought you...I don't know what I thought but not this."

Lola and Cavanaugh started to move toward him, their arms reaching out. Seeing them now, Michael felt the anger rush up from his throat, his brain suddenly on fire, the scene before him cast in red. The boy who had never yelled in seventeen years on the planet, found he knew how to do it.

"GET THE FUCK AWAY FROM ME! BOTH OF YOU!"

His shout stopped Lola and Cavanaugh in their tracks. Michael dropped his arms to his sides. He looked directly at the detective. "Look, I'll go with you. Nothing's going to happen. It already has."

Jaime took in the scene and decided it was safe to slip the pistol back in the holster strapped just below his armpit. "I swear if any of you try to hit me with anything, this pistol is coming back out!"

Colleen walked over, sliding her hand across Jaime's back. "Thank you," she whispered, as she kissed his cheek.

Colleen spun quickly and ran to her father.

"Oh, Daddy!" Colleen threw her arms around Cavanaugh, pulling him into a hug he couldn't manage to resist.

With her face pressed into his neck, Colleen didn't notice the color rushing from her father's face. Cavanaugh wriggled from her grip, taking her arms in his hands and easing them away from him as he backed away, one slow step at a time.

"Honey, it is good to see you. Really. If you'll just wait here.

I've got to pick up something, but I'll be right back. Just, stay here!"

Colleen reached for him again. "Daddy..."

The word hit Cavanaugh like someone had touched him with a live wire. He turned and sprinted across the parking lot toward the boat ramp and the open water.

Colleen watched him for only a second before racing off in pursuit.

"Daddy! Wait for me!"

In the commotion, Lola disappeared into the room. She emerged quickly with her duffle bag. Without a word, she started walking through the parking lot toward the dirt road that led to the highway. She didn't look back.

Watching her go, Michael felt the knot return to his stomach and the world closing in around him. Standing up even a second longer was simply not possible. He crumpled like a rag doll onto the motel sidewalk, leaning his head back against the cinder block wall.

The Way You Walked Was Thorny

—

Of course the Swamp Fiend didn't want to be bad. He was driven by love or desire or some deep instinctual need to find a mate and make caviar. That's what Charlie had told his screenwriter almost six month earlier.

Calling Larry Fletcher a screenwriter was perhaps too strong a description. At that moment, Larry was also Charlie's bartender at Guido's, a high-dollar Italian joint in the Pacific Palisades, a few miles from Charlie's split-level. Guido's specialized in creamy risottos, five-layer tiramisu and hiring aspiring actors and screenwriters who needed actual jobs. Jerome Lefkowitz, who owned Guido's, knew employees with dreams of stardom seldom complained about the hours or the pay.

"You want the fish man and the leading lady to do a little spawning? Kinky. I can give you that," Larry told Charlie as he passed over a Mescal margarita, rocks, no salt. "Give me a week."

Larry had moved to LA after taking a playwriting course at the University of Michigan from the legendary professor Kenneth Thorpe Rowe. Another one of Rowe's students named Larry – actually Lawrence Kasdan – had done pretty well in Hollywood. Larry Fletcher didn't let the "C" Rowe gave him deter his dream, which involved silver BMWs, a split-level in the Hollywood Hills, and a bubbling hot tub populated by a coven of topless starlets, certainly not a one-bedroom apartment in the valley and a bartending gig at a place called Guido's. He had dropped out of UM three years earlier and driven his VW Beetle to LA where he knew he'd soon be famous for writing the next

Body Heat or *The Big Chill.*

Charlie thought the script Larry handed over a month later had more holes than a hunk of Swiss cheese, with language less believable than most soap operas. But a shaky script and clunky dialogue never bothered Charlie. The story included lots of teenage victims dying horribly, plenty of boobs, and some very special sauce: a cross-species, *Beauty and the Beast* love story between the lead actress and the Swamp Fiend.

A part of that love scene was being shot on this bright January morning as Charlie watched from a director's chair with his name on it. Charlie sat right behind the actual director, a lumbering neurotic named Oscar, who moved through life with the resigned sadness of Lon Chaney Jr., the tortured Wolf Man in several 1940s horror classics. As Chaney's character was dying, the gypsy woman Maleva tried to offer some comfort: "The way you walked was thorny, through no fault of your own..."

Oscar didn't turn into a wolf man on full moon nights, but his path through LA had been equally prickly. Two expensive divorces. A daughter in rehab. Some really bad real estate decisions. High-strung on the best of days, Oscar had stopped directing episodic TV after this third nervous breakdown.

At this point in his career, Oscar's specialty was making sure all the scenes on the shot list that day were actually completed. If you only had time for one take, Oscar was okay with that. His mantra, whispered anytime he felt his blood pressure rising, was "this too shall pass." His support system was the bottle of Valium he kept in his fanny pack.

He had used his mantra and his support system several times already this morning. A storm was due in the afternoon and Charlie was pushing him to get a day's worth of shots done before the rains came.

Between takes, Charlie would stand behind Oscar, clapping his hands and shouting: "Tick tock, people. Tick, fucking, tock."

Each time Charlie started clapping and hollering behind him, Oscar unzipped the fanny pack.

The Swamp Fiend's lair was a cathedral of tall cypress trees down a small stream that branched from a black, meandering river. The towering trees were ringed with phallic families of cypress knees. One of the trees in the cluster had grown horizontally instead of vertically and it was along that bench of tree trunk that Dawn's character spent several nights in captivity, trussed in a discarded fisherman's net.

Before shooting each evening, Dawn was laced into the net, a process that took almost an hour.

"Can I get a coffee or something?" Dawn asked. She was in her white lace bikini, swaddled in netting, her almost-bare butt resting on a hidden pillow, the flinty bark of the cypress tree pressing into her back.

"Gloria, how much longer?" Oscar quietly asked the makeup artist.

"Give me two more minutes," shouted Gloria, working at a picnic table a few feet from the cameras. Brad Fishman, the Swamp Fiend, was perched on the table, his flippered feet on the bench below, as the makeup artist spread a thick coating of jell onto his rubber fish mask. The close-up was next, and the jell would make it look like the Swamp Fiend had just shaved with pond scum.

"Tick tock, people!" Charlie shouted again, though he forgot to clap this time. "Time is money. My money."

Oscar quivered in his chair. He pulled the bottle of pills from the fanny pack and quickly swallowed two.

"Yes, please!" Dawn shouted from her tree trunk perch. "Faster! Please?"

———

Chief Billy's motel rooms were covered in plywood painted to look like real wood paneling. Jaime stood back as Michael pinned up his latest scenes, the pins sinking easily into the soft boards. Once they were up Jaime moved in for a closer look, running his finger along the hand-drawn panels.

Michael's latest story was set at the Olympic games in Helsinki, where Dawn was the anchor of the U.S. relay team. The team from Romania had apparently fallen under the spell of a bloodthirsty hypnotist. They were winning gold medals by killing off the competition one by one.

"No. No. No," Jaime said, shaking his head. "It can't be the javelin - that's too obvious. Think about the shot put. It's big. It's deadly. And imagine what a skull would do if it was smashed with one of those."

Michael was standing behind him. "You think so?"

"Oh...no question. Or the pole from the pole vault? What if one end was whittled down to a razor sharp point? No one is expecting that."

Moments before, as they'd sat side by side on the motel sidewalk, Jaime and Michael had bonded over the horror movies Roger Corman made for American International Pictures. Jaime particularly loved Vincent Price, and the aging Boris Karloff and Bela Lugosi, who made cameos in those films. "We didn't have money for first-run movies," Jaime told him. "But every weekend all the kids got piled into the car for a night at the drive-in."

"Remember in *Pit and the Pendulum*, when that razor sharp pendulum is swinging back and forth," Jaime continued. "Anything sharp is scary long before it cuts."

As soon as the words left his lips, Jaime wanted to call them back. Michael's dad had told him how the boy's mother had died. And who found her. "Sorry, kid. Maybe the shot put would be better after all."

Michael returned to the sheet on the wall, holding a pencil and adding some quick notes to the frame. Jaime sat down on the bed. When Michael finished, he joined him there.

"Stories I can figure out," Michael said after a second. "It's only in real life that things don't make any sense."

Jaime patted him on the shoulder.

"If you're talking about that Cuban girl, what can I tell you? Cuban women are like time bombs with tits. I married one. No, wait, they're like land mines. You think all is good, then you take a step and something goes CLICK. You know you shouldn't lift your foot, but you do and – KABOOM! – your whole world goes up in smoke."

"I'm starting to see that." Michael nodded.

"What did my *abuelo* say? 'Women – can't live with 'em; can't kill 'em.'" Jaime turned and looked hard at Michael. "I mean you wouldn't kill 'em, would you?"

"Why is this stuff so complicated?"

"I'm a detective, not a shrink. I don't know."

Jaime looked over at the open door of the motel and the woods and water where Cavanaugh and Colleen disappeared.

"So you're not going to take me to the nut house?" Michael asked.

Jaime turned back to face the boy. "You're a little crazy, but not that kind of crazy. Not killer kind of crazy."

"Just in the movies. I promise." Michael started pulling the pins and taking his drawings off the wall. "So you and his daughter?"

Jaime rubbed an open hand across his face, then pushed it up through his unruly mop of thick black hair. "I guess so. Yeah. And I can't figure that out either, but I've decided not to try. I'm going with it."

Michael smoothed the sheets of paper on the tiny desk, then slipped them into his black binder with the rest of his drawings.

"Two things we have to talk about," Jaime said. "One, let's just say I never found you, okay? And two, ah...don't...you know... kill any actors."

Michael set the binder on the bed. "I won't. I wouldn't. Hey, how about we go try to find them? I really need to talk to her dad."

They crossed the parking lot, walking around Bobby's office toward the trees and the open water. Jaime put a big hand into his jacket pocket and fished out a business card.

"Listen, if you ever need me to find somebody for you ... it's what I do."

Playing Hide
And Seek

—

Watching her father run away from her, Colleen remembered when she was a girl and they'd play hide and seek in the oak-shaded squares of Savannah, before they made the move to Atlanta for Cavanaugh's job as press spokesman for Georgia's Secretary of State.

She cherished those memories: Her father bobbing and weaving among the stately trees, occasionally ducking behind a Confederate statue, grinning devilishly, his hair tousled, as he looked back to make sure she was still in the hunt.

Now her father was running again. This time along the side of a motel, toward a boat ramp and a wide expanse of water, glistening silver in the morning sun. From a distance her father looked like the young version of himself, loose-limbed and lanky. That memory made her smile. Sure he was running from her, but that's what he did. And chasing him was her part. In the hide and seek games they played so long ago, Cavanaugh made her work for it, but he always let her catch him.

She was sure she'd catch him now.

She saw him stop at the edge of the motel building, leaning over, hands on his knees, throwing a glance back toward his daughter. She thought she saw that same sly grin cross his lips. That's when she knew for sure. This was just one more game they were playing before they were together at last and he would take her in his arms and pull her close and call her his Little Sheba. She could see that as clearly as she could see anything.

Cavanaugh ran again, past the boat launch, and out to a grassy meadow beside the water, where clusters of spindly oaks spouted together then arched away from each other, like so many drooping tulips. He stopped under one family of oaks, at a spot where grass was green and thick.

"Daddy," Colleen called to him, as she ran. "It's okay. It's just me. We've been playing hide and seek and now I've found you."

Cavanaugh looked up at her, his face crimson, his chest heaving.

Colleen, a bit out of breath herself, knew the chase was over. She rushed up to her father, arms outstretched, fingers reaching for him.

"You look like a little girl I used to know."

"Oh Daddy!" Colleen wrapped her arms around him. His head fell forward on her shoulder. She could feel his body heaving. Cavanaugh slowly encircled her with his arms.

This was the moment. After so much time and so many tears. Colleen hoped her knees wouldn't give way.

"Daddy. Why did you run away?" Colleen whispered. "Was it me? I missed you so much. Every day."

Cavanaugh raised his head, but still held her close.

"It wasn't you, Little Sheba," he said, between gasping breaths. "It wasn't your mother. It was me. It was always me. Please believe that."

"I do, Daddy. I do."

They hugged for a long moment, then Cavanaugh coughed hard and jerked back sharply, breaking the hug. Colleen tried to grab him, but everything happened too fast. Her father's eyes slammed shut and like a great tree finally giving way to the saw, he tilted backwards, landing hard on the grass, his legs twisting up beneath him.

"Daddy!" Colleen screamed.

She dropped to her knees, frantically straightening out her father's legs until Cavanaugh looked like an old man taking a nap on the soft grass. When that was done, she cradled her father's head in her hands, easing it down onto her lap.

"Daddy...Are you okay? Please be okay. I've come so far."

Cavanaugh's eyes slowly opened but he didn't look at his daughter. He seemed to be staring off into a distance only he could see. Colleen heard steps behind her and turned to see Jaime and Michael walking toward the boat launch. She waved furiously at them to hurry.

Michael got there first and knelt next to Colleen, looking down at Cavanaugh. The old man's lips were moving now, but there were no words, only a foamy bubble of saliva oozing from the edge of his mouth.

"He needs his pills," Michael whispered. "I'll go..."

But Cavanaugh shook his head.

"Michael. Stay here. It's too late for pills, I'm afraid." He was whispering, his eyes moving between Michael and his daughter.

Colleen, still cradling his head in her lap, pulled a tissue from her pocket and wiped the spittle off his lips. Cavanaugh hacked, releasing another dark wad of spittle. As Colleen wiped it away, some color returned to his face.

"The VA doctors told me I was dead two years ago," Cavanaugh whispered. "Since then, every time I've checked my watch it read, 'Borrowed Time.'"

With some effort, Cavanaugh raised his hand and let his fingers brush his daughter's cheek. "You got a raw deal in the father department, Little Sheba. But truth be told, I thought of you and your mom every day. Especially you."

"We've got to call an ambulance. Get you to a hospital." Colleen looked up desperately at Jaime. "Help me carry him."

Cavanaugh reached up, gripping her shoulder.

"NO!" His voice was strong. "Please no. Don't move me now. I don't want to die in some emergency room smelling of urine and Clorox. I want to stay right here, on this soft grass, by this placid water. This is good. Cinematic. Michael will make sure that my remains are spread among the proper Savannah districts."

He looked up at Michael, his voice weak but clear.

"Would you? I know I've let you down, but I think of you as

my friend."

"Sure. Of course," Michael said, bending down to place his hand on Cavanaugh's chest. He could feel the old man's heart pounding furiously.

Cavanaugh slowly turned his head back to Colleen. "In my left pocket, there's a key..."

Colleen eased his head back to the grass and slid a hand into his pants pocket. She came back with the key to the motel room.

"Now come close," he said.

Colleen leaned down so their faces were inches apart. Her father's voice was as soft as a breath. "In my suitcase. A paper bag. It's for you. Now go. I love you, Little Sheba. Always have. Remember that."

Colleen looked at the key, then back at her father. Jaime was kneeling behind her, his hands resting on her shoulders. "I love you too, Daddy. Let us take you to the hospital. Please?"

Cavanaugh coughed and Colleen quickly wiped away more foamy liquid from his lips. Now his words seemed to come from some dark, constricted place deep in his chest.

"Go now. Quickly."

A violent series of coughs shook the dying man. After one final shuddering cough, Cavanaugh was still, then his eyes fluttered open and his face relaxed, a hint of a smile settled on his lips. His right arm seemed to rise magically, his fingers reaching for his daughter. Colleen thought she felt her heart stop.

"Daddy?"

Just before his fingers could brush her cheek, Cavanaugh's arm went limp, dropping like a discarded baseball bat to the grass. His smile tightened and his eyelids ticked down slowly, like a roll top desk closing one final time.

Colleen brushed stray strands of gray hair back off his forehead. She looked toward Michael, then up at Jaime as her face constricted and a low moan, from deep inside her, rose in the suddenly still air. She collapsed on her father's chest.

"Daddy. Oh Daddy." She kept repeating. Loudly at first, then in a hushed whisper. "Oh Daddy. My beautiful, beautiful Daddy."

Standing now, Jaime and Michael looked at one another, their faces grim. After what seemed like ten minutes but was likely only one, Jaime leaned over and gently lifted Colleen off her father and brought her to her feet.

"Come on. Come with me now." Jaime's voice was tender.

Michael stood up too, but continued to stare down at his friend dead on the grass.

"Will you take care of him?" Jaime asked.

Jaime was holding Colleen tightly now, as she sobbed, her face pressed into his shoulder, the motel key clinched in her fist.

Michael nodded blankly.

"You want me to call someone?" Jaime asked. "At the motel, they'll know how to get an ambulance."

"No. I can do this," Michael said, looking up at Jaime. "You guys go ahead. I'll take care of it. It's what he wanted."

Jaime nodded, then slowly turned Colleen around and led her step by step toward the motel.

When It Comes To Women And Money

—

Colleen lifted the old Samsonite bag onto the bed and pushed the two clasps with her thumbs. The silver locks released with a metallic snap. She carefully lifted out some folded white shirts and a pair of plaid slacks, taking a moment to raise each one to her nose, taking in the smell of her father.

Setting the clothes on the bed, she reached in again and came out with a crumpled brown bag, the kind of small paper bag you got from the corner store twenty-five years ago, before everything became plastic.

She looked over at Jaime, standing in the open doorway, the light pouring in around him. She offered a him a weak smile, then slid her hand into the bag, bringing out a battered box of Barnum's Animal Crackers, the kind with a circus wagon on the side, the kind with a handle made of white string. Colleen pressed the box to her chest. When she looked up at Jaime, tears were streaming down her cheeks.

"He remembered me," she whispered.

Jaime stepped inside, closing the door behind him. "He did."

Colleen sat heavily on the bed, the box of crackers clutched to her chest. Jaime let her cry. After a few minutes, Colleen cleared her throat and wiped her eyes. Jaime walked over and helped her to her feet, his arms firmly gripping her shoulders.

Colleen held up the empty box. "Thanks for getting me here. I lost him, but I found him too, you know?"

Colleen stood and Jaime led her toward the front door. As

they stepped onto the landing, Colleen turned back, scanning the empty motel room. It was almost identical to the one where she had discovered Jaime, passed out, in a pool of golden goo. Was that really just yesterday?

Colleen felt like a circle was closing.

"What do you want to do now?" Jaime asked. "Go home?"

"I don't know," Colleen said. "I'm not sure I really have a home at this point."

"I know this isn't really the right time but I wanted to tell you I'm sorry about all the trash talking I did. You know, about love. About families. I hope you'll give me a chance to prove that."

Colleen let her head fall on the soft pillow of his shoulder.

"Sure. Okay," she said. She raised her head. "But Daddy's body? I don't know about leaving him there. Shouldn't I..."

"The boy will take good care of him. I'm sure of that," Jaime said. "Come on. How about I take you to get something to eat? I'm suddenly starving."

Colleen eased her grip and looked up at him. "What about the case? I mean what will you tell the kid's dad?"

Jaime kissed her.

"Would you be interested in dating an unemployed, over-weight Cuban detective?"

——

"This is not how I pictured it. Not how I pictured it at all."

Michael was pacing near his dead friend as a fresh posse of storm clouds hunkered down above Bobby's Indian Village. The stiff breeze whistling from the northeast churned up cascading whitecaps on the water, swirling Michael's already unruly hair.

He paid no attention to the incoming storm. Michael was busy talking to a dead man at his feet.

"I told them I just stood at the door, but that's not true. I went inside. I looked at her for a long time before the maids found me. I didn't cry. It wasn't scary. I just stood there asking her why? Why she did it. Why she didn't love me enough to stay."

He didn't care that Cavanaugh couldn't hear him. He had never told anyone this story and now it just spilled out.

He told his dead friend about the maids pulling him from the bathroom. How Dick Adams, his father's partner, had driven Michael south along A1A to Fort Lauderdale, while the police, the coroner and finally a cleaning crew did their work. Michael wasn't there to see them take his mother's body out of the house in a black zippered bag on a stretcher.

He talked about coming home to find his father crying in the kitchen. How Michael dodged Alex's outstretched arms and locked himself in his room.

"For weeks I felt like I was walking around in some surreal haunted house. Every morning, after my dad went to work, I'd go stand in the doorway of that bathroom. It was so clean. Like it had never happened. I wanted to cry or scream or yell, but somehow I just swallowed it all. I'd open my mouth but nothing would come out."

Michael shook his head, pulling his mind back to the grassy, windswept waterfront. He looked down at Cavanaugh.

"You're wrong, you know. You don't look like a sack of bones. You remind me of how my mom looked. Kind of like she was just sleeping."

He sat down on the grass a foot from Cavanaugh's body, staring off at the open water beyond the boat ramp. On the sandy shore of the small bay, a dozen egrets, also oblivious to the incoming storm, walked with their beaks bent to the shallows, like postulants on a holy quest. A great blue heron, emitting a series of harsh squawks, thumped through the air, just inches above the whitecaps.

Michael followed the flight until the majestic creature disappeared into the horizon. He turned back to his friend.

"I guess we're even. You lied to me and stole my money. I stole your girlfriend. I knew it was wrong but I did it anyway. I'm really, really sorry. "

Michael felt tears stinging his eyes. He roughly brushed them away.

"I wouldn't do it again," Michael repeated. He needed to say it as much for himself as the dead man. "I wish you could know that."

"I bet you'd do it again if you had the chance."

Michael looked around. The whispered words seemed to be riding on the wind. He spun in a slow circle to see if anyone was there. Turning back, he saw Cavanaugh was still stretched out – corpse-like – on the grass, but his eyes were open and his lips were moving. "I know I would."

"Are you?" Michael bent over Cavanaugh, leaning close so he could hear him whisper.

"Not that I'm letting you off the hook, you sneaky little bastard," Cavanaugh said softly. "But one thing you'll learn about life – when it comes to women and money, there are no rules."

"But you're..."

"Is she gone?"

Michael looked back at the motel. Jaime and Colleen were nowhere in sight. "Yeah. I'm pretty sure they're gone."

With a grunt and a sigh, Cavanaugh eased up on his elbows, then sat up completely.

"I think I missed my calling. I could have been one of the great actors. Don't you agree?"

Michael shook his head. It was a lot to take in. Cavanaugh was very much alive; his face full of color; his breathing easy; his body strong.

"I mean the great ones are judged by their death scenes," Cavanaugh said. "I believe mine was award-worthy."

Michael smiled. This wasn't some run-of-the-mill con man. Cavanaugh Reilly was a world-class con man. How could you not love him?

"Actually, I'm not sure they've left the parking lot," Michael said. "Maybe I should check before you get too lively."

Cavanaugh winked at him and lowered himself back to the grass.

"What did you give her? What's in your room?" Michael asked.

Cavanaugh smiled as he stared up at the wind-swept oak branches and the tumultuous gray sky. "Something I've been carrying around for a very long time."

———

Lola didn't look back. She wanted to put steps between herself and the ugly scene at Bobby's.

The dirt road wasn't easy to maneuver in her flimsy sandals, especially with a duffle full of clothes hanging off her shoulder. She had to stop every hundred yards or so to loosen her sandal straps, and shake out the dust and grit. She had stayed in the clinging sundress, thinking a little sex appeal would help land her a ride back to West Palm.

At least I'm not a murderer, she thought. But at the moment, that was the only plus she could add to the ledger of her life. The drugs. The street-corner sex business. Her so-called love life. The Cavanaugh thing was never going to be long-term, but she had feelings for him. Michael too.

And she had ruined it with both of them.

Lola was cinching up the strap on her sandal when she heard the baggie calling from deep in her duffle. Keeping it in her purse had been too tempting, so before she left the motel, she pushed it to the bottom of the duffle. Now, she knelt and pulled back the zipper, rummaging among her clothes until her fingers found the tightly rolled plastic.

Holding it up, she could see the mound of white powder clumped in one corner. Something had to change, she thought. The baggie could make the world seem sweeter, but she always ended up on her ass, sometimes literally, sometimes emotionally and often, like today, both at once.

The wind picked up and the bag flapped as it dangled from her fingers. She knew she'd have trouble getting the powder from her fingernail to her nose.

Turning back, she stared at the dusty road she'd trod, now darkened by an approaching storm. The rain was on the way but the sun hadn't given up completely, the scene shifting from shadow to light as the sun found a seam in the curtain of clouds. The air had a crisp sweetness, a sense of possibility. Out here, so far from the trash bins and monoxided blocks around the Blue 'Arlin, Lola thought it might be time to take another path.

She pulled open the bag and shook out the contents. Some of the chalky powder settled atop the dirt and the rest floated away like puffy buds blown off a dandelion.

Lola didn't like to litter, but she let the bag drop from her hand and watched it flip in the wind, floating off down the dirt road. In the distance, she could see the cars moving east and west along Alligator Alley. She'd get where she needed to go, she thought. She could do this.

———

"Maybe I need to go home."

Michael and Cavanaugh sat side by side on the grass, looking across the open water, now white-capped by the approaching storm. The boy's question was as much to himself as to his companion.

"What about the quest?" Cavanaugh asked. "The demonic damsel who's always in distress?"

"I don't know..."

"What do you want? Really?"

"Maybe I've just been fooling myself the entire time. Living in some fantasy world. Right? And don't lie!"

Cavanaugh put his hand on Michael's shoulder.

"Fooling ourselves is how we all get through the goddam day. I majored in it at Georgia State. Here's the only truth I can muster – at the end of the day, everything we believe in, everybody we love, the whole messy, elaborate ballet - it just rolls out with the tide. Like the man says – all sound and fury signifying nothing. And people hate that. It's too damaging to their fragile egos. So they build big mansions with walls around them. They pray to gods they think will save them. They reach out to central casting for a comforting old president."

Cavanaugh took his hand off Michael's shoulder and gave him a gentle slap on the cheek. "So have some fun, kid. Do what you want. But don't worry that any of this has to mean something."

"What about Savannah? You're dying to get back there. It's your Mecca? Your Emerald City? So you believe in that, right?"

"Even non-believers have to believe in something. We need our illusions like everyone else. It's important to remember that's all they are."

Cavanaugh let his words hang there for a long beat before turning to look at Michael.

"So what do you want to do now?"

Michael shook his head, looking off at the water. The wind was gaining strength. Michael could smell the rain swelling inside swollen clouds. Hearing a flutter of wings, he turned to watch the clutch of egrets rise and circle together, before moving in a floating caravan across the open water.

"I really don't know." Michael said, as much to himself as Cavanaugh.

"I think you do."

Michael returned Cavanaugh's smile. He couldn't be mad anymore. He was happy the old man was alive and they were together. "We've come this far. I mean, we could, right?"

"Right."

Cavanaugh looked off again, deep in thought. After a minute, he snapped his fingers and turned back to Michael. "Please tell me you still have that credit card."

You Haven't Died Properly

—

Jake Messer, half of Swamp Fiend's security detail, was hunched in a folding lawn chair at 10 a.m., struggling to light a fattie. Each time he struck a match, a crisp breeze snuffed the flame.

"Shit, shit and double shit." Jake turned his back to the wind. When he straightened, a dancing blue flame was devouring the paper tip of the joint.

A massive storm the day before had shuttered the Swamp Fiend set, the tropical blitzkrieg toppling light stands and director's chairs, and chasing the cast and crew into the leaky trailers, where a leaden rain pounded out drum solos on the tin roofs. One angry gust stripped part of the roof off Charlie Gray's production shack, prompting the producer – huddled under his desk – to invent an entirely new vocabulary of curses.

But the new morning had dawned sunny and cloudless. The kind of day Jake liked to start with a few hits of Myakka Gold. After releasing a cloud of smoke, Jake hacked up a wad of phlegm, spitting it into the dirt as he passed the joint to his brother Jerry.

Ever since he and his Harley catapulted into the swamp behind the Cypress Knee Museum, Jerry Messer spent his days in a rusting wheelchair, his left leg and right arm cast in plaster, his head mummified in gauze. Inhaling hurt him in more places than he could count, but he took comfort in new reports suggesting that pot had medicinal qualities.

Exhaling into his bandages, Jerry coughed and cursed. Jake peeled the joint from his quivering fingers, snuffing out the flame against the arm of his chair. Tapping his brother's good arm, Jake pointed up the winding dirt road, where fusillades of mud were arcing above the palmetto scrub.

"Somebody's coming," Jake said.

A few seconds later the brothers could see a black limo bouncing in and out of the road's crevices and canyons, potholes Charlie had regularly asked Jerry and Jake to repair since "it looks to me and everyone one else that you're getting paid to sit around on your asses and get high."

The mud-caked Cadillac finally bounced up to the barricade and stopped. A thin chauffeur, in full uniform — tight gray jacket and pants, billed black hat and wrap-around sunglasses — stepped from the car with stiff formality and hustled to open the back passenger door.

A tall figure emerged and when he saw him, Jake felt the color drain out of this end of the Everglades. This was a character from some 1930s Hollywood movie Jake had watched on the black and white set in his family's doublewide. The man was dressed in gray riding breeches, a puffy black shirt, and high black boots, his eyes hidden behind aviator sunglasses. He snapped a leather crop against a black-gloved hand. Each slap only deepened the scowl on his hawk-nosed face. His fierce gray eyes scanned the barricade and passed quickly over the Messer brothers.

Jake stood slowly, not exactly sure what was happening. "Hey! Excuse me but-"

The man, who looked to be in his '60s or '70s, didn't give Jake a chance to say more. "You're not excused. Where's Edelstein?" His voice was deep and regal.

The man strode past the barricade, heading toward a shell path that sliced through the palmettos. At the end of the path, the Swamp Fiend set glowed like a ballpark during a night game.

"Look, mister! Who are you? Do you have a pass?" Jake shouted at the man's back, as he gave chase, lumbering through the mud as quickly as his boots would allow. "Hey, wait up!"

The man paused at the lip of the path, turning slowly, his

scowl still in place.

When Jake was close enough, the man swatted him across the chest with the riding crop. "Dammit! Where's your walkie? Get Edelstein on the horn. Tell him the studio hates the dailies. The concept is all wrong! Jesus! They've forced me to come to this god-forsaken, mosquito-ridden hellhole to set things right."

With that, the old man marched toward the clearing where a dozen silhouetted figures moved around copses of scrub palms and oak trees. Banks of round lights, dangling from spindly metal trees, shimmered like ripe fruit.

The visitor stopped halfway down the path and shouted back at Jake.

"Find Edelstein, now!"

Jake walked slowly back to Jerry, who had turned his wheel-chair to watch the encounter. Jake moved his folding chair around and sat next to his brother. He pulled the remnants of the joint from his front pocket and hunched over to light it. He took a long hit, then held it out to Jerry.

Jerry leaned close so he could be heard through his gag of bandages.

"Who's Edelstein?"

———

With their bloodshot eyes focused on the old man with the riding crop, Jake and Jerry hadn't paid attention to the driver. If they had, they might have noticed he looked too young to be issued a State of Florida chauffeur's license.

Tossing his hat and glasses on the front seat, Michael stepped quickly along the palmetto scrub that bordered the road. Pocked with muddy divots, the dirt road cut straight through the underbrush for about 20 yards, before making a slow curve. At that point it opened onto a wide, shell-covered lot where seven cars, a white van and a Harley chopper were parked haphazardly. A wooden shack sat in the center of the lot, its front porch sagging, part of its tin roof missing. Four sordid trailers were clustered in the back corner. The trailers had been white at some point, but now a mask of mold covered the walls. Instead of tires, the tin boxes rested atop short stacks of concrete blocks.

Michael was shocked that an actual movie set could look this tawdry. Overstuffed trash bins sat outside each trailer, bags and empty bottles and cans piling up around them. The trailers were identified with hand-lettered signs: COSTUMES, HAIR AND MAKEUP, CAST. Michael was pressed against the side of HAIR AND MAKEUP when he got a look at the sign on the fourth trailer – "DAWN KARSTON."

God, I'm so close. What should I do now? What if she's not here?

The door of HAIR AND MAKEUP squeaked open. Michael inched back. A young woman came down the steps, her hand wrapped around what looked like a fluffy Pekingese. Dressed in pink overalls, a white T-shirt, and flip-flops, the girl was gawky and bone thin, with clunky black glasses, her black hair pulled back into a short ponytail.

She ran quickly to Dawn's trailer, skipping up three steps onto a cross-hatched metal landing, just big enough to hold a bristled door mat, now caked with mud.

"It's Gloria!" she hollered, as she knocked. "I got your hair. Oscar says five minutes!"

A female figure eased the door open. All the lights were on in the trailer, throwing the woman standing in the doorway into silhouette. Still, Michael recognized her.

Dawn Karston!

Dawn backed up to let the stylist enter. When the door closed, Michael moved across the parking lot toward the trailer, shells crunching under his shoes. He froze at the foot of the stairs.

This is it, he thought, his mind skittering, his breath coming in gulps. Should I wait? Should I knock? God, if only I could ask Cavanaugh. He'd know what to do.

Michael thought he heard shouting from the set. Cavanaugh's ruse wouldn't last forever. You need to act! His inner voice was insistent but his feet would not budge.

Just then, Dawn's door opened and she stepped onto the landing in a white bikini and white Converse All-Stars, her eyes scanning the tops of the trees. Michael felt like he was observing a wild creature that didn't yet realize a human was lurking nearby.

Dawn was smaller than he imagined, but even more beautiful. Her pale skin was porcelain in the mid-day sun. The swimsuit wrapped the curves of her breasts and hips, but the rest of her body could have belonged to a skinny teenager. As he counted the ridged bones of her ribs, Michael noticed Dawn's chest and shoulders were peppered in pale peach freckles. The blond wig fell in a single wave to a spot just below her dimpled chin, flipping up around the bottom, '60s style. The hair bounced as Dawn descended the three stairs to the shell parking lot, Gloria in step behind her, a can of hair spray in one hand, the other scrunching the flipped end of Dawn's wig.

Stepping onto the shell lot, Dawn finally noticed the chauffeur. Summoning all his courage, Michael took a step forward. He and his movie star were now face to face, just inches apart.

Dawn looked blankly at him, then smiled, radiantly, happily. Michael loved that smile. It was the same one that had launched so many teenagers on ill-fated trips to old campsites, or high school football fields, or deserted soda shops where masked killers lurked.

"Finally, they sent a real limo," Dawn said, turning to Gloria, who took the opportunity to give Dawn's hair a hissing blast of spray.

Dawn turned back to the chauffeur, a grimace replacing the smile. "Now they send a car for me? Where were you all last week? Ben promised me a limo for the entire shoot."

When the young driver didn't answer, Dawn dropped her anger and smiled at him. "Anyway, you're here. It's great. OK, listen – DO NOT LEAVE! When I'm done with this scene, I'm getting out of this hellhole and finding some real dinner."

"Sure, okay," Michael heard himself saying. "Can I talk with you?"

"Not now. Gotta swelter in a swamp for a few hours. We'll talk when I'm done and you're driving me somewhere civilized. How's that?"

Not waiting for an answer, Dawn started to brush past him. The chauffeur grabbed her arm.

"Dawn. It's Michael." Her skin was soft, but firm under his fingers.

Dawn's head swiveled back in his direction.

"Who?" She turned to the stylist. "Do I know this guy?"

Just then, the name registered. Dawn turned back to the chauffeur.

"You're THAT Michael?"

"I'm Michael Donnelly. Did you get the scenes I sent?"

"It's him," she hissed to Gloria.

"You mean, THAT HIM?" Gloria hissed back.

Dawn nodded gravely, her body going rigid, her face constricted into the terrified countenance the audience always saw just before her character died — horribly.

Michael, still clutching Dawn's bare arm, thrust his free hand into the inside pocket of his chauffer's jacket. The rented costume fit him like a wet suit; the gray jacket secured by an angled row of buttons from the waist to the neck. Before buttoning his jacket this morning, Michael had rolled up his latest hand-drawn film scenes and stuffed them into the inside pocket, planning to pull them out at this exact moment.

"I've got something special for you," Michael said, struggling to get his fingers around the shaft of paper. He could feel his body tingling, his nerves sending out sparks.

"Stay away from me," Dawn whispered.

As Dawn stepped back, Gloria reached out, firing a gauzy cloud of hairspray in Michael's face.

"Get back, you!" Gloria barked.

Michael's eyes caught fire. He let go of Dawn and rubbed at them furiously. Dawn quickly backed up the stairs to the landing, almost tripping over Gloria, who was moving behind her, one hand still clutching Dawn's hair, the other holding out the hairspray, ready to deliver another blast if the crazy stalker came any closer. On the landing, one of Gloria's flip-flops got caught up in the muddy doormat. As her arms flailed for balance, the wig came off in her hand, along with the tight beige skull-cap underneath. Dawn's auburn curls tumbled down, falling in waves to her pale, freckled shoulders.

Even with cloudy vision, Dawn's pale beauty took Michael's voice away. He tried to speak, but his mouth writhed oddly. He continued to rub at his eyes, while his other hand struggled to free the rolled up papers stuck in his jacket.

"Stay away, please." Dawn pleaded from the landing. She might have been trying to summon a scary film voice, but what emerged was a high-pitched, girlish quiver.

Blinking furiously, Michael's vision started to clear.

"No wait. Please. It's not what you think. I've got something special for you." He pulled again, but the papers refused to budge. "You're going to be impressed. At least I hope so."

Standing in front of the first step, looking up at her, Michael watched as Dawn pushed out her arms, her fingers splayed, signaling him to STOP!

"No! I don't want to die. Really, I don't." She looked over her shoulder at Gloria. "Please tell him. I don't want to die."

"She doesn't. Really!" Gloria had regained her balance but not her composure. As her eyes searched desperately for help, Dawn's wig slipped from her fingers, plumping onto the landing like a dead pet.

"You don't understand. You haven't died properly." Michael blurted, his voice oddly squeaky. "Let me do it and you'll see. I've had so many ideas. Did you get my drawings? I kept sending them but..."

Jeez, Michael thought, I'm babbling now. After all the time I've practiced for this moment, and now I'm falling apart in front of her.

Just then, Gloria moaned and fainted, the can of hair spray clattering onto the landing.

Michael reminded himself to breathe. I have to regain my equilibrium. I just need to show her my strength. My determination. Explain what we could accomplish together.

He felt the pounding in his chest slow down. Words were rising in his throat.

"I've come a long way," Michael said, his voice now deeper, calmer. "You wouldn't believe how hard it has been to get here."

Michael put his foot on the first step. Dawn's head swiveled, looking desperately for an escape route. Behind her, Gloria was slumped against the door. In front of her, a killer was climbing the stairs. She was trapped.

Finally noticing the stylist sprawled at Dawn's feet, Michael paused on the step below the landing. "What's the matter with her?"

"Please don't come any closer," Dawn pleaded, her cheeks blotched with crimson. "Please. Please. I don't want to die. I really, really don't want to die. I don't! I don't! I don't!"

Michael tried to plant his foot on the narrow landing, which was already crowded with Dawn, a wig, a can of hairspray, a muddy doormat and Gloria's crumped body. Struggling to find his footing, Michael clamped his free hand on Dawn's shoulder.

Just then, with one last desperate jerk, he was able to free the rolled sheet of papers. It slipped from inside his jacket like a sword departing a scabbard, the force sending Michael's arm up and over his head. From a distance, the shaft of paper clenched in his fist might have resembled a long blade about to be rammed into Dawn's chest.

Behind him Michael could hear angry shouts and the splat of feet slapping against mud. He thought he heard Cavanaugh holler – "Better hurry!"

Frozen in place, Dawn's eyes darted from the odd weapon raised above her head, and back to Michael's face, now drenched in sweat.

"Dawn," Michael said, his voice firm and surprisingly deep. "I did this for you."

And then, Dawn screamed!

The sound was primal. Blood-curdling. It likely echoed for miles in all directions. Had it been recorded and filmed, Dawn would have easily won another *Fangoria Magazine* "Scream of the Year" statuette.

The force of Dawn's full-throated shriek sent Michael back-pedaling. His foot missed the middle step. As he fell, the scene shifted into slow motion and Michael left his body. Watching the scene from a distance, like a film director, Michael heard himself call "Action!"

He watched a skinny boy in a chauffeur's uniform tumbling backwards down the stairs, as papers unfurled above him. A pale young woman stood screaming on the landing. The boy's body was airborne a long time, his arms undulating, his legs and feet rising higher than his shoulders. Finally, the boy landed with a thud onto a bed of white shell.

Michael was back inside his body for the landing, his head snapping back against something hard.

He felt no pain. Looking up, all he could see was a perfect close-up of Dawn Karston.

Her cheeks were blood red, her mouth open wide. But there was no sound. In the droning silence, he was able to see beyond her pink lips and her ivory teeth, deep into the dark, quivering cavern at the back of her throat.

What a great angle, he thought. Tight and powerful. Riveting. This isn't some fake B-movie moment, but real, honest-to-God terror! It's the horror film finale I've dreamed of directing! And Dawn Karston is my star!

Michael felt hands roughly encircling him, but as they did, a pulse of pure joy throbbed from his heart, the tingling train surging through every vein and artery, raising the hair along his arms and legs before blasting from his fingers and toes in bursts of sizzling silver sparks.

"And...cut!" Michael whispered, as the scene slowly faded to black.

This Little Cubanita

—

Whoever designed the community room at Palmdale Haven had elevated blandness into an art form. Sand-colored couches – with beige throw pillows – were arranged beside tan coffee tables atop a terrazzo floor the color of Sahara sand, tossed with sesame chips. Michael and the other patients spent the days in loose, khaki jumpsuits and white T-shirts, their feet swaddled in soft slippers in a shade that could be described as *café au lait*. In those outfits, the patients seemed to melt into the background as they pondered jigsaw puzzles, used soft-pointed pens to color in illustrated versions of *White Fang* and *Last of the Mohicans*, or stared absently at the wall-mounted TV droning softly in one corner.

It was as if the imposition of a primary color might ignite slobbering spasms of madness in these docile, medicated guests.

Michael found the bland setting gave him room to think and rethink all that had happened, starting at his Mother's bloody bathroom and spiraling from there to Horror Time Video, to Cavanaugh and Lola, the Cypress Knee Museum, the magical hour with Lola at Bobby's Indian Village, and his final showdown with Dawn.

After Sammi and Sheila deposited him in a spacious, beige bedroom at Palmdale, the whole crazy ride seemed suddenly exhausting. Michael spent the first month mostly asleep. He woke when an orderly brought in the bamboo meal tray topped by a plate of overcooked vegetables over chalky mounds of rice, food even more bland than the décor. After just a few bites,

Michael tumbled back into a dark well of sleep.

When he finally emerged, Michael started twice-a-day therapy sessions with a gray-haired psychiatrist who looked like a refugee from The Lollipop Guild. Elizabeth Kendrick favored girlish dresses covered in tiny flowers and lots of rouge and eye shadow.

"Just call me Dr. Liz." Unlike a movie munchkin, Dr. Liz spoke in a warm alto. Not that she said much. Michael found himself filling the silence with stories, most of them about the years he and his mother had spent in their tight cocoon inside the big house just off Coconut Row.

"Did you ever think you needed to make some friends? Get out of the house?" Dr. Liz asked.

"I got out," Michael insisted. "I went to movies. The video store."

Palmdale had its own video library and most nights Michael watched VCR versions of classic Hollywood movies on the TV in his room. They were the same sweeping period romances (*Gone With The Wind*) and smart romantic comedies (*The Philadelphia Story*) he and Crystal had devoured in the comforting darkness of the Donnelly screening room.

"I'm noticing that you and your mom didn't watch any modern films," Dr. Liz said, after Michael described the two weeks when he and Crystal binged on Frank Capra films. "Why was that?"

"I'd go out to the mall and watch modern stuff, *Raging Bull, Serpico, The Exorcist*. Sometimes I had to lie about my age to get in. But at home with Mom it was mostly classics. Lots of black and white movies. She really liked a happy ending."

"Why do you think she liked happy endings so much?"

"I guess in those movies, things could go wrong, but eventually all the strings wound together and everything worked out. Mom liked that."

Dr. Liz was a patient therapist. In some sessions, Michael's answer to her opening question filled the entire hour. The genius of Bava covered two hour-long sessions. The misunderstood monsters in the James Whale classics took an entire week. The artistic travesty spawned by the blockbuster success of *Friday the 13*[th] — which birthed a legion of mindless killing machines with no depth or character development — he could expound quite a while on that topic.

"I mean can you imagine Jason or Freddy listening to a gypsy violin or playing with an innocent little girl? Frankenstein had depth. The Wolf Man didn't want to go on his bloody rampages. Nobody — even villains — should be all bad or all good. Right?"

"I wonder why you're asking that? In the whole Dawn thing, do you think you were a hero or a villain?"

"Jeez. I guess it depends who you're asking. Dawn apparently didn't see me as a hero."

"Do you have any heroes?"

Michael flashed on Cavanaugh, a guy with plenty of hero and more than a little villain inside him.

"I thought I did. Now I'm not so sure."

"You obviously see a lot of horror films," Dr. Liz asked at another session. "I'm thinking those films don't have a lot of happy endings."

"What can I say? It's a horrible world. Bad things happen. That's why we have horror movies. We need 'em. I just hate it when the story unfolds so predictably."

"Like Dawn's movies?"

"Exactly."

"So could you have predicted your Mom's death? Could you have changed that script?"

"I should have."

"How?"

"I should have seen the signs. I should have loved her more. I should have done something."

"Maybe you could have done all that in the movie version. But don't you think sometimes in real life things are out of our control?"

The sessions provided no life-changing revelations, but three months in, Michael noticed his mental image of Crystal gradually shifting from the dead woman in the bloody bathtub to the sad, beautiful and very alive mother he had loved.

When he conjured her image, it still hit him like a cresting Atlantic wave, strong enough to sweep him off his feet and leave him thrashing in the surf. But Michael found he could hold his ground in those moments, letting the cascading emotions pass over and around him, the sea bottom solid beneath his feet.

On his weekend visits, Michael's dad brought drafting paper and colored pens. Michael found himself brimming with new film ideas. He changed his mind about the horror genre. Maybe he'd been too hasty going down that path. Bava was a genius, he was sure of that, but what about Kubrick?

Watching *Barry Lyndon* on the dayroom TV got Michael re-thinking his French Revolution scenario. Romance, intrigue, lavish costumes, a story of an upstart peasant girl manipulating her way into the French court – there was an idea he could work with. If you needed some blood, there was always the guillotine, but his new film ideas included no butcher knives, deadly shot puts, or sinister killers.

The leading lady in his current sketches didn't resemble any women he knew or dreamed of meeting. Michael was now focused on the story, not the star. Seeing Dawn, hearing her terrified scream as he approached, put a period on something for him.

He looked forward to Saturdays when Alex waited nervously for him in the visitors' center, the tentative hugs at the start, the quiet moments when they didn't have to say anything, the warmth of his father's hand on his cheek as they said goodbye.

In the afternoons, Michael found it peaceful to sit by the large banks of windows, ignoring the tiny metal grids inside the glass that made them shatterproof. He liked to stare out at the manicured lawn, the trimmed Viburnum hedges and the round tile fountain, its single geyser sprouting through the wide, white bulbs floating atop flat, viridescent leaves.

Looking out at that peaceful scene, Michael let his mind wander back to Chief Bobby's Motel and the night when Lola crawled into his bed. He replayed that particular hour in every way he could think of, rolling it back and forth in slow-mo, in fast-mo, in close-up, in tracking shots, even in 3D, ignoring the circumstances and events that came before and after.

The days ran together like that for almost six months. The one exception was the Thursday afternoon in May when his father and Dick Adams arrived unannounced along with Dr. Liz, Sammi, Sheila, and a few other staff members. There was a two-layer vanilla cake and everyone sang and clapped as Michael blew out all eighteen candles.

———

Sundays between noon and three the patients at Palmdale Haven could make collect calls from an off-white pay phone mounted on a wall near the nurses' station. On the Sunday before his release, Michael waited patiently as an emaciated woman of 70 or more, her silver hair teased into a Bride of Frankenstein halo, yelled a string of obscenities into the phone before slamming down the receiver. When she turned to Michael, the anger vanished as if a switch had been flipped. She smiled radiantly, before spinning 180 degrees and skipping away.

Michael stared down at a business card he'd kept with him since that crazy morning at Chief Bobby's. A card he had slipped under his mattress and checked on every week. And now, with his discharge just days away, a card that he was ready to use.

He dialed the number and recognized the Cuban accent on the other end of the line.

"Solano Investigations. Jaime Solano speaking."

"This is a collect call from Palmdale Haven Rehabilitation Center," a recorded voice announced. "Do you agree to accept the charges?"

"Yes, I do."

The phone clicked twice, signaling that Michael could start his call.

"Hey. It's Michael Donnelly....Yeah....No kidding. Look, I want to take you up on your offer to find someone for me....No, no, not her! Someone else."

———

Lola awaited her big moment in a lamp-lit green room, the closed door muting the shouts and claps from the adjacent ballroom, at least a little bit. That suited her just fine. Lola enjoyed being near the commotion of an American Dream rally, but always found the scripted ballyhoo a little much. She preferred the quiet of the small, square room – bare except for four black banquet chairs and a card table holding pots for coffee and tea, cups and saucers, and a standing lamp.

The Dreamers, as the company called its sales force, needed some cheerleading to keep them building their pyramids, but Lola's drive to succeed didn't require a rally or an exuberant emcee in a sharkskin suit. She didn't need to be sardined with 300 believers in a room meant for 200, mainlining potent doses of pure prosperity. She was happy to crack open the door just a bit to watch and listen. The green room was behind the stage, so she could see the back of Sonny James's shiny gray suit, and beyond him, the adrenalized dreamers on their feet, clapping, hooting and stomping, as Sonny egged them on.

"It's anotha' great day in America!"

Sonny 's audience was a cross-section of 1980s America – white, black, Hispanic, Asian, eager twenty-somethings, middle-aged strivers, and a lot of gray hairs looking to enhance a fixed income. Sonny leaned over the lectern, his hand behind his ear, his voice as gooey as a praline on a summer day.

"I cain't hear y'all. I said – IT'S ANOTHA' GREAT DAY IN AMERICA!"

Listening with her eyes closed, Lola thought the roar ricocheting back sounded like a jet was racing down a runway inside the Hilton ballroom. In terms of spirit and showmanship, American Dream's quarterly sales meetings fell somewhere between a high school pep rally and the 1980 Republican National

Convention.

Sonny let the crowd roar for a long minute, before waving them down.

"Thank y'all! Thank y'all! Thank y'all so much."

Lola studied Sonny's pitch like a student prepping for a final exam. The biggest slices of the American Dream pie were served to people who could whip up a crowd at recruitment meetings in rec centers and the back rooms of restaurants. Lola knew she needed to get better at it. And it wasn't just words. Sonny, like all good American Dream MCs, knew how to tap into the dreamers' visceral yearnings: for the seductive scent of chlorine vaping off your polished cedar hot tub; the sweet and sour tang of a frozen margarita sipped on the foredeck of your yacht; the 007-style giddy-up as you piloted an Aston Martin along a two-lane snaking above the Riviera. The dreamers came to these rallies to be shaken *and* stirred. Sonny's job was to convince them that pushing expensive cleaning products on their friends and family could put them in sniffing distance of all their most fragrant financial fantasies.

Like the Catholic Church, the wise men overseeing American Dream Enterprises knew that the set decoration was just as important as the homily. Sonny beamed from behind a lectern decorated with red, white and blue bunting. Beyond him, billboard-sized American flag banners decorated the walls. Portable TVs, on tall rolling carts set every 10 feet or so, channeled images of the American Dream logo - Old Glory flying above a rustic tableau of cleaning products, scrub brushes and mops, and this quarter's sales mantra – "*Don't make the sale. Be the sale*" – and colorful, Rockwellian portraits of George Washington, Teddy Roosevelt, Dwight Eisenhower and Ronald Reagan.

Sonny's opening act was a Dixieland band – four gray-haired musicians from a Lake Worth senior center – offering a choppy, but enthusiastic medley of "The Halls of Montezuma," "Dixie" and "When The Saints Go Marchin' In."

Despite the cacophony, Lola was sure she could hear the staccato beating of her heart. Stage fright. Something else she needed to overcome. She eased the door closed, and went to work making a new pot of coffee, hoping to settle herself before her walk-on. She recalled Sonny's advice: "Just be yourself, little girl. And if that's not good enough, then be somebody else."

Sonny had barged into the green room after the run-thru. Lola watched as he made tea, lacing the cup with four sugars.

"Saving the pipes for the show," he whispered, raising the teacup in a mock toast.

Sonny sat for a moment, his cowboy boots tapping out a march. He had a toothy, well-fed face, framed by a gelled black pompadour and Elvis-style sideburns, a look that fit well with his slow, Southern baritone.

"How did you get here? Doing this?" Lola asked. "I mean, I want to be you. Or be like you."

"Only one of me, but I watched you out there in the warm-up. You're a natural, little girl. Don't worry." Sonny sipped his tea.

"So?"

"Okay, about me? Sure thing. You want the long version or the abridged?" Sonny nervously checked his Rolex. "Never-mind, we only got time for the short one."

Sonny's first on-stage job was auctioning off livestock. "It's a smelly business and the pay is for shit. Or it's a shitty business and the pay stinks."

He had worked his way up to auto auctions before a friend invited him to an American Dream pep rally and now, three years later, he was leading sales rallies like this all over the Southeast.

"So, since it's just us in here – why don't you try to guess where I'm from?" Sonny struck a stoic pose, only his eyes corkscrewing madly in Lola's direction.

"I haven't ever been out of Florida, but I've watched a lot of TV and movies," Lola said. "I'm thinking you're from Alabama or Mississippi. Or wait, I got it – Louisiana!"

Sonny let go of his pose and laughed. He reached out to shake Lola's hand.

"I'm Elliot Janowitz, born and raised in Secaucus, New Jersey,"

Sonny said, his Southern drawl replaced with precise, East Coast consonants. "Tell anybody else that and I'll deny it all."

"You changed your name and your voice?"

"My advice, little lady, is this – if being yourself isn't working, consider becoming someone else. Elliot Janowitz was just a turd in the punchbowl. I needed to slather some honey on myself. Do something special. One night on TV I saw Jimmy Swaggart begging forgiveness and I had my inspiration."

Lola looked blank.

"Jimmy Swaggart? The revival preacher? Jerry Lee Lewis' cousin? Girl, where you been? He's half-sinner and half-saint, and 100 percent grits on the griddle. People just flat eat up that combo platter."

Sonny winked at Lola as he sipped his tea. He stood up, pushing back his shoulders and raising his chin. His next line was spoken like a man fresh from an East Baton Rouge fish fry: "Sonny James at your service, little girl. How can I make you happy today?"

What made Lola happy was that after that sales pitch, Sonny didn't hit on her. And he seemed pleased with his adopted persona – despite his flushed face, the sheen of sweat below his pancake makeup and his speed-freak eyes. Lola figured those parts of him hadn't changed.

Sonny gulped down the rest of his tea and hopped from his chair.

"You're our finale, little girl, so do it just like the rehearsal and Uncle Sonny will take care of everything else. Okay?"

He didn't wait for an answer, slamming the mug on the table and racing from the room like a man who just remembered he was late for his own wedding.

Now, two hours later, Lola watched Sonny walk solemnly to the lectern. The lights dimmed. Sonny leaned close to the silver microphone, his voice a hushed whisper, as if he were talking intimately to his closest friend.

"You know, sometimes I think about my old life in the 1970s. Oh my yes! Those horrible days. Slavin' for a weekly paycheck.

Waitin' in gas lines. Never gettin' ahead. Worryin' 'bout how I was gonna pay for my hair gel and Nik Nik shirts."

He let the crowd laugh at that line, then returned to his stage whisper.

"And I think about those first baby steps I took toward financial freedom and independence! When I said 'Yes!' to the American Dream representative on my doorstep."

His eyes rolling to the heavens, Sonny shifted into his final arpeggio. "I remember that glorious day like it was yesterday. The day I told my American Dream rep that: 'YES! I WANT TO BE SOMEBODY! AND NOT JUST ANY SOMEBODY! I WANT TO BE A RICH SOMEBODY!' What a marvelous, amazing time that was. CAN I GET AN AMEN?"

The crowd rose again, offering a chorus of "AMENS."

Sonny waved them quiet. "Now let's get down to some business. What y'all say?"

As Sonny narrated, the TV screens snapped through a series of new product releases – images of smoked glass jars, the liquid inside all glossy and glowing – and charts bearing the latest county, state and national sales figures. On each chart the trajectory of the arrow-tipped red line was up, up, up!

Sonny welcomed Don Denton, the guy at the pinnacle of the American Dream pyramid in Palm Beach County. A red-cheeked cherub in a plaid jacket and white slacks, Don and Sonny called the names of that quarter's top performers – bringing each one up for a hug, a bonus check tucked in a golden envelope, and a beaming photo op.

"Now we've reached my favorite part of these monthly shindigs," Sonny said. "The time we honor our newest success stories. The young people who threw off the old and jumped feet first into the new. People who said *adios* to the sluggish '70s and *si, si, si* to the fabulous '80s!"

That brought the crowd back to its feet, hooting and clapping.

"Calm down now, y'all. My limo's idling outside and I'm paying by the hour. We gotta wrap this sucker up. I ordered a raw steak and a bottle of Dom from room service at the Breakers." He did a double-take at his Rolex, pulling back his shirtsleeve so everyone could see it glitter. "Should be arriving any minute now. So let's calm it on down so Uncle Sonny can get this thing done."

The crowd slowly settled into silence.

"Thank y'all so much. So what we're celebratin' tonight is a young person who isn't just thinkin' 'bout that ol' American Dream, I'm talking about a young American takin' giant steps to reach the financial promised land. That's right, it's time to celebrate this quarter's District Six Junior Achiever! "

Sonny turned dramatically to the side of the stage.

"Eulene, can I have the envelope please?"

A thirtyish woman, her ample curves tucked into a red beaded "Miss Florida" gown, rushed up on glittering high heels, an oversized golden envelope clinched in manicured fingers.

"Thank you, Eulene." Sonny turned back to the crowd. "Don't she look great! Man, if she was a flag – I'd salute her! Please don't tell my wife I said that! Anyway, on with the show! Our District Sixteen American Dream Junior Achiever for April, May and June of 1982! Ladies and gentlemen, put your hands, your hearts and your hoots together for..."

Sonny made a show out of trying to open the envelope, grimacing as he grappled with it. When he finally managed to tear it open, he scanned the contents, then flashed a buck-toothed smile.

"Miss Lola Fernandez Famosa! COME ON DOWN!"

As the crowd clapped and whooped, the band struck up a Dixieland version of *Guantanamera*. Lola stepped onstage, looking businesslike in a sensible blue pants suit and navy high heels. The hot spot revealed a small woman in full makeup, her lips fire-engine red, her sprayed curls glittering.

Taking her hand, Sonny led Lola to the front of the stage, spinning her slowly around like a dance instructor, in the Vegas-bright spotlight. When they stopped, Lola offered the audience the tight, open-handed wave she had seen Nancy Reagan do on TV.

Sonny brought Lola back to the mic, where Eulene handed her a golden trophy in the shape of a wind-whipped American flag. Beaming, Lola raised it over her head.

The crowd went wild. Sonny eventually hushed them. He took the trophy and bent the metal neck of the mic stand so Lola could reach it on her tiptoes, before leaning down to speak first.

"Little girl, looks to me like you hit the *quinela* – you're beautiful and you're making buck. What you got to say for yourself? Tell us how this feels."

Lola let the room go completely silent, just as they'd discussed at rehearsal. The house lights dimmed, leaving her encircled by the single spot.

"Well, first, when I heard I was getting this award, I thought, it's time to treat myself to two items I've been dreaming about for a very long time."

She signaled the band for the pre-arranged drum roll. As the spotlight followed her, Lola stepped to the front of the stage, her hands gripping her lapels. With a quick two-handed pull, the snaps holding the jacket released, revealing a bra, covered in red, white and blue sequins. Lola's new, silicon-enhanced cleavage bulged from the sequined cups like twin dolphins breaking the surface of the sea.

Holding open the jacket, Lola did a quick, hips-swaying runway walk as the crowd roared. When she had covered the entire stage, she snapped the jacket shut and stepped back to the microphone. On tiptoes, her bright red lips brushing the mic, Lola held the moment until the crowd hushed.

"I have a favorite movie. It's about the South where I grew up. Okay, maybe my South was actually South Florida. But still. This movie has always inspired me, even at the lowest moments of my life – and let me tell you there have been plenty of those. No matter what happened, I'd think about Scarlett O'Hara and how she persevered. How she picked herself up off the floor time and again. How she refused to give up despite every losing hand life dealt her. How she made a promise to herself, and, dammit, she kept it."

Lola turned, taking the trophy from Sonny's outstretched hand. She raised it over her head.

"As God is my witness, this little Cubanita is going to be FILTHY, FREAKIN' RICH!"

The blast from dozens of fluorescents flashing on at once whited-out the room. The Dixieland band snapped into "Happy Days Are Here Again." as hundreds of red, white and blue balloons dandelioned down from the ceiling. Once they regained their senses, the audience rose as one, the decibel level of the hoots, claps and stomps crescendoing to triple-digits. Sonny, Eulene and Don Denton circled Lola, the four of them beaming and waving, like two political couples on the convention stage, who had just secured the presidential and vice-presidential nomination.

Some Kind
Of Crazed Killer

—

Lola pulled off her high heels and walked east through downtown to the wide sidewalk fronting the Intracoastal, just below the Flagler Bridge. She found her favorite spot along the seawall, the one backlit by a single streetlight, the one with a clear view across the dark water to the glittering lights of Palm Beach.

Lola carefully set the trophy beside her on the concrete perch, then pulled a pack of Marlboro 100s and a plastic lighter from her purse. Inhaling, she let her head roll back, the tension of the night leaving her along with the escaping smoke.

She continued to smoke and stretch until half the cigarette was gone, then, without turning around, she spoke to a figure lurking in the shadows behind her.

"You're not some kind of crazed killer, are you?"

She leaned her head forward, brushing the hair off her neck. "Here you go. Bring on the butcher knife. Or the ax. Or the meat cleaver. Whatever it is, let's get it over with."

"How did you know I was here?" Michael stepped slowly into the pale glow of the streetlight, until he was standing behind Lola, both of them looking east toward Palm Beach.

Lola took another slow drag on her cigarette. "You were the only one in the audience who didn't have that American Dream spirit."

"Congratulations. On your award. I did clap."

Lola took another drag, inhaling and exhaling before replying, "Thanks."

Michael wasn't sure what to say. Here he was again, trying to communicate with a woman and blowing it. He had hoped Lola would be glad to see him but when she turned in his direction, her face was blank.

"So, I guess you're okay?" he said, looking off at the lights of Palm Beach and not at Lola.

"I'm fine."

"I worry sometimes."

"Don't."

"You know, about your –"

"My vices? My other career? Don't fret your rich little head. After our trip to the swamp, I gave up some vices – and some fantasies."

"I guess that's good."

Lola took one last pull on the cigarette before looking up at Michael.

"And how are the Donnellys?"

"Lola –" He watched as she flicked the butt into the water.

"And the movie star? How's she doing? I heard there was some trouble on the set."

"She's fine. I think. They're not pressing charges. There's even a studio interested in my ideas. It could be something." Michael hesitated. "But I guess I've given up a few of my fantasies too."

"Like the one about being torn between the slasher princess and the hard-working hooker? That fantasy?"

"I've had time to do a lot of thinking. And there's something I really want to tell you."

"Since you're here, I probably ought to tell you something too," Lola said.

"Okay..." Michael nodded.

"I wasn't faking it."

"What do you mean?"

"That night, in the motel, with you. I wasn't faking it. I meant it. I know it didn't look that way afterwards, but I did ... you know ... mean it."

Lola lit another cigarette. Michael stood awkwardly, the silence like a curtain drawn between them.

"Okay then," Michael slowly turned to go. "Thanks for that. And I'm glad you're okay."

He took a few steps, but Lola's voice stopped him.

"Wasn't there something you were supposed to tell me?"

Michael turned back. "Oh, yeah, damn. I'm not good at this stuff."

"Just say it. Whatever it is."

Michael moved closer. "Well, I used to spend a lot of time thinking about death."

"You don't have to tell me that. That much I knew for sure."

"But now, I mostly think about how I felt when you and I were together."

"And how was that?"

"Alive. Really alive. And even though I didn't know if you ever felt the same way, I needed to find you and tell you that."

Having gotten that much out, Michael again found himself out of words.

"Okay, I guess that's it."

He turned to go but Lola's voice stopped him again.

"How's Cavanaugh?"

Michael turned back. "It's kind of a crazy story."

"I'm sure of that."

"Cavanaugh died and went to Savannah."

"What?"

"It's complicated, but he's fine. And I think his daughter is fine too."

"That's good."

"Yeah. It's all good."

Lola swung off the seawall and came toward him. When she was close enough, she took Michael's arm, leading him back to the seawall.

"Come on, sit down, you're making me nuts. You're over there in the shadows like some kind of slasher in a hockey mask."

She moved the trophy so he could sit beside her, their legs dangling over the edge of the seawall. This time the silence was easier, their eyes not on each other, but focused on the golden lights of Palm Beach.

Finally, Lola spoke: "I'm going to get there, you know?"

"I'm sure," Michael answered.

"And I'm going to do it my way. I don't need anybody else's money. You understand what I'm saying?"

"I have no doubt."

"Somebody once told me it's lonely waking up in those big houses," Lola said.

Michael turned to look at her. She was looking back, a hint of a smile on her lips.

"It can be very lonely," he said.

"I guess it doesn't have to be. If you have somebody to wake up with."

"That could make it better."

"Yeah, especially when the butler brings in breakfast for two," Lola said.

"With silk napkins and the fresh flowers," Michael added.

"And the silver coffee pot and some fine china cups and saucers."

Michael rolled with her fantasy.

"And *The Wall Street Journal.* Two copies."

"And freshly squeezed orange juice in cut crystal glasses," Lola said. "And a sliced grapefruit, sprinkled with sugar."

"And those serrated silver spoons. Really sharp. You know for slicing into the..."

Lola shot him a look.

"Grapefruit," Michael added quickly. "For slicing into the grapefruit."

Lola reached over and took his hand. "Anyway, those two people could tell the butler to call the office and let them know they weren't coming in. Cancel the hairdresser and the masseuse. Let the house staff know not to disturb them for the rest of the day. They've got some serious business to attend to."

"Very important business," Michael tightened his fingers around hers.

"Extremely urgent business," she said.

Lola turned in Michael's direction. Their faces were close.

"I'm not a movie star," Lola whispered.

"And I'm not a businessman."

"I know. You're another dreamer. Just like him."

Michael shrugged. She was right. "So what you're saying is, I'm the wrong guy?"

"Basically, yes. But, you know, when it comes to men, I've got this character flaw."

Lola placed the trophy in Michael's hands, then pushed up off the seawall. She stepped into the white circle of streetlight and started spinning slowly, her arms outstretched. Even in her tailored American Dream pantsuit, Michael thought she looked young and free.

"So what do you think?" She posed briefly, leaning toward him, then tossed off a series of Isadora Duncan spins. "Were you impressed with my new boobs? The best money can buy."

"I was pretty impressed with you from the start."

Lola continued her slow, twirling dance.

Michael put down the plastic American Dream trophy and brought his hands up to frame his shot, mentally recording Lola's dance in a series of cinematic stills.

After a few more spins, Lola danced over and reached out, pulling Michael to his feet. It felt like that night in the Everglades. Their bodies close. Lola's head just below his chin. Her dark eyes staring up into his.

Bending slowly to one knee, Michael raised her hand to his lips, planting a very proper kiss on her butter-soft skin. Lola smiled down at him, her moussed curls glittering in the streetlight.

"Such a pleasure to meet you, Mr. Donnelly," she said.

"Why, Miss Famosa," Michael said, "the pleasure is all mine."

They held that pose for a very long time, as a determined moon broke through the clouds, the couple suddenly incandescent in the arc light.

Michael could picture exactly what a good director would do next.

He'd hold the camera on the moonlit lovers for a long beat, then the shot would rise above the waterfront sidewalk, sweeping up Okeechobee Boulevard, then over the barrel-tile roofs of the cheap motels and half-empty strip centers along Dixie Highway. Picking up speed and altitude, the camera would race above downtown's aging department stores and bank buildings, gazing down on the golden lamps of the Flagler Bridge as it crossed the Intracoastal, before rising up and over the alabaster boulevards, neon-blue pools and the ornate Mediterranean battlements of Palm Beach.

The camera would climb vertically then, into a crystalline stratosphere, where the eastern and western shorelines – now both black as night – became identical shoulders, linked by a necklace of glittering diamonds.

Epilogue

—

The morning is cool and the oak-shaded square is framed by stately brick homes, rising two and three stories, pushed up against the sidewalk like so many gingerbread palaces from a childhood dream.

A few cars wait at a corner stoplight for the right turn that starts the route around the square. A tall, regal figure in a white linen suit and Panama hat limps up to each window, aided by a brass-handled cane. He stands tall, his back straight, only the deep creases on his cheeks and the etched lines around his eyes tell the story of almost seventy years on this slowly circling planet.

The man holds a sign: "Can you help a Savannah boy with a broken heart and a bum leg enjoy a happy homecoming?"

A car window cranks down. A $10 bill comes out. The old man tips his hat as he pockets the cash. This routine repeats – more cars, more limping, more cash disappearing under the flap of the old man's coat pocket.

When a distant church bell chimes the noon hour, the old man limps onto the sidewalk and around the corner. Once out of sight of the street corner, the limp miraculously disappears. He walks with purpose. A young woman in a cotton dress, all flower prints with a swinging skirt, smiles as she approaches. The white-suited gentleman tips his hat and nods ever so slightly.

A few more steps and the gentleman pauses below a wooden sign, secured by four golden hoops screwed into a shaft of polished wood – Hiram Beauregard's Old Town Bar and Grill. He smiles and removes his hat.

Feeling the sun on his shoulders, Cavanaugh Reilly turns in a slow circle, giving his hometown a long and loving look, before slipping inside the dark bar.

———

On 1,500 Cineplex screens, tucked into mammoth shopping malls hunkered beside American roadways running from sea to shining sea, anthropomorphic candy bars perform a kick-line along a snack counter, as a chorus of sodas sings "Let's All Go To The Lobby..."

Afterwards, the screen goes black for a brief beat before turning pale blue: *The following preview is rated PG-13.*

Another black screen gives way to a long shot of snow-capped Alpine peaks. A mountain goat leaps onto a flat rock in the foreground. The creature slowly turns its majestic snout toward the audience as a string of silver letters spin into focus: *Coming this fall from High Peak Pictures.*

Cut to images of Paris and Versailles circa the late 1700s, a skittering harpsichord and violin score running beneath. We see long-shots of elegant peach-colored chateaus; a looming gray Bastille; tight on be-wigged courtiers at a masked ball; tighter still on angry peasants, waving torches and wooden clubs; close on the terrified face of a woman with powdered skin and red lips; pull back to reveal the shining blade of a guillotine slicing toward its destination.

Finally, the camera lingers on a very regal coach – drawn by four black horses – as it rolls through a forest glen at twilight. A mellifluous movie trailer voice intones: "From Marchand and Avery, the filmmakers who brought you "*Stiff Upper Lip*, comes a tale of two star-crossed lovers trapped in the tumult of an approaching revolution."

Tight on the young woman inside the coach, her dress flowered and flowing, the tops of her breasts pushing skyward from a lace-covered bodice.

"Dawn Karston stars as Agnes Stewart, a spirited English noble trapped in a gilded world about to disappear forever.

Leopold Zamara is the man she shouldn't love."

Cut to a horseman emerging from the trees, his black hair flowing to his shoulders. He's clad in rustic, string-tied breeches, his leather jacket adorned with bits of fur, his jaw square, his eyes intensely blue. From atop his mammoth black stallion, the man aims a flintlock at the carriage driver, who jerks back the reins. Four carriage horses whinny and kick.

The young noblewoman steps out of the carriage to face the dashing ruffian standing before her, pistol drawn. The shot tightens on her wide, unblinking eyes, her painted pout of a mouth. His fingers brush her powdered cheek. She looks like she might scream, but instead, as he leans in to kiss her, her lips part and she sighs.

"Ahhhhh..."

The image fades to black as the narrator intones: "Be there this fall when Dawn Karston and Leopold Zamara set the screen on fire in Marchand and Avery's thrilling romantic adventure *Off With Her Heart!*"

Author's note

—

This book is about South Florida as I knew it during the 1980s and 1990s. For much of that time, I roamed the state as a reporter for the *Tampa Tribune* and the *St. Petersburg Times*. The West Palm Beach in the book is the city as I found it when I arrived right out of college as a low-level editor at the Palm Beach Times, a soon-to-be-extinct afternoon newspaper. West Palm Beach always had a picture-perfect waterfront, well-tended neighborhoods and modern suburbs, but like so many American cities at that time, its urban core was hollowed out and desolate. On my first night in town, I stayed at an aging motel on the fringes of downtown. It was dead quiet when I closed the door at 10 p.m., but when I stepped outside at 4 a.m. – afternoon papers started very early – the motel was bustling with merchants and shoppers involved in various aspects of the illicit pleasure industry. Today the city boasts a vibrant, completely legal downtown. On several research visits, I could find no trace of that old motel or the squalid areas that once surrounded it.

Palm Beach remains pretty much as I discovered it during those years, and when I returned to cover numerous stories including the William Kennedy Smith trial. There are newer cars and different restaurants, but the same privileged attitude, polished streets, manicured hedges, and Mediterranean revival architecture.

I loved revisiting the wild and not-so-wild places around Glades County for this project. Despite years of political promises and lots of money, the Everglades remains both endangered and magnificent. I'm sad to report that Tom Gaskins and his Cypress Knee Museum, where I enjoyed many visits – including some memorable lunches with Tom and his wife – are long gone. Chief Bobby is a fictional character, though I did meet Chief Billy in my travels, and the Seminole Tribe continues to operate a casino in Glades County.

And I do believe the real Cavanaugh Murphy found his way back to Savannah, after a long detour through Florida.

For their invaluable help with this book, I want to thank Maxine Swann, Dorothy Smiljanich, Chris Calhoun, Amy Cianci, Joe Hamilton, Chad Mize (cover art), Eva Avenue (comic panels), David Warner, John Huls, Jay Hoff, the Monday night writers table - Nicole, Gloria, Eleanor, Brian and Brian. Also thanks to Savannah and Ben Hoffman, everyone at Tombolo Books and St Petersburg Press, and Eugenie Bondurant, for her love and steadfast support.

About the author

—

Paul Wilborn collected multiple awards from the American Society of Newspaper Editors and the Florida Society of Newspaper Editors during a journalism career that included stints at the *Tampa Tribune*, *The St. Petersburg Times* and the *Associated Press* in Los Angeles. He won the Green Eyeshade Award from the Atlanta Chapter of Sigma Delta Chi, the South's top writing prize. Based on a selection of his writing, Wilborn was chosen for the Paul Hansel Award, Florida's top journalism prize. He was a Knight-Wallace Fellow at the University of Michigan.

Wilborn's short-story collection, *Cigar City: Tales From a 1980s Creative Ghetto*, won the Gold Medal for Fiction in the 2019 Florida Book Awards.

His plays have been produced at Stageworks, Off-Center Theater, Radio Theater Project and University of Michigan.

A pianist and singer, he has led several bands including Paul Wilborn and the Pop Tarts and Blue Roses. He produced and performed in the long-running American Songbook Series at American Stage.

In the 1980s, Wilborn was a founding member of Ybor City's Artists and Writers Group, which created multiple themed art and music events in Tampa's historic district.

Wilborn, a fourth-generation Floridian, is currently executive director of the Palladium Theater at St. Petersburg College and lives in Saint Petersburg with his wife, the film actor Eugenie Bondurant.

Paul Wilborn

CIGAR

CITY

Tales from a
1980s Creative Ghetto

Gold Medal for Fiction
— winner —
Florida Book Awards

Also by Paul Wilborn from
St. Petersburg Press

Cigar City: Tales From a 1980s Creative Ghetto is a collection of linked short stories about the young artists, writers, poets, musicians and actors who inhabited Tampa's Ybor (E-bore) City immigrant district in the 1980s. Drawn by urban authenticity and cheap rents, they created a surreal, chaotic arts scene. The scene drew international artists like James Rosenquist, Jim Dine and dozens more, and mirrored what was happening in New York's Alphabet City. The stories are fictional but they capture the spirit of the place and the people. The book is illustrated with photos by Bud Lee and David Audet.

Paul Wilborn is an award-winning journalist, playwright and musician. He was a founder of Ybor City's Artists and Writers Group. Wilborn lives in Saint Petersburg with his wife, the film actor Eugenie Bondurant

"These stories make the time and place shimmer back to life. If you were there, you'll be glad to remember it all. If you weren't, you might wish you had been."
Colette Bancroft, Tampa Bay Times, page 1 review.

....

"Affectionate but not sentimental and often laugh-out-loud funny, these stories capture the romance and the hard truths of a world we won't likely see again."

David Warner, duPont Registry

www.wilbornwrites.com
www.stpetersburgpress.com
Revised Edition Print ISBN: 978-1-940300-13-9
Available at Ingram (returnable, standard discount)

CPSIA information can be obtained
at www.ICGtesting.com
Printed in the USA
LVHW010303270722
724468LV00002B/180